THE WOLVES OF ST. PETER'S

✛   ✛   ✛

The

WOLVES OF ST. PETER'S

GINA BUONAGURO
JANICE KIRK

HarperCollins*PublishersLtd*

Published by HarperCollins Publishers Ltd

First edition

HarperCollins books may be purchased for educational, business,
or sales promotional use through our Special Markets Department.

HarperCollins Publishers Ltd
2 Bloor Street East, 20th Floor
Toronto, Ontario, Canada
M4W 1A8

www.harpercollins.ca

Library and Archives Canada Cataloguing in Publication
information is available upon request.

ISBN 978-1-44341-745-7

Printed and bound in the United States

RRD 9 8 7 6 5 4 3 2 1

FOR JOHN PEARCE

✣

The wise are instructed by reason, average minds by experience, the stupid by necessity, and the brute by instinct.

MARCUS TULLIUS CICERO

⁜

THE WOLVES OF ST. PETER'S

✦ ✦ ✦

CHAPTER ONE

IT WASN'T THE FIRST TIME HE'D SEEN A BODY PULLED FROM THE Tiber River, but it was the first one he recognized. He could almost hear her voice in the rain. *Calendula. I was named for the flower.* He stopped at the foot of the bridge, watching as two policemen attempted to hook her body with long poles and draw it toward the bank. Caught against one of the bridge pylons, she was barely distinguishable from the garbage and river weeds. Leaning over the parapet, a group of boys shouted instructions down to the policemen, their voices competing with the demented screams of seagulls circling like vultures overhead.

Francesco Angeli shifted his weight from one leg to the other, putrid ankle-deep mud sucking at his boots, the cold, insistent drizzle seeping through his cloak and straight into his bones. He looked up to where the Castel Sant'Angelo, as gray as the sky, loomed at the other end of the bridge and told himself he should go, deliver the sack he was carrying, and save himself the wrath of his master,

Michelangelo. But he couldn't. Even in the filthy water, her hair was still every bit as golden as the flower she'd been named for, every bit as golden as his beloved Juliet's.

The first time he met Calendula, he'd thought she *was* Juliet and had almost called out her name. He'd stood there dumbfounded, disappointed, heartbroken, and Calendula had thought this turmoil was all for her. *You've never seen hair as golden as mine, have you?* she'd asked, winding one gleaming strand around her finger. She affected the voice of a little girl, though she was twenty, the same age as himself. *I have,* he'd replied when he could speak again. *Though not on a whore.* He had meant it to be cruel, but his voice had shaken.

The boys hooted with pleasure as the policemen finally freed Calendula's body from the pylon and dragged it toward the bank. It escaped, turning ever so slowly in an eddy of water, the weight of the waterlogged dress threatening to drag it under the surface.

There was a frantic scrambling of poles as the policemen attempted to snare the body once more, while the boys threw stones at it for good measure. Then, to their amusement, one of the policemen skidded down the muddy bank and found himself sitting up to his waist in the cold water. He pulled himself up and, directing his curses at the laughing boys, yanked off his cloak, threw it up on the bank, and waded out until he was chest deep. Grabbing at the dress, he staggered back to the shore.

Francesco could have left then. But something compelled him to keep watching.

The second policeman went to aid the first, and the two of them lugged the body up onto the bank before dropping it. One of the men pushed aside her hair with his boot, and Francesco recoiled at the sight of her face, battered and bloodied. Her eyes were still open and staring, their blueness shot through with blood. The hair she was so proud of, so adored by men, so envied by women, was matted with sludge, weeds, and the rotten remains of an old sack. And the dress, carefully chosen to reflect the color of her hair, now muddy and torn, twisted around her slender body, exposing a breast the color of a dead carp. Bile rising in his throat, Francesco looked away quickly.

He'd painted her in that dress. Not Francesco, but Marcus. A portrait of the Virgin and Christ Child, with Calendula in a field of yellow marigolds, a child with curls as brilliant as her own resting in the luminescent folds of her dress. *Madonna della Calendula,* the Marigold Madonna. Glowing with an internal light, it was the best thing Marcus had ever painted. A masterpiece by an otherwise mediocre painter—at least in Francesco's judgment. It had been commissioned by a rich shipping merchant known as The Turk, and it had nearly killed Marcus to hand the painting over. *It sickens me to think of that fat prick's eyes on her,* he had said. Calendula was not only Marcus's model, she was his lover, and Marcus was jealous of those who paid for a brief taste of her beauty.

And she was so very beautiful, Francesco thought, every bit as beautiful as the woman she'd reminded him of. But now, with her left arm twisted behind her back, her right splayed out on the bank, fingers curled like claws, it was already becoming hard to remember that loveliness.

He'd seen her just two nights earlier at Imperia's, the elegant brothel that was the favorite gathering place of Rome's artists. With the candles burning bright, Imperia, dressed in a violet gown, had seen to her patrons' comforts, pouring out flattery as generously as she'd poured the wine. A couple of houseboys, five or six years of age, dressed as cherubs complete with gold-tipped wings, held out plates of grapes and sweetmeats while a bare-breasted girl played an ivory lute. And in the middle of the salon, Calendula had held court, a dozen men gathered around her. Seated in a delicate gilded chair in front of the pink marble fireplace, she'd basked in their effusive compliments as Marcus, vying to get closer, made several vain attempts to edge his own chair through the admirers. Francesco, standing a little apart, a little drunk, couldn't take his eyes off her, disoriented by the firelight dancing in her hair, the yellow dress that shimmered with every silken rustle. Only when she'd reached for a grape did he notice the ring, a large amethyst set in a heavy gold band etched with intricate swirls. Marcus, who had finally succeeded in reaching her side, saw it too. *Who gave you that?* Marcus had demanded. *The Turk?*

Someone far richer than you'll ever be, she'd said evasively, torturing him further by planting a kiss on the ring.

It was *The Turk,* he'd said, grabbing her by the arm and attempting to pull the ring from her finger. She'd laughed, freeing her hand from his, and he'd slapped her face hard enough to bring tears to those eyes, as blue as the Sicilian skies she'd been born under, as blue as Juliet's.

There were several startled responses, but Francesco had acted first. Shaken out of his stupor, he'd lunged through the men, knocking Marcus off the chair and smashing his head into the side of the marble fireplace. It had taken Raphael and two others to pull him off the stunned painter. They'd pushed him into the nearest chair and told Marcus to leave. Francesco had shaken them off, saying he'd be the one to go. He'd gulped the rest of his wine and stood up, aware of Calendula watching him, the hand with the ring pressed over her cheek. She hadn't looked at Marcus, only at Francesco, as if to say, *I'm not just any whore to you, am I?* Francesco had thrown his cup into the fireplace and left without another word.

The ring wasn't there now. And not only was it missing, the finger she wore it on was missing too. "Her finger is gone," he exclaimed in disbelief. Clearly this was no accident. Could Marcus have killed her out of jealousy?

"What did you say?"

Francesco turned to see a man standing beside him. A third policeman, this one with a large, pockmarked face and a dripping nose.

"Her finger's gone," Francesco repeated reluctantly.

The policeman looked from Francesco to the body and squinted. "How do you know that?" he asked sharply.

"You can see. There. The middle finger. It's been cut off."

"Must be sharp eyes you've got," the policeman said suspiciously.

The other policemen were dragging Calendula's body farther up the bank, but when the boys from the bridge joined in, one of them grabbing an arm, another a leg, the men stood back and let them do the work. A small group gathered to watch, among them a woman with a crying baby wrapped in a shawl, a man leading a wretched-looking donkey weighed down with bundles of firewood, and a couple of hooded monks.

The policeman at Francesco's side watched too, and Francesco wondered if he'd lost his chance to leave. He knew they wouldn't spend much time worrying about how this woman came to be in the river, and he, standing here watching, was as good a suspect as any. He pictured himself being hauled down to the courts. Once the officials learned he had connections to the man painting the Pope's chapel, they might decide they could extort a nice fine, but Francesco didn't trust them not to first tie his hands behind him and haul him up over a beam to see if they could extract a more interesting story. Not to mention that Michelangelo would hardly feel it his duty to bail out the houseboy who'd failed to bring his meal. Francesco didn't even know if his temperamental employer could be relied on to write his father or tell his friends. Not that Michelangelo knew who his friends were. If he did, he'd condemn Francesco to the gallows for that alone.

Having reached the top of the bank now, the boys dropped Calendula's body facedown just a few feet away. A seagull landed beside her and snatched up the hand with the missing finger in its beak. It flapped its wings as if planning to fly off with the entire body, and one of the policemen kicked at it, his boot thudding into its side. Dropping the hand, the bird backed off, screeching abuse at its attacker.

The policeman beside him pulled up the hood on his cloak, and Francesco could see he was bored and cold. If he'd been calculating before that Francesco looked like a good suspect, he was now thinking it was too much trouble. Francesco, reckoning this marked a conclusion of some sort to the events, shifted the sack with the bread and wine to the other hand and turned to go, the mud sucking at his boots.

"You know her?"

"No," Francesco answered. He wasn't going to risk rekindling the policeman's interest in him. "No," he said again. "Most likely just another whore."

"You're probably right. We'll be stuck with the expense of burying her. I'm sure no one's going to pay to collect her."

"Likely not," Francesco agreed, thinking this would certainly be the case if he failed to tell anyone. But of course he would, and the faster he did so, the faster he could forget. He wouldn't go to Marcus, though, not after the other night. Maybe Raphael. He could trust him. Let him take care of it.

"What's your name?" The policeman asked this not as if Francesco were a suspect, but as if they'd come to this point in their relationship.

"Guido del Mare," Francesco said without any hesitation, giving the name of his greatest enemy, even though Giudo was almost two hundred miles away in Florence. *Find him if you have any further questions,* he added to himself. He made his excuses and got away this time, not looking back until he was in the middle of the bridge. He watched one of the policemen bend over the body. *He's closing her eyes,* Francesco thought, and he cursed himself for not having had the courage to do it himself.

✢ ✢ ✢

WHEN Francesco entered St. Peter's Square, thousands of men were at work. Every day they got up from their beds and came here to labor, and it was said the basilica consumed men as hungrily as it consumed stone. Mostly it appeared to Francesco as if they were moving things around. Stacks of timber, piles of stone and brick, mounds of gravel, crushed marble, lime, and sand—everything moving from one place to another to make way for yet more piles of timber, stone, brick, gravel, marble, lime, sand. Pickaxes, shovels, and mallets rang and scraped against stone; men shouted and cursed. In the center of the square, a group of old women wrestled a large iron cauldron onto a fire, ready to make the day's soup, a slop made of rotten onions and rancid meat scraps that, along with the barrels of vinegary wine, fueled the men.

Teams of oxen stood ready and harnessed to begin the work of dragging the giant blocks of limestone transported by river from quarries north of the city. Yet more teams would cart the rock mined from Old Rome: the Palatine Hill, the Forum, the Colosseum.

The old St. Peter's was being demolished as the new one was being built, and little remained but the facade, which was dwarfed by the four giant pillars that would hold the new basilica's dome. By latest count (the architect Donato Bramante's design grew grander by the week), the basilica would cover tens of thousands of square yards, the dome itself over three hundred feet high. Greater than even the greatest visions of the ancient Romans. It was His Holiness Pope Julius II's way of saying, *We're back, even more glorious than before!*

Pope Julius's ambitions also extended to the old Sistine Chapel, and the man he wanted to paint its twelve-thousand-square-foot ceiling was Michelangelo, but getting the sculptor to accept the commission had been no easy task. For years, Michelangelo's heart had been set on securing the commission for Pope Julius's tomb. Declaring himself a sculptor and not a painter, Michelangelo had fled Rome for Florence and evaded the Pope and his request for two years until, seeing no other option and fearing for his life at the hands of papal spies and assassins, he had acquiesced and agreed to start at once.

But Michelangelo knew almost nothing of fresco. Instead of applying paint to a canvas or dry surface, pigment was applied to wet plaster that absorbed and sealed the colors as they dried. The mixing of the plaster was akin to alchemy in its difficulty, and Michelangelo required assistants not only to do the tedious preparatory work but also to familiarize him with the process. Suspicious by nature and not trusting any Romans, he'd hired his helpers from his home state of Florence.

Francesco had come with them, though not because he had any artistic expertise. Up until two months ago, Francesco had been a

8

lawyer in the court of Guido del Mare, a powerful Florentine land-owner and his family's longtime patron. Francesco's father, Ricardo, had been the del Mare family's personal priest and trusted humanist adviser for decades. But when Francesco made the mistake of falling in love with Guido's wife, Juliet, Ricardo sent him to Rome to keep him safe while he attempted to soothe their vengeful patron's injured pride. To punish his son for his sin of arrogance, Ricardo had struck a deal with Michelangelo, paying the artist handsomely to take Francesco on as his lowly houseboy.

When Francesco finally reached the Sistine Chapel, he climbed the forty-foot ladder to the scaffolding that spanned the width of the ceiling, where the assistants were waiting for him. Michelangelo was far down at the other end, engrossed in studying the expanse of white ceiling. The scaffold had been Michelangelo's own design, and after six months of work, it was virtually his only accomplishment. It was by anyone's reckoning a brilliant piece of engineering. Michelangelo had built a series of bridges anchored into the walls, the design allowing equal access to all parts of the arched ceiling. The bridges, stepped on either side and flat at the top, reminded Francesco of the bridges he'd seen in Venice when he was seventeen, having just finished his law studies in nearby Padua.

But the Venetian bridges weren't suspended at such terrible heights. Looking down through the cracks between the spans of Michelangelo's scaffold would have been dizzying save for the canvas that had been hung from the underside to catch falling paint and plaster. As Masses were still performed in the chapel, it served to protect the worshippers below, but the canvas also worked as a screen, hiding progress—or lack thereof—from curious onlookers. While he had nothing much yet to show, Michelangelo guarded the ceiling closely, convinced that at any time his enemies would steal his ideas and replicate them elsewhere before he'd completed his project. Little did he know that Francesco amused Raphael and the other artists who gathered at Imperia's brothel with regular reports of his failures.

Today it was obvious that another failure was in the making. Yesterday Michelangelo's first fresco, depicting Noah and the Flood, was finally nearing completion after a month of agonizing work, but today all that remained of the scene were buckets full of colored chunks of plaster.

"Don't ask him what went wrong," whispered Bastiano, one of the assistants, as Francesco handed around the loaves of black bread from his sack and poured cups of wine. "Be glad you weren't here when he arrived this morning. It's a wonder he didn't murder us and tear the entire chapel down. A new priest was saying Mass, and Michelangelo was smashing out the plaster and screaming damnation on the whole of Christendom. I could just picture the faces down below. I'm sure for a moment they thought they were about to suffer every terrible punishment God has ever doled out."

"Did the priest complain to His Holiness?"

"No, but Cardinal Asino and Paride di Grassi did."

Paride di Grassi was the papal master of ceremonies. He looked after the running of the chapel, checking the quality of the incense and candles and the cleanliness of the priests. He enforced silence during services and kept his ears peeled for anything in the priests' sermons that could be construed as heresy. He and Michelangelo had hated each other from the beginning, and while the master of ceremonies made little headway with his objections to the noise and dust, he still complained every chance he got.

Cardinal Asino and Michelangelo's mutual dislike was more material in nature. Asino, like all the cardinals, felt himself a victim of Pope Julius's giddy overspending. Rebuilding the Vatican, his plans for St. Peter's, the construction of new roads, and his military campaigns throughout Italy to expand the Papal States were depleting the Church's resources, and the twenty-five or so cardinals in Rome had seen their allowances sharply reduced.

Francesco had been in Rome long enough to know that a life fit for a cardinal was scarcely less grand than a life fit for a king. It took a household of at least 150 people to run and maintain a palace, and it was hard to know where to cut corners and still be able to live and entertain in a fitting manner. So while Asino resented the Pope's projects and everyone associated with them for robbing him of his luxuries, Michelangelo felt more could be spared for him if these cardinals weren't such expensive parasites on the Church.

"What happened after they complained?" Francesco asked.

"His Holiness came with that boy of his, and Michelangelo had to apologize in front of everyone. If I were di Grassi and Asino, I'd be checking my bed for water snakes." The other assistants snickered as they cast guilty glances toward their master.

"But what was wrong with the scene? It was almost finished."

The assistants all shrugged, clearly annoyed. "Who knows?" Bastiano whined, scratching furiously at his long, tangled hair. "All we do know is that he took one look at it this morning, declared it an abomination, and went berserk. No consideration at all for how long we've been slaving away at it." Bastiano was the most experienced and talented of the lot, but also the most disgruntled. He made no effort to hide his dissatisfaction that, despite all his skill, he was still not only an assistant but a grossly underpaid one at that.

"Stop gossiping like an old woman and bring me my food!" Michelangelo's voice echoed around the cavernous chapel, and

Francesco, rolling his eyes at the assistants, left them and crossed the spans with the two remaining loaves and the wine.

"You're late," Michelangelo grumbled. "What took you so long?" Francesco decided the truth was as good an excuse as any. He didn't give a name or say he knew her, only that a woman's body had been found in the river and he'd stopped to watch.

"Just another whore, I'm sure," Michelangelo said, echoing Francesco's own words. "If I had a ducat for every whore who found herself floating in the Tiber, I'd be a rich man. There are four thousand priests in this city and two whores for every one of them. Not that all their tastes run to women. Rome would be wise to remember the fate of Sodom and Gomorrah."

If Michelangelo had been a friend, Francesco might have warned him against expressing such an opinion of the clergy too loudly, even if it were true. But he wasn't, so Francesco said nothing as he reopened his sack and pulled out the jug of wine. He might also say a few rumors were circulating around Michelangelo's own tastes when it came to desires of the flesh. People had seen his sculptures of strong, virile men and drawn their own conclusions. While sodomy was a crime punishable by burning at the stake, Francesco was of the opinion that in Rome it was largely overlooked. Francesco had already made the acquaintance of the Vatican painter Il Sodoma, "The Sodomite," a man who wore his nickname as openly as his collection of frocks, a collection that Imperia said was the envy of every courtesan in Rome. Still, Francesco doubted Michelangelo shared any of Sodoma's tastes. A follower of the Dominican friar Girolamo Savonarola, Michelangelo was too prudish and afraid of eternal damnation to involve himself with women, let alone men. *It's a pity*, Francesco thought, as he wrenched the cork from the bottle. *It would almost make this misery worth it, to see Michelangelo wearing a fine gown!*

The wine had leaked around the cork and soaked into the remaining loaves of bread, but Michelangelo didn't notice. He didn't care what he ate and took no pleasure in food. However, probably out of spite for Francesco's lateness, he declared himself hungry and took Francesco's loaf too, all the time ranting on about di Grassi and Asino. Francesco only half-listened as Michelangelo chewed the bread, washing each bite down with wine he first swished around his mouth. He gestured like a peasant as he talked, his hair and beard were matted and dirty, and his squashed face was grimy with several days' worth of plaster dust and smeared paint. His ill-fitting clothes were in no better condition, and Francesco thought a swim in the Tiber, as filthy as it was, might do him some good.

"Did you send my letters?" Michelangelo asked, wiping his mouth with his dirty sleeve.

"Letters?" Francesco repeated, momentarily confused. "There was only one on the table, and yes, I sent it."

"There were two letters. One to my father, another to my brother." Having exhausted his venom for the papacy, Michelangelo was back to the one other earthly thing besides his art that consumed him: his family and how they misspent his money.

"I sent the one to your father. I didn't see one to your brother."

"Find it and send it. It is hard to believe that a man of twenty cannot perform the tasks usually entrusted to a boy of ten."

Francesco would have liked to remind him that Ricardo paid Michelangelo well to put up with him, but he couldn't risk Michelangelo sending him back to Florence out of spite. He was in exile and would remain so as long as it pleased his father, not to mention that Guido del Mare still wanted to kill him. So instead, Francesco looked up to where the scene of Noah and the Flood had been chipped away and asked in his most innocent voice, "What happened?"

The response was every bit as apocalyptic as the assistants had warned.

✤　✤　✤

THE house Francesco shared with Michelangelo had once opened onto the Piazza Rusticucci, close to St. Peter's. But long ago, someone had blocked the front door by building a lean-to, and now they were forced to navigate the narrow alley that ran behind the row of houses to the back door in order to get inside.

These additions to buildings were common throughout Rome, a cheap way to add a room for housing animals or to earn some extra rent. Rumor had it Pope Julius would soon issue a decree to have them knocked down, since they made many of the streets impassable to carriage traffic. Francesco didn't care about the carriages, but he did wish he could use their front door. He also wouldn't mind getting rid of the lean-to's current tenants, a soap-maker and his wife. With their hands and faces burned and scarred by lye, they were an evil-looking pair whose nightly arguments could be heard clearly around the edges of the door. Two or three times a week, they collected rancid fat from the butchers and boiled it over a fire in the square, sending up a stink that permeated the entire neighborhood. Today was one of those days, and as Francesco picked his way through the debris-choked back alley, he could still smell it over the vile stench of the outhouses. *In Rome, even the soap is dirty,* he thought, not for the first time.

This row of outhouses, he'd already learned, was favored for the disposal of unwanted infants—those born to the too young, the unwed, slaves, servants, whores, the poor with too many mouths to feed already. His first week in Rome he'd found a newborn girl wrapped in rags, weakly whimpering outside one of the doors, the baby's mother perhaps unable to bring herself to drop her into the filthy hole, where she would quickly, or not so quickly, drown.

He couldn't bear to pass the child by and so, taking her back to the house, laid her on the hearth. *Would have been more merciful to leave it where it was,* Michelangelo had said, looking up from his drawings. *You're only prolonging its misery.* Francesco had known Michelangelo was right. Hell was full of good intentions. The girl was just hours old, already dying from starvation and exposure. *There should be some other recourse . . .* Francesco had said, but he knew not what that could be. They didn't have milk, so he'd mixed some water with wine, but the child breathed her last before he could even get it to her lips.

Today there were no other horrors in the alley but the smell itself, and he'd just about reached the house when he saw Susanna looking over the gate into Michelangelo's yard. Her back was to him, but he knew it was her from the long dark plait and brown dress she held up to keep it from dragging in the filth. Sure she hadn't seen him, he quickly stepped out of sight behind one of the neighboring sheds. Feeling a little foolish for hiding from a girl, he waited there for a moment, watching a lizard climb a sickly-looking lemon tree, before peering around the corner. She was still there. He pulled his head back again and sat down on a stump to wait a few more minutes.

He wasn't in the habit of avoiding her. If it hadn't been for the events of the morning, he would have been happy to see her. Susanna's presence usually meant she had brought him something to eat or come to beat the fleas out of the bedding—and she might even be persuaded to slip into that same bedding with him for a while. But right now, he really just wanted to find that letter and get over to Raphael's. Maybe once he'd passed along the news of Calendula's death, he could shake the image of her mangled face from his mind.

It started to rain again, and he shifted on his seat to avoid the drip from the shed roof while he waited for Susanna to go inside. Francesco had met Susanna on his third or fourth night in Rome after opening the wrong gate, surprising her as she picked her way across the yard from the outhouse. She was the maid to Benvenuto the Silversmith, whose house and workshop consisted of a jumble of sheds adjoining Michelangelo's. Francesco had been out wandering the streets until night had fallen, hoping to avoid Michelangelo, who'd been in a particularly foul mood. When he told her this, she'd laughed. Then, taking him by the hand, she had led him inside the house, where a feeble fire with more smoke than flame burned inside the gargantuan fireplace.

Benvenuto had been in Florence on business, and Francesco said he was from Florence too. She'd given him wine and sympathized with his forced exile. Michelangelo, she claimed, could scare away demons with his scowl. Francesco had drunk her wine and, deciding that even with a blackened front tooth she was not unattractive, had started to tease her, telling her she talked like the gypsy girl who collected rags with her mother near his home. She'd slapped him for the comparison, but he'd caught her hand and, kissing her fingers, explained that he'd always thought the gypsy girl very beautiful, with her dark eyes and hair like a raven. She forgave him, letting him kiss more than her fingers.

He'd spent the night in her bed, waking in the morning with his cheek against her breast. It was infinitely better than the restless nights he spent next to Michelangelo, who snored and kicked him with the boots he often wore to bed. Francesco had made up the bit about the gypsy girl, but he did like Susanna's dark eyes, as, unlike Calendula's, they didn't confuse him or remind him of what he'd lost. Maybe that was why he'd found her so easy to confide in.

His story had made Susanna incredulous. *You fell in love with your employer's wife? And you're still alive? You're a very lucky man.*

As miserable as he was to be separated from the woman he loved, he knew he was indeed lucky to have escaped with his life. If Guido had taken one moment to think that afternoon in Florence, he wouldn't have gone after Francesco himself. He would have sent his bodyguard—a brute of a man named Giovanni, although everyone had long forgotten that and called him Pollo Grosso, "Big Chicken," for the bright red hair that stuck up like a comb from his big square head. If Guido had sicced Pollo Grosso on him, Francesco would have been dead for sure. Because despite his cowardly sounding name, Pollo Grosso was a vicious dog who did his master's bidding without thought or remorse. He was as devoid of feeling as he was of articulate speech, and his only pleasure was to kill.

When Francesco looked out again from his hiding place, Susanna was still peering over the gate. *What's so interesting,* he wondered, *that she'd stand outside in the rain?* Deciding that he wasn't going to wait her out, he walked up behind her.

"What is it?"

"There you are," she said accusingly. "I've been waiting for you. There's a chicken in the yard. I don't know what to do."

"A chicken?" he echoed, looking around for the bird. How odd. He'd just been thinking of Pollo Grosso and now a real chicken appeared. "I would think it obvious. Kill it for my dinner. Where is it?"

Most of the yard was filled with the giant blocks of marble Michelangelo had chosen for the Pope's tomb, blocks he refused to sell just in case His Holiness changed his mind. Now stacked with firewood and covered with vines, they had taken on the quality of a ruined monument, and it was from out of this that a mottled brown-and-white chicken emerged.

"Is a chicken with three legs a good or bad omen?" she asked as the bird blinked up at them.

It was on the tip of Francesco's tongue to tell her she was mad, but she was right. The chicken had three legs: one dead-center and one on either side. It stood on two of these legs, listing to the left while the third leg stuck out from the opposite side, looking like a useless appendage until suddenly it gave a funny little hop before coming to rest on the third and center legs, listing now to the right. Francesco laughed for the first time that day.

He told her omens were superstitious nonsense, but Susanna was insistent, and as the bird did its little dance for them, tilting from one side to the other, she rhymed off a litany of strange sightings. "But what about the two-headed calf born in Tivoli only three days before an earthquake? There can be no other explanation. And last year, just before the Tiber flooded its banks, a dwarf was stillborn not far from here. And the day before that terrible storm swept through Ostia and knocked down my father's house, a bat with red eyes flew down the chimney." She grabbed his sleeve. "They say too the day before the Castel Sant'Angelo bridge collapsed and all those people died, a donkey—"

"Enough," he interrupted, wondering if gypsy blood actually did run in her veins. "Look at it. It's too ridiculous to be anything bad." Indeed, if there were any bad omen that day, it was the discovery of Calendula's body.

"Well, a good omen then," she rebutted. "The day before you came, there was a giant blue moth on the window ledge. That's how I knew when I met you that you were a good man."

"Is that why you slapped my face?"

"That was just to get you to kiss me."

He kissed her now—even considered more, as it would be hours before Michelangelo returned—but all he could think of was Calendula's bludgeoned face and missing finger, and he changed his mind again.

He needed to find Raphael.

"Well, don't kill it then," he said, backing away while trying to maintain the glib tone. "Maybe this will bring you another man. A rich one this time. But you better put the chicken in your yard, because Michelangelo will see it only as an omen he is about to have dinner."

He tried to make his escape, but Susanna insisted on his help in catching it. In any other case, she would have swept the chicken up by the legs and carried it upside down. The third leg made this awkward, however, and Susanna was afraid of hurting it, for fear it could turn against her, changing it from the good omen she was now convinced it was into a bad one. In the end, Francesco opened the gate and propped it open with a rock while Susanna attempted to herd it out with her shawl. Only the bird refused to leave. Instead, it stopped short at the gate and, evading the shawl, flew to the top of the stone wall, where it recommenced its dance, its head bobbing from side to side in time.

"Forget it," Francesco said after two more failed attempts. "I don't have time for this right now. It'll just have to take its chances with Michelangelo. I must find Raphael."

"Now?" Susanna asked, her disappointment palpable. "Come inside with me instead. It's raining, and I have a fire."

He still didn't want to tell her about Calendula. And he wasn't sure why. Maybe because he liked the simple companionship he had with her, the distraction from the dark regrets that found him even in his dreams. But he couldn't avoid the subject forever. She was going to find out, if not from him then from someone else. News traveled fast in Rome. "It's one of the girls from Imperia's, Calendula," he said a little more matter-of-factly than he felt. "She's dead, I'm afraid. I just saw her body pulled from the Tiber."

Susanna looked unfazed, and *just another whore* echoed in his brain. "Was she murdered?" she asked.

"It appears she was."

"I thought so," she said with a certain amount of satisfaction as she attempted to steer him toward the silversmith's yard. "The way she went around flaunting herself and that new ring. It was bound to happen."

He was annoyed with her. He didn't expect grief—he wasn't even sure he felt that himself—but this bordered on glee, the kind reserved for watching your enemies humbled. He had to wonder why. Because she was jealous? "Aren't we the lady then," he said mockingly as he pried her hand from his sleeve.

"More than her," she responded haughtily.

"And I suppose all you do for the wages Benvenuto pays you is mend his clothes and cook his breakfast?"

She aimed a blow at his head, but he was ready for it and dodged it easily, telling her to piss off, which made her even angrier. "Well, at least I *know* now the chicken is a good omen," she yelled as he kicked open his back door.

"Of what?"

"Of one less whore in this city!"

He tried to slam the door, but, because everything in the house

20

leaned, it jammed against the floor instead, leaving a gap just wide enough for a three-legged chicken to slip through. Francesco swore and attempted to shoo it back out again, but it flew onto the shelf over the room's one window and gazed down at him, unperturbed.

Francesco gave up and hunted for Michelangelo's letter. Impatiently, he sifted through sheets of paper filled with sinewy, muscular males he hoped Michelangelo wasn't thinking of painting on the Pope's ceiling. But the letter wasn't there, nor was it on their only chair. The room was dark, which made the hunt even more difficult, but there really weren't too many places to leave a letter other than the table and chair. He looked in the fireplace, wondering if Michelangelo, in a bad moment, had thrown it in there and forgotten about it. Not that it would have burned. The grate hadn't seen a fire for several days, because Michelangelo was engaged in a feud over prices with the man who delivered the wood.

Feeling more irritable with every passing minute, he searched the bed, tearing off the coarse woolen blanket and the tanned hides that covered the straw mattress. He opened the small trunk that held Michelangelo's extra clothes: a pair of breeches, two stained shirts, and a jacket of unusually fine brocade Francesco had never seen him wear. There was nothing among the bottles of tonics and cures for Michelangelo's many ailments, ailments Francesco was sure were all either imagined or feigned, no doubt to add to his image as a long-suffering martyr.

Francesco was at the point of admitting defeat, concluding that Michelangelo had either dreamed up this letter or taken it with him to the chapel that morning, when the chicken started its little dance again on the shelf over the window. It was the only place Francesco hadn't searched, since Michelangelo would have needed the chair to reach it. And why he would have hidden the second letter there if he wanted Francesco to send it was even harder to fathom. But there it was, and he pulled it out from under the chicken just as it gave one of its little hops. "You might have some use after all," he said. "That is, if Michelangelo doesn't lop your head off before I return. The bastard probably hid it up here just so he'd have something to complain about."

Francesco tucked the letter beneath his cloak, fastened his dagger at his waist, and, wishing the chicken good luck, went back out into the rain.

Thankfully, there was no sign of Susanna.

CHAPTER TWO

WITH HIS FEET SQUELCHING IN HIS SODDEN BOOTS AND HOSE, Francesco followed the streets that were by now familiar to him. First came the squalid Piazza Rusticucci with its little church of Santa Caterina. The soapmaker had covered his cauldron of fat with old boards to keep out the rain, but underneath the pot a fire still smoldered. From the Piazza Rusticucci he entered the maze of streets, if they could even be called streets, choked as they were with stalls, lean-tos, and overhead bridges that connected the upper stories of facing houses. Outside the butcher's, three sheep huddled together, waiting their turn for the axe, while a dozen crows fought over the entrails of their brothers. Pope Julius, in an attempt to minimize the foul smells, had decreed that all offal was to be thrown in the Tiber, but the law was largely ignored. Francesco dodged the beggars, the whores, the fishmongers, the rag sellers, the children, and the livestock, all while attempting not to step in the worst of the filth or the ever-deepening puddles.

Just a few minutes away, the Piazza Scossacavalli was significantly more elegant. Here the slaves and servants of the rich who lived in the square's imposing palazzi chased out unwanted business and traffic. But the city couldn't be kept out completely, and a beggar wrapped in rags grabbed Francesco's sleeve, imploring him for a few coins. Francesco shook his head.

"Not even a crust of bread?"

"No," Francesco said as he kept on walking. "I could use some bread myself." And it was true. If it hadn't been for Calendula, he could be with Susanna now. She would not only have bread, but cabbage soup too. She always saved him the marrow from the soup bone, and he thought of it now, longing for its greasy smoothness on his tongue.

In the middle of the square, one of the city's self-proclaimed prophets, a man looking not much wilder and dirtier in appearance than Michelangelo, kept up a tirade against Pope Julius that would no doubt have him dragged away and burned at the stake in no time. "And he may call himself a man of God, but he is the Antichrist, a man of sin, the last leader of fornicating popes and pederastic cardinals, the eighth head of the beast. But God, the true God, will cast him into a bottomless pit, where he shall be consumed by a seven-headed snake, and his cries of agony will be ignored . . ." Yes, Francesco would have liked to wager how long the man would last and even entertained a quick fantasy of Michelangelo being hauled off in a case of mistaken identity.

He rapped on Raphael's door, realizing as he followed the houseboy upstairs that he'd been so preoccupied with the prospect of telling Raphael about Calendula and dreaming of bread and marrow that he'd forgotten to send Michelangelo's letter.

Raphael's studio was a complete contrast to the hovel Francesco shared with Michelangelo. Michelangelo knew this, and it was one of the grudges he bore against his rival. For one thing, the door fit into its frame, and inside, a fire chased off the damp of the day. Even the stink of the city couldn't permeate its walls, and it was here that Francesco was most reminded of the luxuries and comforts of his childhood home outside Florence.

Two tall windows with clear beveled-glass panes opened to the south, and two more to the north. On a sunny day, the room was flooded with light, and even on this very dark one, it was still bright enough to work. Canvasses waiting to be completed leaned against the walls. Francesco caught his reflection in a gilt-framed mirror and almost didn't recognize himself in the rough clothes, his black hair longer than he ever remembered, his face thinner, making his brown eyes seem disproportionately large. An inviting settee covered with velvet cushions faced the fire. A big oak table dominated the center of the room, loaded down at one end with pots of paints, brushes, and boxes of candles, at the other with sheets of paper covered in sketches, their corners held down by heavy books. In contrast to the anguished bodies featured in Michelangelo's drawings, these figures were as graceful and peacefully composed as their creator. In the middle of the table was a jug of wine, and beside it a heel of bread and an end of cheese. Francesco eyed the remains of the midday meal jealously.

"Take it," Raphael said, turning from his easel and wiping his brush with a rag. Francesco thanked him and poured wine into one of the pewter cups on the table, dipping in the heel of bread to soften it. He was grateful for the food and also the diversion. Now that he was here, he didn't know where to start. He took a bite of bread. It was good, as was the cheese. "Alfeo's sister," Raphael said, indicating the houseboy who was stoking the already roaring fire, "brings in cheese from their farm. It is the best in all of Rome, do you not think?"

His mouth full, Francesco could only nod. Alfeo beamed at the praise. Like everything around Raphael, Alfeo, a slim boy of about ten years, could only be described as beautiful, and Francesco knew that by the time Raphael finished the Vatican apartments, Alfeo's cherubic features and dark curls would be reproduced in the face of at least one angel. Francesco handed him his damp cloak, and the boy almost disappeared beneath it as he took it to hang by the fire. It was humbling to think that in Rome he, Francesco, was this boy's equal—a houseboy to an artist. In Florence, as Guido's lawyer, he'd been very much Raphael's equal, if not his superior.

Raphael had lived intermittently in Florence and had once dined with Francesco and his father. Francesco had attempted to introduce Raphael to Guido, but Guido had refused. Infatuated with the work of Leonardo da Vinci, he had failed to recognize the much younger Raphael's genius, an oversight Francesco knew he later regretted. Francesco had sought out Raphael upon his arrival in Rome, catching up with him at Imperia's. It was the same night he'd first met Calendula and been stunned by her resemblance to Juliet. Although Raphael had noticed his shock and confusion, he hadn't pressed him to elaborate, nor did it appear to color his opinion of him. Francesco couldn't help but think his exile here would have been much more pleasant in Raphael's employ, no doubt something his father had taken into consideration when determining his son's punishment.

"You have caught us on a quiet day," Raphael said as Francesco chewed his bread. "My assistants are preparing the walls of the Pope's apartments, a job I am pleased I can leave to others. And how is Michelangelo coming in his work? I can see he is still starving his help."

"Not well," Francesco said. Had his master been anyone else, he would have felt like an informant, but as Michelangelo made no attempts to hide his animosity toward Raphael, he felt no guilt. "He's torn away everything he started and is beginning anew. He is still begging to be allowed to work on the tomb. In the meantime, he writes letter after letter to his father and brothers and sends me to find their way to Florence." He was babbling now. "He never gives me enough money, and I am left to pay the rest out of my own pocket." He pulled the letter out. "See? And I've already sent one today." As he looked at it, he felt even more ridiculous. Just a few months ago, his days were taken up with overseeing the sales of great tracts of land. He'd been paid for his services in pouches of gold, and now he was whining over a few small coins.

Still, Raphael laughed sympathetically and offered him more bread. "It is as if he is determined to make everything so difficult for himself. His Holiness is punishing him not only for his disobedience, but also for his lack of courtly manners. I fear if one behaves like a mannerless peasant, one is treated as such, and only in Heaven is there a disregard for outward appearances. Should he display a little charm and humility along with his genius, not only would he find His Holiness to be more generous, he might even have some friends."

Francesco could only agree. Raphael was a painter, an artist, a position no higher than Michelangelo's, and yet since Raphael's arrival from Florence a few months ago, he had found an exalted place for himself in the papal court while Michelangelo, in his workman's clothes and with his slovenly habits, was still so much the outsider. And while Michelangelo had to beg for every papal ducat, Raphael was a rich man. He lived and worked in these elegant rooms, ate fresh food from the countryside, dressed as well as any of his patrons, and was generous with all his many friends. He was generous too with young artists, and they sought him out, becoming part of his growing circle of admirers. He was in every sense a true courtier.

But these weren't the only reasons Michelangelo despised Raphael. As Raphael picked up a piece of glass and held it up to the feeble light to appreciate its muted colors, Francesco thought no two men could ever look more unalike. While his master was squat, with a face like that of a bulldog kicked too many times, Raphael was tall, with fine handsome features that turned the heads of the most beautiful women in Rome. He had a reputation as a great lover, though Francesco had yet to see evidence of this. Although charming and gracious to everyone he met, and surrounded by people who adored him, Raphael seemed to carry an air of loneliness about him. Perhaps Raphael and Michelangelo had that much in common, though one ranted to Heaven while the other prayed quietly.

Francesco finished the bread and wine and set the cup back on the table. "Now that I have saved you from starvation for another night," Raphael said with a smile, "is there anything else I can help you with? Something must have brought you out on such a day."

Francesco nodded. There was no way out now. "Yes, and it is not good news." He glanced toward Alfeo. "May we speak privately?"

"Of course." Taking the letter and reading the address above the seal, Raphael turned to the boy. "Alfeo, take this to Marcello's. It is for Florence, and he leaves for there in the morning."

Alfeo accepted the letter with a nod as Francesco emptied the purse at his waist. "I hope this will be adequate."

Raphael waved away the money, opening a wooden box on the table and extracting several coins. "Keep them for yourself," he said. He handed the money to Alfeo and told him to use the remainder to buy himself a sausage for his dinner.

Francesco thanked them both and watched Alfeo put on his cloak and make for the door. Sighing, he turned his attention back to Raphael, who was now watching him with a look of concern, lines marring his smooth forehead. "It's Calendula," Francesco began, his voice faltering slightly over her name as he again pictured her mutilated face. "I saw them pull her body from the Tiber this morning. I believe she was murdered. Not that I told the police that. Her finger was missing . . . and so was the amethyst ring. They have taken her body to the mortuary."

"Murdered?" Raphael exclaimed. "Calendula? Marcus's Marigold Madonna? Are you certain?"

"I know what I saw."

Raphael walked to the window overlooking the Piazza Scossacavalli. "This city is a cursed place. Violence finds people here so easily and for so little reason." He was silent for a moment before facing Francesco again. "Does Marcus know?"

Francesco shook his head. "I came to you first. I thought you'd know what to do. And after the other night . . ." He let the words trail away.

"You suspect Marcus did this?"

Francesco shrugged. "I don't know."

Raphael walked back to the table and poured them both cups of wine. He indicated the settee to Francesco, who stretched his legs out in front of him in hopes of drying his wet feet. Raphael took the poker and pushed a log further into the flames. "First of all, you were wise not to tell the police anything. I fear they are more interested in extracting fines and confessions than uncovering the truth." He laid the poker on the hearth and sat in the chair. "But Marcus? It is true he struck her the other night. However, I think he has lived in misery ever since, and so I believe it was an act uncharacteristic for him."

He looked at Francesco, who knew what was coming next: his own uncharacteristic act of that evening, for he was not known as a man of violence. "Do you want to tell me what happened? We were all shocked by Marcus's actions, and I have wondered what might have happened if we had not been there to stop you. A man's skull is no match for a marble fireplace. And to defend Calendula? It is no secret you bore her a great deal of animosity. I have never heard you direct a kind word to her, and yet you do not treat the other women there, who are members of the same profession, with similar disdain. What was it about her that elicited such," he paused, searching for the word, "contempt?"

Francesco stared into the fire, feeling chastised and ashamed. Though when he thought about it, he'd been ashamed all along. He felt foolish too, telling Raphael the truth, but knew he had no choice. "She reminded me of someone else, while at the same time being a complete mockery of her. It made me angry."

"And yet, when Marcus struck her, you came to her defense."

"I don't know what came over me. I was confused. The wine, the heat from the fire . . . For a moment she was . . ." Juliet's name almost escaped his lips. "I'm sorry now for my cruelty to her. I certainly didn't want this to happen."

"And I am sure Marcus even less. We will tell him ourselves. Poor man. He was in love with her but could never take her for a wife. A man like him needs a dowry. And I cannot see him defying his father and marrying so beneath himself. Still, even knowing that, he was very jealous."

"Do you know who gave her that ring?"

Raphael shook his head. "No, but it seems she might have been murdered for it. While I am neither old nor wise, I have learned that in many ways people are simple and do things for uncomplicated reasons. Love, hate, guilt, greed. Calendula was bold, and no doubt flaunted the ring unwisely."

Susanna's words echoed in Francesco's head. *The way she went around flaunting herself and that new ring. It was bound to happen.* Words almost identical to Raphael's, if not as graciously put. But then how did Susanna even know about the ring or that Calendula was flaunting it? He was sure he hadn't told her.

"So you think then it was theft?" Francesco asked. "Just greed?"

"It is as good a place as any to start."

Alfeo returned then, declaring that the letter would be on its way to Florence by morning. Francesco eyed the sausage the boy prepared to roast on the fire and decided to buy one for himself that night with the money he no longer needed to spend sending the letter.

Church bells began tolling for vespers, and Raphael asked Francesco over the din if he would like to come with him to Imperia's.

Francesco nodded and put on his cloak, comparing its woolen simplicity with Raphael's cloak of velvet trimmed with ermine. He'd once had such a cloak, but his father had forbidden him to take it to Rome, insisting that the one he now wore was better suited to his humbled position.

Alfeo held the lamp and led the way down the stairs to the door. Outside, darkness was falling, and the drizzle gave no sign of letting up. They stood for a moment in the open doorway, watching the light rain fall on the square, as Alfeo waited to bolt the door behind them. The damp was insidious, creeping through Francesco's cloak and hose, and despite the warmth of Raphael's fire, his feet were still wet. A nun clearly late for evening prayers ran by, slipping and nearly falling on the greasy stones. There was no sign of the prophet who'd been ranting earlier, and Francesco envisioned him suspended by his elbows between two soldiers, earnestly proclaiming His Holiness's righteousness as he was led away. Or maybe he was merely at home having dinner with a long-suffering wife who secretly wished he'd be led off to the stake so she could have one evening of quiet.

Imperia's house faced Raphael's across the square, and in moments, they were standing before her door. "Tell me," Raphael said as he raised his hand to the knocker. "The woman you were reminded of when you looked at Calendula—is she the reason you are in Rome?"

"Yes," said Francesco without elaborating.

"Do you want me to tell Marcus?" Raphael asked next, and Francesco nodded, as thankful to be relieved of the task as he was not to be pressed further on his past.

The door opened, and they found themselves staring into the chest of one of the near-giants Imperia employed for this duty, their size a warning to anyone who might have come with violence on his mind. Francesco recognized him as the man who supplemented his income by wrestling brown bears at street fairs. He protected Imperia and her girls with the same ferocity. Wherever Calendula had been when she'd met her fate, it hadn't been with this man beside her. The giant recognized them and, uttering a low grunt, stepped aside to let them pass. Francesco followed Raphael along the hallway, laughter and the sound of a lute spilling from the candlelit rooms.

The salon was warm and bright. A fire roared on the hearth, and candlelight made the gold-threaded tapestries and Persian carpets glow. He looked around the room, waiting for Calendula's laughter and a glimpse of her golden hair, but he realized almost in the same instant that he would never hear or see her again, and the memory of her battered face momentarily overwhelmed him with unexpected sadness.

Seated in richly upholstered armchairs in their preferred corner were half a dozen of Raphael's group. They may only have been apprentices and assistants, but Raphael paid them well, and they emulated their master with their fine dress and courtly manners. Legs encased in finely knitted hose stretched languidly in front of them, while their arms, clad in velvet sleeves trimmed with lace cuffs, were draped over the bared shoulders of their favorite girls.

The painter Sodoma had the men laughing with one of his stories. He was as well-known for these as he was for the lascivious drawings he sold on the side, making no secret of the fact that the Roman clergy were among his most enthusiastic buyers. Tonight he was wearing one of his favorite gowns, of vivid aquamarine, and as he talked, he punctuated his story with flutters of a painted fan.

The apprentices and assistants rose when they saw Raphael, and one of them gave up his chair and took another. They greeted Francesco too, though no one was willing to give up his chair for him, so he brought a straight-backed one from beside the fireplace and included himself in the circle. Normally he went straight to the tall glass-fronted bookcase that held Imperia's valuable collection of more than twenty-five books: Greek and Latin classics bound in leather and edged with gold. He caught the enticing aroma of roast chicken, and his thoughts briefly turned to the three-legged chicken and its uncertain fate in Michelangelo's hands, concluding that it was probably safe so long as his master found the bread and pot of cabbage soup on the hearth.

He took the cup of wine Raphael handed him as Sodoma repeated his story for Raphael's benefit. "You told me to seek him out for the burnt sienna I needed. You said he had the best, but you didn't say he also had the largest wife in all of Rome. You must warn me of these things! You know it's difficult for me to maintain my composure and keep from laughing in these situations. But I did my best, though I had to feign a fit of coughing. Then she took me to see her husband, who she said was working on a commission for a very important ambassador. It was a Madonna and Child, and he had taken a chicken, all plucked and ready for the pot, and sat it up on the table. He was using it as a model for the Christ Child!

"I only bought half the pigment I needed because I must go back so I can see the finished painting. For right now, the Madonna—who I tell you is no beauty herself—has a headless chicken in her lap! Drumsticks instead of legs, with the most deformed feet! I was trying to picture Our Savior walking among the masses with legs like a chicken, curing the sick and infirm . . ." Sodoma was laughing too hard now to continue, while Francesco, wondering at the appearance of so many strange chickens in one day, laughed too, as did Raphael, though with the terrible knowledge of Calendula on their minds, their laughter was more subdued than the rest.

Also present was Colombo, a goldsmith whose work was favored by the Pope. He played the lute and, over the preceding six months, had written 182 songs celebrating Calendula's beauty. Francesco had heard many of these, sung to her on evenings not unlike this one, though he was hard-pressed to tell the latest from any of the others. Colombo praised her eyes, which were as blue as the sky or the sea, her hair, golden like wheat or the sun or gold itself, her voice, as melodious as an angel's song, a babbling brook, a meadow lark. *Marcus*, Francesco thought, *won't be the only one to take Calendula's death hard.*

Then there was Dante. He was one of the finest wood-carvers in all of Rome, but with every full moon, he would undergo a transformation and believe himself to have changed form. Ever since Francesco had been in Rome, Dante thought himself to be a bat, coming out only at night, wearing a black-hooded cape. He would still join them, though, crouching on a chair and clutching his cloak around him. He voiced his fears that he would never be human again and was forever doomed to fly by night around the city walls. He hadn't always thought himself a bat. Sodoma had informed Francesco that, for one stretch of the full moon, Dante had imagined himself to be a jar of olive oil. Francesco asked how he'd behaved as a jar of olive oil, and Sodoma laughingly told him it was much the same way as a bat, only instead of crouching on a chair, he kept trying to get on the table. He had also been on other occasions a dog, a chariot, and a coat rack, which Sodoma declared to be his favorite because Dante had stood still for an entire night with Sodoma's cloak hanging over one outstretched arm.

The architect Bramante was missing from Imperia's that night. Like Raphael, he was from Urbino and had been instrumental in convincing Pope Julius to hire his still relatively unknown compatriot to paint the Vatican apartments. Present, though, was Imperia's Sienese lover, Agostino Chigi, whose considerable wealth was in part due to his position as Pope Julius's treasurer. Chigi was building a villa along the Tiber between the Vatican and the district of Trastevere and knew that the best artists to decorate his estate were those gathered around Raphael. In the short time Raphael had been in Rome, he and Chigi had become good friends. It occurred to Francesco that Raphael's connection to the Pope's treasurer had probably helped him secure his generous income, and he marveled not for the first time at how Raphael had such powerful friends and yet the humblest of demeanors.

As was her custom, Imperia came in to greet Raphael. It was clear to everyone that her interest in Raphael was more than professional. Still, Chigi bore him no ill will, for what woman would not be charmed by Raphael? And although Raphael's frequent visits to the brothel had added to the rumors of his virility, Francesco was sure he did not share Imperia's bed, or anyone else's, for that matter. Raphael's pleasure at Imperia's was an aesthetic appreciation of beauty, of which there was no shortage. He sought out models from among her girls, transforming each one of them on the canvas from a prostitute to the Holy Virgin herself, an irony not lost on anyone. Besides, as the smell of roasting chicken reminded Francesco, no one in Rome had a better cook.

This evening, Imperia wore a gown of lavender, cut low over her bosom, with an overcoat and matching sleeves of purple velvet. It was the costume of a noblewoman, not unlike something Francesco had seen Isabella d'Este wear. But an accident of birth had made one a patroness of the arts and the other a whore. Raphael told Imperia affectionately that she grew more beautiful every day. She smiled with pleasure, standing close to his chair while resting one of her fine-boned hands on his shoulder. As she leaned over to kiss his cheek, a wave of her dark hair escaped from its jeweled comb.

Francesco knew they could not delay the news any longer. Imperia had to be told; it was cruel to engage her in witty conversation while in possession of such a horrible truth. Indeed, Raphael stood and was offering his chair to her when Marcus burst into the room.

Marcus was clearly in an anxious state. "Have you seen Calendula?" he demanded breathlessly. "She was to meet me hours ago at my studio. Is she here?" His eyes darted around the room as if she might be hiding in the corners.

"I haven't seen her all day," Imperia said. "I thought she left with you last night."

"It wasn't me. I left by myself." He raked his fingers through his hair. "How about you?" he asked, addressing Raphael. "You were still here when I left. Who did she go with? Did you see him?"

Raphael shook his head. "No, but I do have something to tell you all. I am afraid it is bad news."

Francesco watched Marcus's face carefully as Raphael explained that Calendula's body had been found in the river. He didn't reveal that Francesco had seen her, or the terrible mutilation, saying only that he was very sorry she was dead.

It wasn't Marcus who reacted first but Imperia, who let out a low moan and fainted into Chigi's arms. Dante whimpered and, tucking his head down on his chest, pulled the black cape that served as bat wings over his head, becoming utterly silent and immobile. Colombo, so little color left in his face, let out a gasp and looked as if he might follow Imperia into a faint. He clutched his lute tightly, and Francesco wondered if Calendula's death would staunch the flow of Colombo's songs or unleash a new torrent of them.

Marcus seemed genuinely stunned. *Not the reaction of a guilty man,* Francesco thought. Francesco knew the world was full of good actors—those who could pull off the most convincing of deceptions to cover up the most heinous of crimes—but he didn't think Marcus was one of them. He was a skilled painter but not an imaginative one, and Francesco was sure *The Marigold Madonna* would remain his only masterpiece.

Sodoma had helped Chigi lift Imperia onto the settee and, with his sleeves fluttering wildly, frantically attempted to cool her with his fan.

"How did she die?" Chigi asked quietly.

Raphael's reluctance to answer seemed to draw Marcus out of his stupor. "Answer him, man!" he demanded. "What happened to her?"

Francesco felt it was time to reveal his role. Sooner or later, it would come up. "I saw her," he said carefully, "when the police pulled her from the water."

"You?" Marcus's tone was quiet but accusing. "*You* saw her?"

"She'd been hit over the head—"

"She was murdered? And you think *I* had something to do with it!" Marcus glared at him, his voice shaking, and Francesco wondered if there was going to be a replay of the other night's violence, only this time with Marcus attacking him. There was an uncomfortable shuffling in the room, and Francesco could see a few other curious guests now standing in the doorway, including Cardinal Asino and Paride di Grassi, who had given Michelangelo so much trouble that morning, as well as Michelangelo's assistant Bastiano. Francesco wasn't surprised to see Asino and di Grassi here—Imperia's brothel was as popular with the clergy as it was with artists—but he was surprised to see Bastiano. If Michelangelo knew Bastiano was here, where Raphael and his group gathered—let alone with di Grassi, the bane of his very existence—he would fire him immediately, no matter how much he needed him. The same went for Francesco himself, of course, and Francesco tried to catch Bastiano's eye in a show of solidarity, but the assistant turned away quickly.

Raphael stepped in at this point. "Not at all, Marcus," he said, not quite truthfully. "Francesco came to me to ask what should be done. And the first thing to be done was to tell you as gently as possible."

Marcus's anger dissipated as quickly as it had erupted. He

trusted Raphael, as they all did. "Where is she now?" he asked, sinking onto one of the chairs beside the fireplace, looking as if he were about to cry.

"At the mortuary," Raphael said. "And someone must collect the body without raising any suspicions from the police. I do not think it wise for you to go, Marcus."

"She didn't have a family," Marcus said quietly. "Well, not in Rome. She had a mother and a sister in Sicily."

Imperia had come to her senses and was now sitting up with Chigi's help. He called for wine, and it was brought. As he gently updated her, it almost seemed she would faint again. "I'll collect the body," she said finally. "I thought of her as a sweet younger cousin, and I will say as much. I'll take my father with me. With his connections at the papal court, we'll be safe." Imperia's father was a favored singer with the Sistine Chapel's choir.

"I will pay any fee they ask," Chigi offered, "and for her burial as well."

Imperia thanked him and then asked the question Francesco had expected from Marcus. "Was she still wearing her new ring?"

Francesco shook his head, glancing reflexively at Raphael for help.

"Damn that ring!" Marcus said bitterly. "That's what this is about. She started acting strangely the moment she got it. Who gave it to her? Was it The Turk?" he demanded of Imperia. Francesco could see he wanted to know now more than ever.

"She refused to say. But she was very proud of it. She would not take it off. How sad that maybe she died for it."

"Someone here has to know who gave her that ring!" Marcus insisted. "She must have told someone!" He glared at the spectators gathered in the doorway, and collectively they shrank back. Francesco saw that Asino, di Grassi, and Bastiano were no longer among them.

"Calm yourself, man!" Raphael commanded. It wasn't often that Raphael raised his voice, and Marcus obeyed, stepping back and sinking onto the settee next to Imperia, looking utterly defeated.

So far they'd avoided revealing that the finger was missing along with the ring. Francesco thought this fortunate. It could be a wise idea to hold something back, something only the murderer would know. Still, he should prepare Imperia and spare her the shock of discovery. He would tell her to keep it in confidence.

It was almost an hour before he was able to talk to Imperia alone, an hour in which Colombo, tears running down his cheeks, sang new songs to Calendula's beauty. These were not at all unlike the others he'd sung, only this time in the past tense. Her hair *was* as golden as the sun, her voice *was* as melodious as a lark, and on it went. Marcus slouched on the settee, Sodoma fanned himself, and Dante stayed wrapped in his cloak, though he emerged long enough to eat some roast chicken. Francesco ate hungrily too, grateful now that he wouldn't have to spend his coin on a sausage, and if the evening didn't take on the usual gaiety, at least a measure of normality returned. One of the girls recited a sad poem about a medieval knight who'd lost his love in a raging storm. They listened and then clapped, though not too hard, and Marcus looked like a grieving man should: utterly bereft.

Though Francesco watched for him, there was no further sign of Bastiano. It bothered him that Bastiano had turned away when he tried to catch his eye. He should have been forming an alliance with Francesco. *I won't tell if you don't.* And what was he doing here with Cardinal Asino and Paride di Grassi? He couldn't help but think Bastiano was up to no good.

When he finally found his opportunity to speak with Imperia, she took the news of the missing finger calmly and swore not to tell anyone. She gave him a torch when he left, and he used it to light his way between the large, stately square that was Raphael's world and the small, squalid one that had become his own. It was well after midnight, and the relentless drizzle spluttered in the torch's flame. He checked to make sure his dagger was still at his side and walked as quickly as the choked streets would allow, suppressing the urge to cast glances behind him, knowing that with every backward glance he would grow more suspicious.

It didn't help that he could hear what sounded like wolves in the distance, a yipping and howling that seemed to come from the hills beyond Trastevere. Could they even be inside the walls? He had never known a wolf to carry off anything other than a sheep, but he was sure the local wolves, like everything here, would be bigger and meaner. He imagined them with ribs protruding under matted coats, blood and saliva dripping from gleaming white fangs as they slunk along in the rain. It was, as Raphael had said, a cursed city. *Violence finds people here so easily and for so little reason,* he'd said. People were murdered here every day. Men drew their daggers without provocation. The smallest slight or affront to honor, whether real or imagined, could mean death, and an amethyst ring was as good an excuse for murder as any. Everyone in Rome was a Guido del Mare.

He heard what sounded like footsteps behind him and, pulling out his dagger, reeled around. He swung his torch from side to side, showering the alley with sparks, but saw nothing more than a cat. It dashed in front of him and disappeared over a wall. *A black cat,* he thought, his heart pounding, and chided himself for this lapse into superstition. All cats looked black in the night, and even if it were truly black, it foretold no ill will. Still, he held his torch high, willing himself to see into dark doorways. But nothing else moved, and so he resumed walking, turning into the alley behind Michelangelo's house and disturbing a rat as he carefully navigated the rubble.

From somewhere close by came a dog's anxious bark, followed by the muted wail of a baby. He paused at the gate, looking longingly at the path that would take him to Susanna's bed. He now regretted being harsh with her. It would do him good to stretch out beside her and sleep well into the morning. He couldn't remember ever feeling this tired before, not even that night only a brief two months ago when he had fought Guido del Mare. But that night, his heightened passions and fears had kept him going, and tonight there was nothing but sadness and unease.

Torch still in hand, he could hear Michelangelo's snores even before he pushed open the door. The room was deathly cold and damp. The hearth had not seen a fire for another night, and the cabbage soup pot was now collecting drips from the leaky ceiling. The candle on the table was burned down to a stub, and Francesco could see that Michelangelo had been sketching out a new version of *The Flood*.

In the drawing, naked figures huddled together on a rock, clutching each other as they waited for the rising waters to carry them away. In the middle of the picture, more naked figures clambered toward a capsizing boat, while in the bottom left-hand corner, more heavily muscled people struggled up a mountainside, bringing with them their babies, their elderly, their household belongings. But they wouldn't be safe there, either. They had not been admitted to Noah's ark, and they would soon all die as the waters engulfed them and filled their lungs. The ultimate price for incurring God's wrath. Whatever Michelangelo's reasons for tearing out his original fresco of the scene, this sketch showed that what was to replace it would be infinitely better.

Francesco lifted up the drawing and found another beneath it showing a bearded man straining under the weight of a seemingly lifeless younger man. He traced the outline of the muscled thighs, erotic, beautiful, and frightening in their power. It was as if Michelangelo had taken all the desire he was too prudish to fulfill in life, dipped his brush in it, and spread it across the canvas.

Michelangelo snorted in his sleep. Francesco looked up from the drawings and, raising the torch, saw him lying on his back, hands under his head, with his elbows jutting out. The chicken roosting on the headboard over Francesco's side of the bed appeared to be asleep too, if not snoring. It listed to one side, the unused leg sticking out into the air on the other. Michelangelo rolled over, and Francesco feared the light from the torch might be waking him. But he was soon snoring again, and the chicken did its little hop, changed legs, listed to the opposite side, and shat on Francesco's pillow.

Cursing under his breath, Francesco went back outside and, standing beneath the eaves, where there was some cover from the rain, planted the torch beside him. Above him, the sky was black and heavy, with only the slightest smudge of gray indicating where the full moon was hiding. No light was visible at Susanna's. No light was visible anywhere but for his torch, which fizzled every time a drop of water circumvented the eaves' dubious protection. He wondered what would happen if he knocked on her door. Would he be greeted with kisses or curses? Probably the latter. Maybe he'd just stand here all night in the rain, listening to the wolves howling as if their hearts had been rent in two. Perhaps he could join them, adding his cries to theirs until Heaven took heed of their demands. Wind caught at the rain and whipped it under the eaves and into his eyes. Shivering, he peeled a wet leaf from his cheek and pulled his cloak tighter.

One clear night only a few weeks ago, he'd stood out here with Susanna. A little drunk with the wine he'd bought, he'd placed his arm around her shoulders and pointed out the autumn constellations, the same stars that shone in the Tuscan sky: Cassiopeia, Cepheus, Lyra, Cygnus, Pegasus, Hercules. For a few moments, he'd almost believed it was Juliet beside him. He had looked down, expecting to see starlight in her blue eyes, disappointed to see Susanna's dark eyes looking back at him. But that had been then. He wouldn't be disappointed to see Susanna now.

Scarcely had he thought this when he heard the scrape of a door and footsteps in the yard. She came up beside him, only the leaning fence between them. She was wearing her cloak pulled over her head, one rough hand at her throat, holding it tight. In the feeble light of the torch, he could barely make out her face, with its gypsy eyes.

"Do you hear the wolves?" she asked, ever so timidly for Susanna.

It was a test, he knew, to see if he would speak to her again after their fight this afternoon. Either he would answer her or else she would go back inside and he and his foolish pride would perish in the rain. "So it is wolves," he said. "I thought it must be, but they sound so close to the city."

"Not just close," she said with a relief that obviously had nothing to do with wolves. "They're right inside the city walls." She rested her free hand on the fence close to his side. "His Holiness's armies camp in the hills outside the city. They hunt game there, but they're under orders from His Holiness not to kill the wolves. So now there's no game for the wolves to eat, and they come here and steal livestock."

"Why would the Pope tell the soldiers not to kill wolves?"

"It would be bad luck for Rome."

"*His Holiness* said it would be bad luck? Is it not sinful for a pope to believe in such superstition?"

It may only have been an effect of the flickering torchlight, but he could have sworn Susanna looked frightened. "His Holiness does not sin," she said in a whisper.

He was about to add that this was maybe proof he did, then decided against it. He didn't want a repeat of this afternoon. "You're right," he said in his most contrite tone. "It's me who's sinned. Tell me, though, why it would be bad luck to kill wolves."

"Because the she-wolf is the mother of Rome, of course," she said, as if it were perfectly logical for the descendant of St. Peter and head of the Christian world to worry about appeasing the gods of ancient Rome.

"I see," he said carefully. "Still, superstition aside, isn't it a problem that the wolves steal the livestock? Why not close the city gates?"

She laughed a little as if it were a foolish question. "The walls leak worse than these roofs. There are plenty of holes for wolves to get through. They come inside the sheds and drag the sheep right out from under the farmers' noses. At first, the farmers chased them away with their torches. But the wolves are so hungry they always come back, so now the farmers leave offerings for them. Old sheep and cows and chickens. They tether them to stakes away from their sheds. Then the wolves are happy, and there's no harm to Rome."

Attendite a falsis prophetis, qui veniunt ad vos in vestimentis ovium, intrinsecus autem sunt lupi rapaces . . . Beware of false prophets, which come to you in sheep's clothing, but are inside ravenous wolves. Francesco turned this over in his mind, thinking how a smart enemy of Rome needed no such disguise. Wolves were safe here.

There was a sudden volley of yelps and then complete silence. Francesco suppressed a shudder as he imagined a wolf running back up into the hills, bloodied pieces of sheep hanging from its jaws, a gore-stained piece of hemp rope the only evidence of the sacrifice that had just taken place.

"One night last week, a wolf stole a farmer's baby right out of its cradle." Susanna spoke now in hushed tones.

"I suspect the cradle was conveniently situated," Francesco said, realizing now why the outhouses along the lane had been quiet of late.

"No, it was truly stolen," Susanna whispered earnestly. "And they say that the leader of the wolves is pure white."

Francesco laughed, shaking off his gruesome imaginings. "Is that all? Are you sure they're not werewolves too? There's a full moon under all that cloud."

"Don't make fun of me or I won't let you in."

"Then I won't make fun of you anymore," he said with a sincerity that became truly heartfelt when she opened the gate. "How do you know all this?" he asked, extinguishing the torch in a puddle and following her inside the house.

"They talk of it in the market." She drew off her cloak and, taking his, hung them both over a chair in front of the fire, filling the air with the smell of wet sheep. Two candles burned on the mantle, and although the room was hazy with smoke, it was warm. "If you listen in the market very carefully, you can learn things."

He paused for a moment but decided it was worth the risk. She wouldn't throw him out now. If she did, he would drown in the rain and let the wolves devour his body—anything but go back inside with that man and that chicken. "Is that how you knew Calendula was wearing a new ring? You heard it in the market?" he asked carefully.

"Of course," she said, leading him to the bed. She pulled off his wet boots and set them on the hearth before sitting down beside him. His hose left puddles on the plank floor.

"Did you hear who gave her the ring?"

"No. Though I did hear your name as a possibility. I hear you gave Marcus quite a thrashing when he hit her." She pulled the blankets over him as he protested. "You'd do the same for me, right?" She wasn't looking for an answer, and, although he did have more questions, it was so warm beneath the blankets, Susanna's hands and lips even warmer, he couldn't bring himself to speak up.

And when he did fall asleep, he didn't dream of Calendula or anything else that had happened since he'd arrived in this wretched city. Instead, he dreamed of being a child again, of fields painted with poppies and running half-naked with his little sisters through endless sun-drenched days, gathering summer in their outstretched arms.

CHAPTER THREE

FRANCESCO WAS THE ONLY SON OF RICARDO VENTIMIGLIA, A Florentine priest, and Fiorella Adamo, daughter of a sheep farmer, which made Francesco a bastard. He had two sisters, Angelina and Adriana, who of course were also bastards. They were first christened with the surname of degli Angeli, "of the Angels," soon changed simply to Angeli, making them angels in their own right. It was an early indication that, despite being illegitimate, theirs was to be the most privileged of childhoods.

Ricardo Ventimiglia had been a practical man from the beginning. He was the youngest of three sons of a wealthy landowner, and his vocation had been chosen for him by his father. Ricardo had accepted this with good will and, with his enthusiasm for the arts and sciences, had become a humanist in the del Mare family court, first as the personal priest and adviser of Guido's father, then of Guido himself. When Ricardo's father and two elder brothers died of fevers, Ricardo inherited the family villa just outside Fiesole, in the hills overlooking Florence.

It was a stone farmhouse perched on a hilltop, reached by a winding lane shaded with black-green cypress trees. From the high windows, one could see groves of olive trees, vineyards, fields of wheat, forests, and far below to the red-tiled roofs of Florence. Green shutters were kept closed against the heat of the day and opened to let in the cool breezes of the evening.

It would have been a sin for one man to live in such a house, Ricardo often told his three children, so he invited Fiorella to live with him, not even demanding a dowry as he couldn't marry her anyway, and set her up in charge of the household. She supervised everything from the maintenance of the house to the collection of rents from the tenant farmers.

Fiorella's father had been pleased with the arrangement, willing to overlook its sinfulness in exchange for having rid himself of a daughter without having to part with any of his sheep to make a dowry. In addition, Ricardo saw to it that he found a good price for his wool, until in time he owned his own wool shop. Fiorella, too, was happy and prayed every day to the painting of the Madonna that hung in her bedchamber, thanking the Virgin for her good fortune. Besides her skills as a landowner's "wife," she was remarkably beautiful and a devout mother, refusing to send her babies to a wet nurse and keeping them always at her side. Francesco's earliest memories of her were warm and sweetly scented like the jasmine sachet she kept tucked in her bosom. And after she died, hemorrhaging from a miscarriage when Francesco was eleven, it was the scent of jasmine that brought her back to him.

Ricardo believed in a superior education, even for his daughters, convinced the female sex was almost as intelligent as its male counterpart. And so the trio not only spoke the language of Petrarch and Dante but also French, Latin, and Greek. While his sisters wrote letters in all these languages to their father in exquisite hands, Francesco had learned mathematics and logic as well.

Of course, none of this entered his dream that night. Instead, Francesco heard his sisters calling his name from the graveled path below the classroom window. It must have been a Saturday, when lessons ended early. He looked expectantly at Maestro, not at all surprised to see him dressed in Sodoma's aquamarine gown. Maestro closed the geometry book and waved him away with a flick of his lace-edged handkerchief. *Ah, to be so young and able to run like the wind,* he was saying as Francesco put away his books and instruments. *But then, I was never strong like you and your sisters.* Maestro dabbed his handkerchief at his cheeks, even more heavily rouged in Francesco's dream, as if he were a comic actor playing himself on the stage, with every effeminate gesture exaggerated. *A weakness of the lungs. Still, it did keep me studious.*

Francesco promised to be studious too before running out of the room and along the hall to the great stairs. Chasing him was his sisters' puppy, Bibi, who barked and nipped at his heels before Francesco slid down the banister—something the children were strictly forbidden to do—and flew up onto a cupboard. Francesco took the oak steps two at a time and ran across the cool flagstones of the entrance and out onto the gravel drive, where his sisters waited for him in their matching pink silk gowns with sashes tied behind them in bows so enormous they looked like flamingos ready to take flight.

They didn't have to discuss where they were going and so talked of other things as they half-ran down the hill, Florence shimmering far below them. Angelina, who was eleven, had taken to sighing over Petrarch's lines to Laura, and she quoted him now:

By grief I'm nurtured; and, though tearful, gay;
Death I despise, and life alike I hate:
Such, lady, do you make my wretched state!

She did her best to look wretched as she said them, and Francesco teased her. *You'll have legions of men writing you sonnets. There won't be enough paper in all the country to hold them.*

What about me? asked Adriana, who was only nine. *I want sonnets too.*

And sonnets you shall have, said Francesco, feeling vastly older at almost thirteen. He was going to Padua soon to study law.

But all the paper will be gone, she complained.

Then they'll have to come and sing them under your window at night. There will be so many brave, noble men singing songs to you, they'll use up all the notes in the world.

Adriana thought on this before telling her brother it was impossible to use all the notes in the world, and he replied that he would talk to their father, as she was the one who should be studying logic with Maestro. She laughed and, putting on a high, affected voice, waved an imaginary handkerchief in front of her. *Tell me, Adriana,* she imitated, *Aristotle's ten categories. I would list them myself, but I am afraid it would make me sneeze.* And at that Adriana let out a delicate *Achoo! Achoo!*

A half-dozen tenant farmers were scything hay in a small field. Wearing long, simple tunics with either bare legs or hose worn out at the knees, they bowed low to the ground as the children passed, the sisters giggling and curtsying in return. Francesco could have sworn he spotted Aristotle himself among the farmers, but it turned out to be Bastiano instead, busily painting rainbows across the farmers' noses.

The children crossed terraces planted with grapes, still tiny and green on the vines, past the silver olive trees, down the grassy path through the patch of laughing sunflowers, and lastly through the field of poppies to the copse of trees that overhung the bubbling spring, warm and white with minerals from the rocky ground. Francesco removed his embroidered doublet, pulling at his hose, mindful that his mother (still alive in his dream) would scold him should he tear the knitted fabric, until he was finally down to his linen chemise. His sisters untied their silk sashes and helped each other out of their gowns until they, too, stood in their chemises.

How he wished his dream could have continued this way, drawing on those summer afternoons of swimming in the spring until, happy but tired and hungry, they would dry themselves in the sun before dressing and climbing back up the hill through the long shadows of cypress trees, but here the dream started to go wrong. The spring was gone now, mysteriously dried up, the only sign of it a coating of white mineral dust over gray rock. Above them, the sun was a white, hazy ball, and he wondered what had happened to the trees, now a forest of blackened sticks. He was suddenly very hot, and salty sweat ran down his forehead, stinging his eyes.

They each pulled a bare branch from the trees and were poking among the rocks when Francesco saw a big furry animal. *A wolf,* he thought, going over to it, the rocks scorching his feet, the grass needle-sharp. But it wasn't just any wolf. It was a fearless white dream wolf with a tail of iridescent green and purple stripes. The tail moved. The green and purple stripes shimmered.

What is it, Francesco? Angelina asked.

A wolf, he said. *Stay where you are.* He sensed something evil in the sun's heat. His throat was beginning to burn.

No, we want to see, his sisters said in unison, and they scrambled over the rocks, gasping at the sight of the wolf with its tail striped like a gentleman's hose. And why should he think that, stripes like a gentleman's hose? Whose hose?

Attendite a falsis prophetis . . . Beware of false prophets, which come to you in sheep's clothing, but are inside ravenous wolves, Adriana translated. She carried her stick over her shoulder, and off the end hung a bat with red eyes. The very one that would fly down the chimney of Susanna's father's house before it fell down in the storm.

The wolf regarded them without interest and blinked. *Do wolves blink?* Francesco asked his sisters. They glanced at each other and shrugged.

What's that sticking out the side of its mouth? Adriana asked.

It's a tail, observed Angelina calmly at first, until she guessed the tail's owner. *Oh no!* she shrieked, backing away. *It's Bibi's tail. The wolf has killed Bibi!*

No! said Adriana. *Look. Bibi's tail is still moving. He's still alive. Do something to save him, Francesco!*

But Francesco barely heard them. His eyes followed the green and purple stripes along the rock across the dry grass to where the wolf's tail had now indeed turned into a gentleman's hose. His eyes traveled upward past the enormous codpiece to where the hose met a doublet of purple belonging to a man gazing down at them from a big white horse. But not just any man on a horse, for Francesco knew him. Guido del Mare. And another day in Rome he would tell a policeman it was his own name as they watched the body of a woman with golden hair being pulled from the Tiber.

What are you doing here? Francesco asked. *It's too early.* Blinded by the sun, it was hard to see Guido's face, but he knew it well, or would know it well. He peered beyond the prancing horse to see if Juliet was there with him, playing with the combs in her hair as she was wont to do when she was being coy, but it was impossible to see with the blinding sun.

But Pollo Grosso was there, at Guido's side as always, and in the dream he really was a big chicken, a white one, sitting astride his horse, wearing nothing but his dagger, big orange chicken feet sticking out on either side of the horse. He held the reins with his wings, and his red comb shone brilliantly in the sun.

The problem with you, said Guido to Francesco from high up on his horse, *is you're a boy, not a man.* The light bounced off the steel shaft of the sword he carried in his right hand, while with his left he held the horse's reins. Francesco shielded his eyes with his hand, seeing now the scar that ran from the corner of Guido's eye to the corner of his mouth.

I did that, Francesco said, pointing at the scar.

And a lot of good it did you. Now do what your sisters asked. Save Bibi, you little boy.

I can't. It's too late for Bibi.

The man raised his arm, and the sword hung over them all. Francesco watched it come down, the blade glinting in the sun. Guido would kill the wolf and save Bibi, because Francesco was a cowardly little boy and because he was starting to sneeze and Susanna was shaking him awake . . .

"What were you dreaming, Francesco? One minute you're screaming like you've seen the Devil, and the next moment you're sneezing. You're sick. You're burning up with fever, and you're staying in bed. I'll take Michelangelo his bread this morning."

Francesco sat up. His head felt as if it were made of stone. It was true he had a fever. His throat burned, and even his eyes were hot. His dream was still there, his heart still pounding from the sword swooping through the air.

"I have to get up," he insisted. "I have too much to do."

"You have nothing to do," she scoffed. "Send a letter. Deliver some bread. Drink with Raphael. That's about it."

"No." He sneezed again, the force of it making his head pound in earnest. "I have to go home. To Florence. I have a score to settle. If not, I'm as good as a dead man."

Susanna glared at him. "A dead man? Nonsense. It's just the fever talking. You got all worked up after what happened yesterday and made yourself ill. You can't go home anyway. You're in exile, remember, from trying to settle that foolish score. Honestly, the way you fly off the handle sometimes reminds me of Michelangelo. Maybe you two deserve each other." She put on her brown wool cloak and pulled the hood over her hair. "When I get back, I'll make a plaster for your chest to draw the fluid from your lungs."

She opened the door, and Francesco could see it was still raining. Was it ever going to stop? No wonder he felt so awful. He remembered how cold his feet had been in his wet boots as he stood in the rain and listened to the wolves. No wonder he had dreamed of them. He had to get out of here. Forget Guido del Mare—the rotten weather in this city was going to kill him. Many a man didn't wake from a fever, and he had the sense he might still be close to finding out what the afterlife had in store for him.

"I almost forgot," Susanna said, turning around in the doorway. "There's a rumor going around the city that Michelangelo stabbed someone so he would know how to draw the muscles of a dying man. Is it true, do you think?"

Francesco struggled to sit up, and everything in the room swam around him. "I doubt it, though I don't see any reason not to repeat it. Serve the miserable bastard right. And I'll thank you not to compare me to him again." He was sitting on the edge of the bed now.

"Give me my boots," he demanded, reaching out a hand to where they rested, mud-caked but dry, on the hearth.

Susanna shook her head. He stood up and made a dizzy step toward his boots, but she was too fast for him. She swooped down and, tucking his boots under her arm, disappeared into the rain. He called her name, and then he called her a few other names, and when she didn't answer, he fell back onto the bed. He stared up at the soot-encrusted ceiling beams, images from the previous day now struggling for precedence over the strange dream, questions fighting to form in his boiling brain. "To Hell with it all," he started to say, but he was asleep before the first word escaped his lips, and this time his dreams were even crazier.

✜ ✜ ✜

WHEN he opened his eyes, it was dark. He thought for a moment he had slept the entire day away, but what he believed to be night was only a cloth over his eyes. He pushed it away and found himself looking up into Susanna's face. In the dim light, her black tooth made it look like she had a big gap between her teeth. He could hear the steady dripping of rain into the pail beside the chimney.

"I'm still alive then?" he asked her, surprised that, while his throat was dry, it no longer hurt.

He tried to sit up, but she pushed him down again. "No, you're in Heaven among the angels." She gave him a fierce smile. "If you were going to die, it would have been last night. I was worried you were going to burst into flames and burn the house down, you were so hot. Now lie still while I take the plaster from your chest. Then I'll get you some water."

He did as he was told, waiting until she'd brought him a cup full of water before sitting up. He still felt weak, and his skin was hot and red where the plaster had been, but his fever had abated. "How long have I been asleep?" he asked after draining the second dipper of water.

"It's only afternoon."

He groaned. "I didn't take the bread and wine to Michelangelo. He'll have me hanged."

"Don't worry. I took it over. He asked me if you had any boils. He's terrified you have the plague. Not that he's worried about you. He's just afraid of getting it himself. I assured him you had no boils, only a fever."

"You should have told him I was covered with them."

"He's scared enough. He's drinking some horrible-smelling stuff out of a bottle." She held out a cup of wine and a chunk of bread. "Think you can eat this?"

"Yes. I'm as starved as those wolves last night." He had the faintest memory of something about wolves in his dreams too. His sisters were there, and his mother was still alive, and it was very hot, but that was probably the fever. The bread was almost as soft and white as the bread he'd eaten at Raphael's the day before, much better than the loaf Susanna usually bought. "Did you buy this especially for me?"

She laughed. "You can thank Imperia's cook for that. I don't buy from the Frenchman—his prices are too high. But it's only the best for Imperia and her whores," she said loftily, as if she had completely forgotten a similar statement had started their quarrel of the day before. But Francesco didn't bite this time. He didn't have another fight in him today, and he wasn't going to risk his bed for the night. Besides, she was looking so pleased with herself he would have laughed if he'd had the strength.

"Imperia's cook bought me the bread? Why would she do that?"

"No, silly boy. Imperia's cook was talking to the Frenchman. She bought ten loaves twice the size of this one. Do you want more?" she asked, waving a couple of flies off the small loaf on the table.

He nodded, and she broke off another piece, brought it to him, and sat down on the chest beside the bed. While he doubted she had much to tell him, she was clearly enjoying making him wait. "And you thought she might be talking about Calendula?"

"Of course. Today the market is very busy, though mostly the talk is of the wolves and the rain and whether the Tiber will flood. I didn't hear anything about Calendula, probably because it isn't so strange here to find a prostitute in the river. But then I spotted Imperia's cook chatting with the Frenchman, and I knew if anyone was talking about Calendula it would be her, so I went and stood beside her. When the Frenchman asked me what I wanted, I couldn't say *nothing* and make it look like I was just eavesdropping. So I bought the bread and took so long to find my money in my basket they went back to talking. And a good thing or I would have missed the most important part."

"And what was that?" he asked when it became apparent she was going to make him beg.

"She said Imperia went with her father to get the body, but when she got there, the body was gone. Someone else had already taken it."

"Did she say who?" He was genuinely interested now.

"No. Only that Imperia was crying. The cook says Imperia was very fond of Calendula."

I thought of her as a sweet younger cousin, Imperia had said. He himself had seen little of that sweetness.

He took down his clothes from where they hung by the fire and pulled on his warm shirt. His hose were no longer caked with muddy water, and he assumed Susanna had washed them. He would have thanked her, except he found his purse to be emptied of coins and assumed that was thanks enough. He knew now who had paid for the French baker's expensive bread.

ANY other day, Francesco would have been tempted to go by the Tiber and see just how high it had risen, but by the time he'd reached the square by way of the alley, he was already tired, and the stench was making him nauseated. He pulled his cloak up over his nose, but the wool reeked of dirty sheep, so he pulled it down again and concentrated on sidestepping the most vile-looking of the puddles. At least the soap-maker had given up trying to keep a fire going in the rain, and his cauldron remained covered.

At the first turn, he found his path blocked by the butcher and his very pregnant wife, attempting to lead a donkey loaded down with greasy sacks that no doubt held the remains of one of the sheep he'd seen tied up here the day before. "Tiber's going to flood," the butcher said. "Maybe even tonight. We're going to my cousin's shop on the Capitoline Hill. That is, if I can get this lazy beast to move." He put his shoulder to the donkey's behind and pushed with all his weight while his wife at the head pulled the rope. The animal fell to its knees before staggering up again, and in that way, the couple proceeded down the street. Push. Pull. Fall down. Get up. Push. Pull . . . Lucky for the Christ Child, Mary and Joseph's donkey had been a little more understanding or they would never have made it to the stable. This lowly child would be lucky not to be born in a puddle by the next corner. Only knowing he didn't want to be there if it happened, Francesco wished them best of luck and edged past.

At the brothel, Francesco was met by one of the giants and soon was led up to Imperia's private apartments on the first floor. Dressed this afternoon in soft azure silk, Imperia lounged on a settee placed before the wide windows. "Francesco, I'm glad you came. It has been a most disturbing morning. I sent my maid in search of Raphael, but he's not to be found." He kissed her outstretched hand and could see that her eyes were red with crying. She dabbed at them, staining her Venetian lace handkerchief with rouge. He took the chair next to hers. In the perfumed air, he could smell the filth rising from his boots, the combination threatening to bring bile to his throat. She poured some wine from the decanter at her elbow and handed him the cup. He sipped it gratefully, and the queasiness subsided.

"I fear I already know the cause of your distress. A friend overheard your cook this morning telling the French baker Calendula's body was not at the mortuary when you arrived."

Imperia's faint laugh was tainted with sarcasm. "A servant's discretion is something that cannot be bought at any price. But yes, it's true. My father and I arrived this morning only to be told the body had already been claimed. They were very happy to tell me she had fetched them a good price—far more than the whore was worth alive." She let out a long breath. "We live in a sad world, Francesco."

"It is that," he said resignedly. "Did they say who paid so much?"

"No. They didn't give a name, just that he was fat. I can think of only one person."

"The Turk," Francesco said without hesitation, though he had never met the man. Surprising, really, as The Turk was a frequent visitor to Imperia's and an admirer of Calendula.

She nodded. "Yes. Though I'm still surprised. He came last night after you left. Marcus was not the only one searching for her. The Turk was most distressed. When I broke the news to him, it took both my guards to keep him from destroying my house. As it is, the carpenter has been at work all morning on half the chairs in the salon, and there was a crack in one of the panes of the bookcase. But when he finally calmed down, I told him of my plan to collect the body with my father, and he agreed. Maybe he forgot. Or perhaps he changed his mind."

Francesco was silent for a moment. "Did you tell him about her finger and the missing ring?"

Imperia shook her head. "And it wasn't because you said to keep quiet about it. I was worried it would make his rage even more fearful. I suppose if he took the body, he knows now." She sighed. "At least about the finger. I don't know if he even knew of the ring."

"Marcus thinks The Turk gave her the ring."

"It's not rare to receive gifts from an admirer. The girls usually sell them to the Jews in hopes of raising a dowry or to help their families. And it's no secret The Turk admired her. But had it been from him, I don't think she would have kept it a secret."

"Not even for the pleasure of torturing Marcus?"

"Yes, she did seem to enjoy that. But only with the ring. She didn't behave that way before with him. She always flattered him, as was expected. And I do think she was genuinely fond of Marcus, though perhaps not as fond as he was of her. I think Marcus assumed she would sell the ring and use the money to marry him. He was very hurt when she didn't give it a second of consideration.

Even his father might have been persuaded by a little money, for no one else had made an offer, or so he said. But Calendula wanted more than to be the wife of a craftsman toiling like a servant. She wants . . . or wanted . . . to be a lady. She used to be a noblewoman, you see, albeit a poor one.

"When I questioned her on the night of the incident with Marcus, she told me she wouldn't be here long. She seemed to think there was far more on offer than just the ring. That's why I don't think it was from The Turk. The Turk has a wife. A very rich one, and I don't believe The Turk, as fond as he might have been of Calendula, would want to return his wife's dowry to her, even if he could procure an annulment."

"So someone else?"

"She had many admirers, but I can't think of anyone who has shown her particular attention beyond a few of the clergy, and she wouldn't be leaving here to go with any of them. They cannot take their pleasure in the marriage bed, nor make her a lady."

"And so you're sure none of them gave her the ring?"

"It wouldn't be kept a secret. She seemed to think whoever had given her the ring would marry her. Whoever it was, I'm sure she didn't meet him between these walls. I would know."

Francesco helped himself to more wine. "Have you looked in her room?"

"For what?"

"More gifts. Letters, perhaps. Anything that might indicate this man's identity."

"We can go and look. She didn't read or write, so I wouldn't expect to find letters."

Imperia led him down the hall past two young houseboys carrying steaming pails of water destined for baths. It was siesta time, and the girls were resting and preparing for the evening's entertainments. Through an open door, Francesco glimpsed two naked girls entwined together on the bed. Another, dressed only in a chemise, sat at a dressing table, combing her hair. Smiling invitingly at Francesco, she beckoned him to join the girls on the bed. He smiled back, shaking his head and blushing slightly at their boldness and his own unexpected excitement. He didn't look into any more rooms after that, and the sounds that reached him as he walked by were ordinary enough to subdue him: a request for hot water, a few lines of song, furniture scraping over the floor, the tolling of bells in the square.

Calendula's room was only a few square yards. This was not the room in which she entertained, only the one in which she lived, and if it held any secrets, they weren't forthcoming. A tiny window revealed a warren of tiled roofs, and the room's only furnishings were a narrow bed with plain linen sheets and a dressing table, its stained surface scattered with cheap combs, pins, and pots of face paint. He opened the drawers of the table and found much the same, along with a few handkerchiefs in various states of cleanliness and some ribbons and lengths of lace. He searched for a hidden drawer, but Imperia told him there were none, since all the girls' dressing tables were the same. Francesco wasn't surprised to see a yellow dress quite similar to the one Calendula was discovered in, the spare pair of sleeves hanging on either side, making the garment appear as if it were intended for a woman with four arms. The only other object in the room was a Madonna, poorly executed on wood that had long ago cracked. He touched her faded face, and the paint came off on his finger as readily as the rouge had come off Imperia's cheek. As Imperia suspected, there were no letters, but tucked into the frame of the Madonna was a small piece of paper that was inscribed with one word: "Calendula."

They sat on the edge of the hard bed. Imperia took the paper from his hand and, placing it on her lap, smoothed it as gently as if she were stroking a child's hair. "I wrote this out for her so she would know how her new name looked. She had others, her given names and her married name, but she wanted to forget all that, to start anew. She insisted I call her Calendula, and that's how I came to think of her. You see, Francesco, I didn't just think of her as a younger cousin. She *was* my younger cousin. You're the only one besides my father who knows this."

"Why?"

"It seemed best to keep it that way." Imperia sighed, glancing down at the paper again. "I know you didn't see it, but she could be a sweet girl. At least, that's how I remember her, when we were both young, before she married, before she tried to bear children. That—and this place—hardened her." Imperia faltered, and Francesco was struck at that moment by how much she reminded him of his mother. It was in the tilt of the head, perhaps, or the fine skin, or maybe it was the tone of her voice as she spoke lovingly of Calendula. Or perhaps it was the fleeting scent of jasmine. He wondered if, like his mother, she kept between her breasts a little sachet, one that released its calming scent with every beat of her heart. His mother would have been about the same age as Imperia when she died, and Francesco had a sudden compulsion to lay his head against Imperia's breast and rest it there for a while to see if he could recapture the feeling of his mother's touch. Imperia caught his eye, and he quickly averted his gaze, fearing she would misread what she saw.

"I was much surprised the day I found her sobbing on my doorstep," Imperia continued. "Her husband, who was a cruel man, had thrown her out when she could not bear him a live child, let alone a male one. This is one place where that's an asset for a woman. She had no family to return to. And so she came here, to her next closest kin. I could offer her means to live. She gave herself a new name and insisted I keep her history a secret. If she could have raised a dowry and found someone to take her, I saw no reason anyone should ever know her past. But it no longer matters."

"And if she didn't bear a son for a new husband?"

"She was willing to take that chance." Imperia briefly put her hands over her eyes. "If only I knew who took her body. I wanted so much to bury her in our family vault. I had my father's consent, although he took some convincing. When I reminded him I was no better than she, he relented. But now I would be content just to know she was buried properly and not left for the wolves to tear apart."

"So if The Turk took her body, you would be content with that?"

She nodded, and more of her rouge transferred itself to her handkerchief.

"Then I will go and see The Turk."

"Thank you, Francesco. Tell him you have come on my behalf. He will be sure to see you then." He got up from the bed, but she didn't let him go quite yet. She had, as he'd feared, misinterpreted what she'd seen. "If you want to stay for a while with me, Francesco, I would be pleased."

He didn't know whether she was thinking of her own pleasure or his, or whether this was merely a bartering of services, but he couldn't, not after thinking how much she was like his mother. So instead, he thanked her and, kissing her cheek, stepped past her into the hallway.

He stopped at the salon on the way out, in hopes of finding Raphael. Raphael wasn't there, but the room wasn't empty, either.

Huddled on a chair in the corner was a dark, wobbling shape. Too big for a cat or dog or rat, it made Francesco pause. It was, of course, Dante, waiting for the cover of night to begin his prowls about the city. It was quite surprising that no violence had as yet befallen Dante, given his strange ways.

Francesco was about to move on when out of the black cape appeared a pale face. "Francesco?"

"Yes, it is I."

"Did you find Calendula? Imperia can't find her. She said a fat man took her away."

It suddenly occurred to Francesco that Dante must see a lot of strange things in his nightly prowling. "Do you know who the fat man was?" Francesco asked. "Was it The Turk?"

"He's not The Turk," Dante said. "His name is El Greco. The Greek. They only call him The Turk because he killed real Turks. He took his sword with the rubies in the hilt and killed three hundred Turks with it. And he's not a Greek, either. He's from Naples. And Calendula is not Calendula. She told me. But only I know, and I can't tell. Not the Madonna of the Marigold, either. Only the same beautiful hair as *The Marigold Madonna.* Are you truly Francesco? Or are you someone else too?"

Clearly, Imperia wasn't the only one who knew Calendula had changed her name. No doubt Calendula felt it was harmless to tell Dante, as everything Dante heard became confused in his mind and no one took much stock in anything he said anyway. Dante asked him again if he was really Francesco, and Francesco confirmed he was, though he could have told him he didn't always feel like the same Francesco from Florence. Dante was content, however, with his answer and bade Francesco good night before sinking back into the folds of his black cloak.

The glass-fronted bookcase looked none the worse for The Turk's rage. Not even on close inspection could he tell which pane had been replaced. It held a new volume too, the latest work from Erasmus, a philosopher Francesco greatly admired. He wrote in the purest of Latin, and in Francesco's opinion had well earned his title as the Prince of the Humanists. Had the glass doors not been locked, he would have been tempted to pull the volume out and settle in the corner with it until he had finished.

The giant at the door let him out into the square. He'd taken only a few steps when he heard Imperia calling his name. He turned to see her standing in the doorway, so tiny in her azure gown against the bulk of the giant. She held out something wrapped in cloth, and he went back and took it from her. It was bread.

"Take it. You need to eat, and this is good bread from the Frenchman." He thanked her and handed the cloth back. It was the second time that day he had eaten the Frenchman's bread, and while this time it hadn't cost him money, he felt he might be paying for it all the same.

✟   ✟   ✟

THE rain was holding off, though the skies were heavier and blacker than in Michelangelo's depiction of the Flood. Francesco wondered if the butcher and his wife had made it to the Capitoline Hill or if, as he'd predicted, she'd stopped to give birth along the way. Taking a bite from the loaf, he looked longingly across the square to Raphael's. Although The Turk may not have killed three hundred men with his ruby-encrusted sword, his reputation was not a gentle one, and Raphael might be willing to accompany him. Or even better, he could forget the mission entirely and, with a cup of Raphael's excellent wine, stretch his feet before the fire and discuss other matters. He sighed, telling himself he was a coward, and turned out of the square in the direction of The Turk's. The faster he completed this mission, the faster he could return to Susanna's, where there was sure to be a pot of cabbage soup bubbling on the hearth.

Although he had never been there, he knew The Turk lived above the New Port in the hills close to where Chigi was at work on his villa. Indeed, it was one of Chigi's goals to outdo The Turk in every aspect of the villa's design: its size, its frescoes, its gardens. And when Francesco saw The Turk's palace, he hoped his taste too. He walked up the wide path of crushed gravel between the rows of potted cypresses to doors so large two Trojan horses could have slipped through abreast without difficulty. Francesco pulled a chain that hung to one side, and the door was soon answered by a Moor darker than any Francesco had seen before. He stated his desire to speak to The Turk and stressed he was here on business for Imperia.

The Moor told him to wait and left him standing in the immense atrium. All around him the walls were frescoed with lush scenes of gardens and classical ruins. At the center of the far wall, in between the doors that led to the inner courtyard garden, itself decorated with ancient Roman statuary, was a gigantic depiction of what could only have been The Turk himself. Resplendent as any sultan in rich, jeweled garb, he was surrounded by both male and female slaves of exotic origins presenting him with great platters of fruit and meat, a boar's head with staring black eyes on one, an enormous silvery swordfish on another. As Francesco looked around, real servants came and went through the doors of the atrium, bearing food and linens or baskets and barrels. They were as varied and exotic-looking as the figures that peopled the portrait, and he realized they were slaves too. Francesco knew The Turk controlled not only the boat traffic on the Tiber but also much of the slave trade in Rome. Slaves who started out working on The Turk's ships often ended up as domestic servants for Rome's patrician classes.

It might have been the aftereffects of his illness, but Francesco found himself feeling a little dizzy, as though the painting had taken on life and the people he saw coming and going through the doors were emerging from and reentering the painting itself. He cringed as, out of the corner of his eye, he glimpsed a lion ready to pounce, and was truly confused when two very much alive peacocks of the purest white wandered in from the garden, milled around for a moment, then wandered out again. Still the servants came and went, taking no notice of him until Francesco wondered if they thought him just another addition to the painting.

Nearly a half-hour passed this way, and just when he thought he could bear it no longer, the Moor reappeared. He wasn't alone, but he wasn't with The Turk, either. Cardinal Asino and di Grassi, in their crimson robes, walked ahead of him, their heads tilted toward each other in whispered conversation. Francesco bowed as they passed through the enormous doors, but his presence went unnoticed by either man. What business could they have with The Turk? Perhaps they were only here on a mission for Pope Julius in much the same way he was here on a mission for Imperia. Perhaps this had something to do with the shipping of materials for the new St. Peter's. But as obsessed as the Pope was with his project, sending a cardinal and the master of ceremonies for the Sistine Chapel to order bricks seemed excessive.

Francesco soon forgot them as the Moor led him through the atrium to what he supposed were the offices of The Turk. His wait was not as long this time, and he wondered if he'd been given just long enough to be duly impressed by the wealth of The Turk's eclectic collection. Vases, water pipes, sarcophagi, lamps, all dripping with gilt, jewels, tassels, and beads, filled the room as though it were a warehouse belonging to an eccentric genie. There were so many tapestries and carpets, Francesco had to wonder if there wasn't now a shortage in the Orient. He pictured sultans explaining to their sand-encrusted harems that it could not be helped, as The Turk had taken the last rugs right out from under them and there wasn't another one to be had in the whole Muslim world.

The Turk also had a penchant for strange beasts. Stretched out on a table of some twenty feet and supported by the preserved legs of at least two unfortunate elephants was a stuffed crocodile. Its mouth was propped open with a wooden stake, and Francesco was examining its rows of deadly teeth when what had to be The Turk's voice boomed out from the doorway. "You like my crocodile, I see."

Francesco turned and was a little surprised to see that The Turk wasn't dressed like a sultan, complete with turban, but as a well-dressed nobleman should be, with a brocade doublet in reds and blues. His white muslin sleeves were finished with double layers of fine lace so deep it covered the ends of his fingers. His right hand rested on a cane of black ebony tipped in ivory, its handle of gold an eagle with spread wings. He was also considerably larger than his portrait, the doublet stretching out over an enormous belly, and his legs, housed in gray hose, were like the legs of the elephants that held up the table. "I brought him from Egypt. I killed him myself." He mimed bringing a sword up under his abundant chins. "He came lunging out of the Nile. If I hadn't been fast, I'd have ended up as Turkish delight." He chuckled here, the dark little eyes in his big, bald head expressing genuine mirth, and Francesco

71

knew it wasn't the first time he'd told this joke. Francesco laughed obligingly. He wouldn't have thought The Turk could move with speed, however great the danger. Perhaps his expertise with his sword predated his size. "Have you ever seen a crocodile of such rare dimensions and beauty?" The Turk asked with almost paternal pride. Francesco answered that he had never seen a crocodile until today, other than in drawings.

"Then this is a lucky day for you. I have a man from Egypt who developed his own unique method of preservation. He guts them and stuffs them with special herbs. My hope is to acquire some of the species from the New World. And not just to preserve, like this crocodile, but a live collection to keep in my gardens. I have heard accounts of snakes so large they can swallow a man whole. Imagine that, boy. So big they can swallow a man whole. I should like to see that. But enough of my interests. I understand you are here representing Imperia. Indeed, one of my favorites among God's lovelier creatures. Is there any way I can be of assistance to her?"

"Imperia would like to know if you claimed the body of Calendula this morning."

The Turk looked genuinely puzzled. "I'm confused. It was my understanding that Imperia and her father were to collect the body. Has she changed her mind?"

Francesco didn't realize until now just how fervently he'd hoped this would be simple. But it seemed nothing ever was. "When she went this morning, she was told the body had already been claimed," he explained. "She thought perhaps you had changed your mind."

"No. I was quite happy to leave it to her. A very valuable shipment arrived this morning from the East, and with the Tiber rising so fast, I had to ensure my boats in the port were secure. But surely the police told her who claimed the body?"

"Only that he was a . . . ," Francesco said, thinking quickly, "a well-built man who paid handsomely."

"Then it is understandable she should think it was me. There was a painter here earlier this morning from whom I'd commissioned a portrait of Calendula. He came wanting to buy the painting back but said nothing of this. It was most peculiar. He stoically accepted my refusal to sell it at first, only to go quite mad, shouting that she was to marry him. I had to have my Moor throw him out. Poor besotted soul. I felt sorry for him—until he attacked me. I would suggest that he claimed the body, though I don't think he could be described as 'well-built,' as you so prudently phrased it."

"No, I think not." He hoped the Moor hadn't done Marcus too much harm. "Besotted soul" described him perfectly, but then, wasn't The Turk supposed to be another besotted soul? He seemed to be far less distressed than Imperia had made him out to be. He found it hard to believe this was the same man who, in his grief, had thrown furniture around Imperia's brothel.

"Would you like to see the portrait, boy? It's a remarkable likeness." Of course Francesco would like to see it; in fact, he felt an urgent need to do so. And so he followed The Turk through several more rooms, oblivious now to their riches. *The Marigold Madonna* hung in The Turk's dressing room. He'd draped it in black as if it were the Virgin herself who had just died. "Didn't I tell you it was a remarkable likeness?" The Turk said as he drew back the black curtain, and it was like opening the shutters on a glorious summer's day.

"It is," Francesco whispered, stunned all over again. And not just of Calendula. He used to stare at the painting to summon the memory of Juliet, but now it wasn't Juliet he was trying to summon but Calendula herself, to erase from his mind the image of her being pulled from the Tiber, to remember her face as it had been, in all its beauty.

73

"Have you ever seen hair of such a rare color?"

"No, never," Francesco lied, Calendula's eyes mocking him. There was no reason to tell The Turk about Juliet.

"How that hair fascinated me. How is it that I didn't think to cut a lock of it for myself? The first time Calendula saw the painting, she nearly fainted away. 'What is it, girl?' I asked her. 'You've never looked at yourself in the mirror?' I have several, boy. The biggest mirrors Venice has ever made. But she told me it wasn't that. I told her modesty was for ugly girls and that she could come every day and stare at herself. And so she did."

The Turk continued as Francesco held Calendula's gaze. "I once brought back from the East a very rare tiger. A vicious beast, to be sure, but of the purest white. It died before I reached port and was too far gone to be preserved by my Egyptian. I had to throw it overboard to the sharks. It broke my heart, but *è la vita*—that is life."

Just when Francesco was thinking The Turk's biggest regret seemed to be not having Calendula's body to stuff like that of a tiger or crocodile, The Turk leaned his cane against an ornate ebony chair and, raising his hand, stroked the hair of the portrait. "Bella Calendula, such a rare flower." There was tenderness in his voice, and Francesco recanted some of his cynicism. Maybe The Turk really did feel something for this woman, beyond being just another curio. There had to be another man. A third man. Not The Turk. Not Marcus. Another lover. The mysterious fat man? Was he both Calendula's lover and her killer?

But before these thoughts could fully take shape in Francesco's mind, the deep layers of lace fell away from The Turk's hand, displaying fingers curiously delicate for a man of such size. As The Turk stroked Calendula's hair, Francesco saw what Marcus must have seen.

What must have turned him from stoic acceptance to rage, what had turned everything The Turk said to lies. Francesco swallowed hard, determined not to make the same mistake as Marcus.

He was suddenly aware that The Turk had asked him something and, willing his voice not to waver, he apologized.

"I asked you what you do, boy. Surely you have a master to be getting back to."

Francesco nodded. In other circumstances, the answer had been that he was a humanist lawyer in the court of Guido del Mare. Schooled in Padua from his thirteenth year. A follower of Erasmus. Literate in Italian, Latin, Greek, French, logic, chemistry, astronomy. But none of that existed. Not here. And especially not now. He forced himself to keep looking at the painting. "I'm a houseboy to an artist, sir."

The Turk laughed a little derisively. "A houseboy? At your age? What are you, eighteen?"

"Twenty, sir," Francesco mumbled.

"Twenty? Twenty, you say? By your age, Julius Caesar was the first emperor of Rome."

"You mean Augustus, Caesar's heir," Francesco mumbled on. "Caesar was dictator, but never emperor. Augustus was the first emperor—"

"Never mind," The Turk interrupted him. "You must apprentice as something that will give you a future. A houseboy is fine for a boy of eight, maybe ten. Get a trade and catch a girl with a good dowry. Many a man has launched his fortune with a good dowry. Did it myself. But," he warned, lowering his voice, "watch out for the ones with the golden hair. They'll break your heart."

They did, Francesco thought as The Turk reached up and dropped the black curtain over Calendula, and Francesco saw it again. The ring. Calendula's amethyst ring. And Calendula's face looking up at Marcus with those blue, blue eyes, and Marcus asking, *Who gave you that?*

Someone far richer than you'll ever be, she'd said, and she'd kissed it. And Marcus had struck her, and he, Francesco, had dived across the table, wrestled Marcus to the ground, and smashed his head against the fireplace.

"Yes," The Turk said, still smoothing the black cloth over the portrait. "Such beautiful hair . . . But such is life." He turned to Francesco and was suddenly all bluster again. "You must be tired of listening to the ramblings of a sentimental fool. Come with me. I shall take you to the kitchen and have the cook give you some meat. You have a hungry look about you. Like the wolves up in the hills. You've heard them at night?"

Francesco nodded.

"It makes me laugh. The peasants flee the water and run right into the wolves' jaws. It's a funny world, no? And remember what I said about finding a trade. You'd do well to listen to me." He put one arm around Francesco, the hand with the ring now resting on Francesco's shoulder, and picked up the cane. The cane topped with a gold eagle, its wings spread to form a handle—heavy enough to smash a skull, sharp enough to rip it open.

CHAPTER FOUR

THE SKIES OPENED JUST AS FRANCESCO REACHED ST. PETER'S
Square. The rain swept down the hills from the direction of
The Turk's, a wall of water that advanced with the rage of
an invading barbarian army. He dove for the nearest portico. Running up the steps with the rain at his heels, he reached the
top, slouching against the back wall to catch his breath. The water
poured off the roof with such fury it was like viewing the square
through a waterfall.

On most days, even at this hour, workers still lingered in the
square, but tonight only a few remained. Francesco watched as, bent
against the onslaught, the workers hastily bundled their tools and
scattered, leaving him, as far as he could tell, completely alone. He
wished he could keep going. In another few minutes he could be
beside Susanna's fire. But he couldn't go there. Not yet. Imperia was
waiting for him to tell her whether The Turk had claimed Calendula's body, and he still didn't know what he was going to say.

He could say The Turk hadn't claimed her body and didn't know who had, or he could say he thought The Turk was lying and that not only had he claimed the body, he'd killed her too.

He could already hear Imperia's exclamations of disbelief. *He was most distressed,* she'd said. *When I broke the news to him, it took both my guards to keep him from destroying my house.* And he wasn't sure he had an answer for her. Why, for example, would The Turk go to the trouble of cutting off the finger to make it look like a robbery? Or, for that matter, throw the elaborate scene of grief at Imperia's? Why these elaborate measures to cover his tracks when he was so clearly displaying his guilt by wearing the ring?

And then there was the ring itself. Imperia seemed convinced the ring was not from The Turk but from a secret someone. What if Calendula had flaunted the ring in front of The Turk, telling him it had come from someone richer than even he, someone who was going to marry her? Could The Turk have killed her in a jealous rage, cut off the ring and kept it?

Still, was The Turk one to be jealous? He clearly knew of Marcus's existence. He knew, too, that Calendula was a whore. If he was so fond of Calendula, why leave her at the brothel? Why not take her to his house or another of his properties and keep her there as his mistress, as many a rich man did? The Turk's wife lived in Naples, and was by all reports happy for the distance between them. And surely if anyone was to keep a harem it would be The Turk, so carefully had he cultivated the image of a sultan. Or maybe The Turk had been agreeable to sharing her and only had a problem with losing her permanently, especially to a man much wealthier than himself. Francesco pictured Calendula showing off the ring, taunting him as she had Marcus. *Someone far richer than you'll ever be.* But while Marcus had struck her across the cheek with his hand, The

Turk had struck her with his eagle-topped cane, the golden wings ripping through her face. Had he panicked and cut off her finger to make it look like robbery, only to decide on reflection it was unnecessary? After all, Calendula was only a whore.

Maybe making it look like a robbery hadn't been The Turk's intention at all. He was a collector, and perhaps the ring was more than he could resist. A souvenir of the crime. Still, Francesco found it hard to believe The Turk would mutilate what he found so beautiful. *I once brought back from the East a very rare tiger. A vicious beast, to be sure, but of the purest white. It died before I reached port and was too far gone to be preserved by my Egyptian. I had to throw it overboard to the sharks. It broke my heart, but such is life.* But then again, once her face was bashed in, surely he no longer found her so beautiful.

Francesco felt he was just going around in circles.

Or maybe The Turk stuffing her full of his Egyptian friend's herbs wasn't so farfetched. The Turk had thrown the tiger's body overboard because it was rotten, but Calendula's body would have been fresh. He imagined The Turk taking the missing finger from his pocket and giving it to his Egyptian friend to reattach. Somehow he would be able to repair her face too. If The Turk couldn't have her alive as part of his collection, perhaps he could have her dead. Francesco pictured her propped up in a corner, her eyes replaced with blue glass, her stitched-together face like leather, only the golden hair still radiant in the light.

"Mother of God, Francesco," he said aloud, his voice lost in the pounding rain. "What morbid imaginings!" And it couldn't be true. The Turk had said he regretted not cutting a lock of her hair. Would he say that if he had taken her entire body? And would he have thrown her body in the river in the first place if he'd wanted to keep it? It was only by chance it had been found so soon and not months later in a fishing net far downstream, an unrecognizable horror of rotten flesh.

The rain showed no sign of abating. The square was a lake now, the ground so saturated it could no longer absorb the water, and indeed here and there the water seemed to be boiling up from underneath. It flushed out the rats from their holes, and like the figures in Michelangelo's *Flood*, they scrambled onto the stacks of stone and marble now serving as islands. An especially large one with a scabby tail staggered almost drunkenly up the steps and stopped for a moment to look up at Francesco with its evil little eyes before crossing the portico and disappearing through a chink in the stone. Francesco, who felt he would never get used to Rome's overabundance of rodents, shuddered.

Across the square he could see dim light through a window of what he knew were the Pope's apartments. He imagined His Holiness with his boy at his side, reassuring them both that God had promised Noah that He would never again send a flood to destroy the earth. Why should he think of the boy now? Of course—he was the Christ Child in *The Marigold Madonna*, his hair every bit as golden as Calendula's. Had Marcus approached His Holiness with a request to paint him? The Pope was known to be quite protective of the boy, and Francesco wondered if he might be a nephew or bastard son. He was said to have a daughter somewhere, so why not a son? Though Francesco wouldn't put it past the man to be keeping some enemy's child hostage. He had no idea what the boy's name was. Everyone referred to him as "the Pope's boy."

Francesco could just make out the bulk of the Sistine Chapel, soon to be blocked from view by the new St. Peter's. How was Michelangelo's fresco faring with all this rain? He imagined the fresh plaster darkening with mold and falling to the ground with a damp thud that wouldn't so much as summon an echo. Michelangelo's *Flood*, destroyed by a flood. A fitting end Susanna would see as an omen of something even bigger and more terrible. Maybe not the end of the world, but something close in scale.

Christ! He didn't want to go to Imperia's. In just a few minutes he could be at Susanna's, stripped of his wet clothes, bundled in blankets, and eating the food The Turk's cook had given him. He pulled it out from under his doublet. The wrapping was fragrant with grease, and inside were not one but two very fat roasted legs of pheasant. He held them up to his nose, and his stomach decided the next move. Imperia could wait. There was nothing to be done anyway. Calendula was dead. Her body was gone. It would still be gone in the morning. He would take the food and share it with Susanna. He stored the pheasant back under his doublet and, pointlessly pulling the hood of his cloak over his head, stepped out into the deluge. Yes, he concluded. Imperia could wait until morning. Let her believe the rain had kept him away.

✛   ✛   ✛

IT wasn't until he pulled the gate and it didn't open that he noticed the scarf tying it shut. It was their prearranged signal that the silversmith was home. He kicked the gate and swore. Why tonight of all nights? Now his only recourse was next door with Michelangelo. Maybe he should go to Imperia's after all. But he was soaked through and his teeth were chattering, making him fear a return of fever. Besides, it was too dark to find his way and too wet for a torch. How he wanted to be beneath Susanna's blankets, sharing the roasted fowl. Instead, the silversmith Benvenuto was there, grunting away like an old boar. *Shit.*

He kicked the gate again, then turned to his own door, giving it the usual boot only to have it swing easily inward. Thrown off balance, he lurched into the room and almost landed on Michelangelo's lap. With a piece of charcoal poised over a sheet of paper, Michelangelo didn't flinch at the interruption, and neither did the three-legged chicken, who blinked calmly at Francesco from the other side of the table.

Michelangelo had fresh paper. Expensive, heavy paper and new candles. One was lit, and three new ones lay beside it, the chicken perched next to them as if keeping guard. And there was a fire. It wasn't roaring, but it was a fire nonetheless, and the room felt almost warm. "We have firewood!" Francesco exclaimed as he untied his wet cloak and let it drop to the floor. He felt his spirits lift almost instantly.

"And you're still alive, I see," Michelangelo said, as though the knowledge had ruined his evening. "Your little friend told me it wasn't the plague." Still, he adjusted his chair a bit farther away as if he didn't trust Susanna's diagnosis. He picked up the sheet he was working on and studied for a moment what seemed to Francesco but a series of arcs and lines, before turning it ninety degrees to the right and setting it down again.

Francesco shook his head. "A fever. My mother always warned me against wet feet."

"It's not wet feet," Michelangelo said, looking up at him from his drawings. "It's worms. Worms so small they can't be seen. They live in the swamps. If you swallow them, they make you sick."

Michelangelo's theories, if bizarre, were not peculiar to himself. "You've been reading Varro Reatinus," Francesco said.

"Who?"

"Varro Reatinus. He supported Pompey against Caesar but was pardoned by Caesar and oversaw the library in Rome," Francesco said, thinking how it seemed to be his day to give lessons in Roman history. "He was a great historian, admired by Cicero, and he was also said to have warned against the swamps. He claimed they contained tiny creatures that floated through the air and made men sick."

"Not flying creatures," Michelangelo said, sounding not at all impressed. "Worms. Worms too small to see. He was right about swamps though. And Rome, being nothing but a giant swamp, is full of worms. They get on everything. Here, if you wish to live, it is wise to drink only wine and eat only bread."

Francesco didn't remind him that he'd eaten plenty of Susanna's cabbage soup of late. He doubted Michelangelo could sustain this regimen anyway. He simply put in his mouth whatever was at hand to keep him from starving.

"Wine and bread don't have worms?"

"They're the food and drink of our Savior, so they're safe."

One had to wonder how genius and ignorance could coexist so comfortably within the same person. It was all Francesco could do to stop himself from asking if drinking wine and bread was going to get him nailed to a cross too. But Michelangelo was looking quite pleased with himself, and it was probably a good idea to leave it that way, since Francesco just wanted to get out of his wet boots and hose before his fever returned and eat his roast pheasant in front of the fire. Besides, constantly appealing to reason was a thankless task and best left to his circle of humanist friends—although superstition tugged at even their minds.

"You have a point," Francesco said finally and without sarcasm. "Enough talk of worms. I see you've made the wood seller understand things your way as well."

Michelangelo gave one of his laughs that sounded as if he were choking and poured a few drops of wine on a heel of bread. This he placed before the chicken, who shifted legs before taking a peck. Francesco wasn't sure whether Michelangelo was fattening the bird up or whether he was actually thinking of the chicken's safety from invisible worms. He certainly seemed to be developing an attachment to it in the way some men were attached to their dogs.

"The old cheat came around today and offered a bundle at half price," Michelangelo said. "I told him that didn't change the fact I'd paid full price for green, wet wood and still expected to be reimbursed in full."

"And did he reimburse you?"

Another laugh, more choking than the last. "Of course not. He was here looking for money. Utterly desperate. I paid half price for one bundle, and he left the other two to replace the green wood. Don't burn it all at once. And, oh yes, he repaired the door too."

"I'm surprised the Pope hasn't appointed you his treasurer. You'd squeeze the clergy until they squeaked for mercy. Though I hate to think what you'd pay the painter who replaced you in the chapel." He couldn't be expected to forsake all jabs at Michelangelo. "And where did you get the new paper and candles? Did you shake them out of the wood seller too, or did His Holiness cough up a few coins?"

Michelangelo looked up at him and snarled, "What are you doing here anyway? Why aren't you with your little whore?"

It annoyed him to hear Michelangelo call Susanna a whore, even though he'd occasionally done the same.

"Don't let her hear you say that," Francesco said. "Benvenuto is home."

"Is he?"

"She tied a scarf around the gate. It's our signal."

"In truth? You'd think I'd have heard them at it by now. He usually has a good go at her the minute he comes home. Then again after dinner. Can hear them grunting and squealing right through the wall. Makes it hard for a man to sleep." He turned his paper ninety degrees again, forcing the chicken to hop out of the way. "I don't recall you ever getting such a reaction from her."

Francesco knew Michelangelo was retaliating in kind. He could accept the slight against his manhood—Michelangelo was hardly known for his prowess with women—but the image of the wizened old silversmith on top of Susanna bothered him more than he cared to admit, especially to Michelangelo.

"Don't think you can get a rise out of me, old man. I know what you're up to. And having Benvenuto home is not without its benefits. I was going to share my roast pheasant with her, but now I have it all to myself." He pulled the bundle out from under his doublet and showed it to Michelangelo. "I'd offer you some, but I wouldn't want you to get invisible worms."

Michelangelo bent lower over his paper. "I only hope I get the chance to say I told you so before you die. And pick that cloak up. I'd call the houseboy, but if I recall correctly, that would be you."

"Consider it done," Francesco said, scooping the cloak off the floor and hanging it on a hook beside the fire. He tossed his dagger onto the mantel. "Though I should remind you that my father is paying you quite handsomely. I wouldn't be surprised if, in the end, you'll be paid more for putting up with me than you will for frescoing that whole damned ceiling. So I don't see why I shouldn't be just as much trouble, if not more."

"At least that bloody ceiling doesn't talk back at me."

Francesco pulled his boots off and, draping his hose over them, placed them as close to the flames as he dared. *Really,* he thought, *this isn't turning out to be the worst evening of my life.* A fire, enough roast pheasant to actually fill his belly, and Michelangelo was even in a passable mood, thanks no doubt to his victory over the wood seller and whatever windfall had resulted in candles and paper.

As Michelangelo was occupying the only chair, Francesco sat on the edge of the bed and unwrapped the pheasant. He peeled off a strip of fatty skin encrusted with salt and rosemary and sighed as he took a bite. He was going to have to tell Imperia her cook was no longer the best in Rome.

He dropped the leg back on its wrapping and went to pour himself a cup of wine from the pitcher. Not the usual cheap swill Michelangelo invariably bought. It truly must have been a good day. Maybe that brother of Michelangelo's had finally repaid some of the money he owed. Francesco took another draught before topping his cup up again and sitting back on the bed. The chicken gave another little hop out of the way as Michelangelo turned his paper yet again.

"Where'd you steal the meat?" Michelangelo asked.

"I didn't steal it." He hadn't intended on telling Michelangelo he'd been to The Turk's, but it could be interesting to learn what Michelangelo knew of him; he'd be sure to have an opinion. Francesco took another bite. "The Turk's cook gave it to me," he said as nonchalantly as possible.

Michelangelo looked up sharply. "What were you doing at The Turk's?"

"Just an errand for someone. Nothing important. I saw your friends Paride di Grassi and Cardinal Asino there. What business do they have with The Turk?"

"Don't call them my friends! Not even in jest. And any business they have with The Turk is bound to be trouble. If there's any providence, they'll wind up on the wrong end of his famous sword."

Topping off his cup again, Francesco finished the wine. He was decided on one thing: he would get drunk. Drunk and full of lovely, greasy pheasant. "You don't believe that story about the three hundred men he killed with his sword? He seems like too much of a buffoon for such slaughter."

"He may seem like a buffoon, but if he has business with Asino and di Grassi, that makes him dangerous. With or without a sword, as long as you're under my roof, you're forbidden from seeing any more of him." This warning was delivered with all the stern counsel of a parent, and Francesco couldn't help but laugh.

"I didn't know you cared so much for my skin. In honor of your concern, I'll obey your wishes . . . Papa."

Michelangelo picked up his paper and held it close to his face, as if suddenly nearsighted. "Don't test me, boy. Or I'll feed you to The Turk's crocodile myself." It was a threat, but Francesco was sure that behind the paper, Michelangelo was hiding the slightest smile.

Francesco couldn't help smiling himself and, resuming his seat on the bed, ate slowly and meticulously, picking off every piece of meat and skin and sucking the bones for every last drop of fat before tossing them on the fire. It wasn't until the final bone had hit the flames with a sizzle that he realized what Michelangelo had said.

"How did you know The Turk had a crocodile?"

But Michelangelo didn't answer, as he'd already fallen asleep, the stick of charcoal still in his hand. Francesco was about to blow out the candle when he saw what Michelangelo had been working on. The paper was packed with sketches Francesco recognized as studies for the ancestors of Christ, to be painted on the vertical sections below the vaulted ceilings. He was about to lift the top sheet when he spotted what looked like a medallion of the size put out by the Vatican's mint. Inside a border of leaves and berries was a chicken—a three-legged chicken. Francesco laughed quietly. "Look at that," he said, addressing the bird, who was now perched on the headboard of the bed. "You just might get your portrait on the Pope's ceiling." The bird blinked back.

His benevolent feelings for the bird soon vanished with the discovery of a fresh, slimy spot on his pillow. "Not again," he said, turning the pillow over. "You shit on my pillow again, you stupid bird, and I'll have you for dinner tomorrow, and Michelangelo can find himself another three-legged chicken to model for him."

He'd get Susanna to wash his bedding. That is, if the silversmith had left. What if Benvenuto decided to stay on for a while? He listened carefully, but there wasn't so much as a squeak from the other side of the wall, though he could hear a fight brewing between the soap-maker and his wife. *Christ*, he thought. He sat up and, after putting on his still-damp boots without his hose, went out through the back door, closing it quietly behind him, which was now possible to do.

The rain had subsided to a steady drizzle. A wolf howled and another answered, but it wasn't the incessant yipping of the night before. He shook his head and went to Susanna's gate. The scarf was still tied around it. He gave the gate an angry tug. No light seeped from the house. He was tempted to sneak over the gate and look inside, but of course he wouldn't be able to see anything in the dark. It was a stupid idea anyway. What was he going to do? Give the silversmith a thrashing? Honestly, he was acting like a jealous lover. What did he care? He should be thinking about Juliet. She was the woman he loved, and for all he knew, Guido was having his way with her right now. He closed his eyes and tried to picture this, but instead saw Calendula watching him from the portrait with her mocking eyes.

✦ ✦ ✦

FRANCESCO was awakened twice the next morning, once when Michelangelo threw his boots at him, and again when Susanna pinched his nose. Michelangelo he told to fuck off, but Susanna he caught by the hair and pulled onto the bed.

"What are you doing here?" he asked, barely containing his relief at seeing her again. "Where's Benvenuto?"

"Gone," she said, struggling to sit upright.

Francesco kept his grip on her. "Then there's no reason for you not to linger here with me for a while."

"God in Heaven, is that all men think about? That and food. Let me go," she said, laughing all the same. "I'm just about worn right out."

"But I doubt your wheezy old silversmith did this for you," he said, pulling at the strings of her bodice.

The silversmith clearly hadn't, and she responded generously, leaving Francesco in a much better mood than when he'd started the day.

She'd brought bread and two eggs, and they ate in bed while he told her about his meetings with Imperia and The Turk.

"So now what?" Susanna asked.

"Nothing. I'll tell Imperia what The Turk said, and that'll be the end of it. Even if I don't know why, I'm sure The Turk killed Calendula. But Imperia won't confront The Turk and risk being the next whore pulled from the Tiber." He shook his finger at her. "And no gossiping about this."

"I'm not stupid," she said haughtily. "Besides, I bet Marcus has already gone back to Imperia's and told her everything."

He nodded. "You're probably right. I'm surprised I didn't think of that myself. You're very smart indeed. But I gave Imperia my word I'd be back. Once I do that, I've fulfilled my duty."

"Still, you're a lawyer. Aren't you supposed to want justice?"

"You can't take down The Turk and live to tell of it. Especially if he's protected by the likes of di Grassi and Asino. Justice might be the ideal, but it's not attained easily or safely. And right now, I just want to get out of this city with my skull intact."

"And leave me here all alone."

"You have your silversmith," he said teasingly.

"Stop it," she said, hitting him with a pillow. "You know I have a dowry to raise. I save every coin I can and have it all safely hidden away."

"And do you have someone to marry once you've saved enough coins?"

"Why, should I make you an offer? I'll wash your pillow for you."

"I might be open to an offer," he said with mock seriousness. "Just how much money can you steal from the silversmith? And why don't you have a dowry already? Your father's a farmer. Why doesn't he provide one?"

She sighed impatiently. "He did. I was supposed to marry the miller. He died a week before the wedding, but my father had already given him the dowry."

"Then according to the law, your father can get the money back."

She shook her head. "The son has the money. He said if we went to the law, he would tell them I'd killed his father and he had two witnesses who would testify that I said I would do so."

"But they'd be lying."

"They're friends of the miller's son. But since my father heard me say the same thing, he felt it best not to pursue it further."

"So did you kill him?" he joked.

She laughed. "You silly goose. You think I'd tell you if I did? I'm sorry my father lost his money, but I'm not sorry about the miller. Mean old bastard."

"How did he die?"

"He was kicked in the head by a horse."

"Well, then, you didn't kill him. A horse did."

"His son said I spooked the horse."

"And did you?"

"He was easily spooked and hardly needed my help."

The little witch, he thought. Her eyes as she told him were as sweet and guileless as Juliet's had ever been, but he was certain she'd done it. He'd bet his next meal on it. Though strangely, it didn't worry him. He found himself almost proud of her for not letting herself be pushed around by a brute. A little excited too, but that might be explained by the kisses she was now bestowing beneath the covers.

✤　✤　✤

IT was midmorning before they left the house for Imperia's. Despite the insistent grayness of the day and the dreary nature of their mission, he was in a fine mood. Although it was out of their way, Susanna insisted they first go to the bridge at Castel Sant'Angelo to see how high the Tiber had risen overnight.

At the bridge, they stopped and watched the water swirl through the arches. "How is it on the other side?" Francesco asked a man carrying a pack. His clothes were crusted with mud, and his face was not much cleaner.

"Arenula and the Campo dei Fiori are underwater," he said, sticking his finger in his ear as if to remove the water lodged there. "High as your waist in some spots. Mules sunk up to their tails. Still, not as bad as I've seen it, but when it recedes, there'll be nothing but mud everywhere. And then you know what happens."

"What?"

"Plague. Seen it before. That's why I'm leaving. Not the water, the sickness. You just wait and see. I'm going to my brother's beyond the Aventine Hill. Had to cross here, since I couldn't get any farther. Just hoping I can cross back over at the Cestio Bridge. His Holiness can kiss his new road good-bye, if you ask me. The whole thing's been washed away."

"Where has everyone else gone to?"

"A lot of people moved up to the Capitoline and Palatine hills in the night, before the water got too high, but some wouldn't on account of the wolves. Said they were safer on their roofs." He laughed disdainfully. "That is, until the water washes the houses right out from under them. There'll be bodies in that mud, and lots of them."

Susanna pointed out a dead cow in the river. Bloated up like a ball, it floated on its back, legs sticking straight up as it approached the bridge. The legs snagged momentarily on the arch before the pressure of the water forced the cow down, its hooves scraping against the underside of the bridge. Screaming gulls circled overhead, and Francesco remembered yet again Calendula's body being pulled from that same river, the policemen turning it over to reveal her mutilated face, a seagull grabbing at her hand. Was that only two mornings ago?

The man laughed, revealing a mouth full of black stumps for teeth. "That one looks like it's been dead for a while. When I was a boy, my brother and I found one all puffed up like that in a field. He stuck a knife into its belly, and the stink came rushing out of the hole so fast it whistled louder than the Devil playing the pipes. Made my brother fall to the ground, the smell was so bad. He got a good whipping for that one. Must remember to tell that one to his wife when I see her." He left them then, still laughing.

"He'll still be laughing when he arrives at his brother's," Francesco said.

"I didn't know the Devil played the pipes," Susanna said.

"Neither did I, but I think men give the Devil whatever attributes they want."

"You're talking foolishness again," Susanna said, giving him a quick swat. "I'm sure the Devil does whatever he likes."

Francesco held his arm and howled in mock pain, earning another swat for his teasing. He really didn't know why being with this silly girl had put him in such a fine mood. After all, nothing about his situation had changed. Instead of pleasant evenings sitting by Imperia's fire, talking with Raphael and his circle, he now seemed to be on an impossible mission to make sense of a prostitute's death.

There was no question of Susanna entering Imperia's by the front door with him, but she could go through the servants' door and mingle with the kitchen staff with no harm to her reputation. "The kitchen is almost as good as the market for gossip," she told him. "You watch. I'll be wiser than you when we leave here."

Francesco found Imperia as he had yesterday, stretched out on the settee in her azure silk, her feet in matching embroidered slippers resting on an ottoman. But today she wasn't alone, and he greeted Raphael, surprised to find him here at such an early hour. "Come in, Francesco," Imperia said. "I was just about to send someone for you." She removed her feet from the ottoman and gestured for him to sit before pouring a cup of wine from the decanter. A greenish yellow songbird warbled cheerfully in a small cage. It hadn't been there yesterday. A gift from a client, perhaps?

Francesco could see Imperia had been crying, and he felt guilty for not having come the night before as promised. "I'm sorry I didn't come earlier. It was late when I left The Turk's yesterday, and the rain—" The excuse sounded feeble even to his own ears, and he was grateful to Imperia for raising a hand to stop him.

"There's no need for apologies," she said. "What did you learn from The Turk? Please tell me he has Calendula's body."

Francesco looked to Raphael, feeling guiltier still, but there was no condemnation in Raphael's face. "I am sorry this fell to you, Francesco. I was kept occupied at the Vatican yesterday."

"I wished to be of help. I would have come earlier, but I was sure Marcus would have already told you. He had left The Turk's not long before I arrived . . . or rather, The Turk had thrown him out."

"Thrown him out?" Imperia looked alarmed.

"Marcus had gone to buy back his painting. The Turk said Marcus took his refusal to sell it quite calmly at first but then became agitated and attacked The Turk. He had his men remove Marcus from the house. He said they didn't hurt Marcus, though."

"And you thought he would come here?"

Francesco nodded, knowing that until Susanna had suggested this, it hadn't occurred to him at all. But it did make sense for Marcus to seek out the people who knew Calendula and tell them what he'd learned. Indeed, now convinced of this, he started to worry about the man.

"Is there something you are reluctant to tell us?" Raphael asked. "It does not surprise me that Marcus would be very upset he could not have the painting back. He came to me about it, and I advised against him going. I worried such a thing would happen."

Francesco took a draught of wine. "It's not that. He seems to have initially taken The Turk's refusal to sell in good stride. Though I can only give you The Turk's version of events."

"And you have reason to doubt them?" Raphael asked.

"I'm afraid so, and it is why I delayed coming here." He looked at Imperia, his guilt resurfacing. "Please believe it was your feelings and safety I was worried about."

"I want only the truth, Francesco. Please tell me what happened and put me out of my misery. Did The Turk claim Calendula's body?"

"He says no. And he seemed very surprised to be asked. He said he was happy to leave it to you and your father, as he was very busy."

"Then who took it?"

"He said he didn't know. That was when he mentioned Marcus's visit. He discounted Marcus as the man who took her body, as he didn't fit the description you were given, but offered no other suggestion as to who might have. I was ready to believe it was perhaps another of her lovers. The one who gave her the ring, maybe. Perhaps this mysterious lover is the fat man." Pausing here, he took another drink of wine. Imperia looked as though she was about to cry again, and the whole time the bird in the cage trilled its merry song. *Singing, singing like the village idiot while his home burned,* Francesco thought. Or was it more like Nero singing while Rome burned?

"I would have gone away believing this," he continued, "until I saw what I'm sure so angered Marcus." He feared putting in a dramatic pause, like an actor in a Greek melodrama, but it was happening anyway. "I'm afraid The Turk was wearing the amethyst ring. Calendula's ring."

95

Imperia let out a cry, and Raphael rushed to her side. "Are you sure, man? The very same ring?"

Francesco nodded.

"But what does it mean?" Imperia implored. "Surely, The Turk didn't . . ."

"I've been over many possibilities in my mind, but in the end all I know is this: The Turk was wearing Calendula's ring. The rest is speculation. Perhaps she flaunted the ring to The Turk, as she had with Marcus, and The Turk killed her in a fury, taking the ring as some kind of spoils before throwing her body in the river."

"But why would he wear the ring," Imperia asked, "when it so clearly marks him as the murderer?"

"Arrogance," Raphael said bluntly. "What can we do? He is wealthy and has friends in very high places. He makes a point of seeking out the most rich and powerful in the Church and among the Roman establishment. I know not what favors he performs for them, but I am sure he can rely on them being returned."

"Oh, I can't believe The Turk would kill her," Imperia said. "He seemed generous in his love of Calendula and so genuinely upset when he learned of her death. But he must have claimed the body, although I don't know why he would lie about it. If only I knew she was buried like a Christian."

Francesco nodded. "It's a strange thing to lie about, since claiming the body doesn't point to guilt, whereas wearing the ring does." He said nothing about his strange theory. If she was now part of The Turk's collection, there would be no Christian burial.

"We may never know," Raphael said. "And what troubles me most right now is Marcus. You know how rashly he can behave. While you have wisely weighed out the possibilities and dangers, you can be sure Marcus has not."

"You're right, Raphael," Imperia said, dabbing her eyes with a lace handkerchief so dainty it seemed designed for ladies who wept but a single tear. "And you, Francesco, were right to think he would probably have come here. He consults me—" She broke off, her face suddenly lighting up. "Dante! Dante has seen him. How could I have forgotten? It's just, with Dante, one's never sure what's real. The poor man. He seems convinced he'll stay a bat forever."

"Did he say where he saw Marcus?" Francesco asked.

"He said so many things. But he is here. In the salon. He won't go out during the day, and he won't go home, either. He says it is too light. I don't know how long I can let this go on, but today it's perhaps fortunate."

They went down to the salon by the great staircase, avoiding, to Francesco's relief, the rooms the girls shared. That, of course, made him think of Susanna, and he imagined her growing impatient. In the feeble light from the windows, the salon seemed empty, but Dante was still there, huddled on his chair, his black cloak pulled over his head.

"Dante," Imperia said gently, "could you speak with us, please?"

Slowly, Dante poked his head out of his cloak. Francesco thought he couldn't have looked more despondent if he'd been Prometheus, just informed that every morning for eternity his liver was to be pecked out by an eagle.

"Just call me the bat man," he said sorrowfully. "I'll never be Dante again. Don't make me go away, Imperia."

"I'm not going to make you go away," she said with a sigh. "Do you remember this morning? You said you saw Marcus. Where did you see him?"

If possible, Dante looked even more distressed. "No. I was to say I didn't see Marcus. That is what he told me to say. You didn't see me. But I said, I do see you. I'm a bat, and bats see in the dark. They must, because they always fly in the night, and they don't fly into things. I didn't fly into Marcus."

"Where were you when this happened?" Raphael asked gently.

"Oh no, this is a trick. It's another trick to make me tell you. I cannot fly in the rain, and it rained and rained and rained, and my wings were too heavy to fly. He said Calendula was there on the ship. He tried to go on it. I'll kill you! I'll kill you! He took her there."

"Who took her there?" Francesco asked. "The Turk?"

"He is not The Turk." Dante was talking at a furious pace now. "He is The Greek. The Turk is The Greek, and Calendula is not Calendula. The Madonna is not Calendula. But Marcus paints Calendula, and it is not Calendula anymore, it is the Madonna. She was making a fool of him with her yellow hair. Stop! Stop! Or I'll kill you! I'll kill you!"

"We will not let Marcus kill you," Raphael said kindly. "He says things he does not mean. Did you go on the ship? Was it in the port?"

Dante shook his head and started to cry. The eagle was circling ever nearer, his eye firmly fixed on his morning feast of liver.

✠   ✠   ✠

"THERE you are," Susanna said. "I was about to get one of those giants to drag you out."

"It was more complicated than I thought," Francesco said. "Marcus hasn't been here. But Dante says he saw him at the port. If any of what Dante says can be believed, Marcus seemed to think

The Turk had Calendula's body on his ship. He might have gone aboard to look."

"So we're going to the port now, are we?"

"Well, I am. Don't you have to return to your silversmith and cook his dinner?" She looked at him as if he were speaking to her in a foreign tongue, and Francesco felt a twinge of fear for the man he had been ready to thump the night before. "Did he get kicked by a horse?" Perhaps that's why it had been so quiet.

"What? Kicked by a horse? Like the miller? I didn't kill him, if that's what you're asking," she replied indignantly. "He's gone on to Ostia to his family, to avoid the flooding."

"Well, then, come to the port if you wish," he said, not quite sure if he believed her.

"Of course I'm going to the port with you." She pulled an apple from her pocket and handed it to him, along with a piece of bread and a slab of cheese. "I took these when the cook wasn't looking."

"You know what Dante—the writer Dante, not the bat man— said Hell had in store for thieves, don't you?"

She snickered. "No. But rich or poor, that's where we're all going. Because everyone's a thief in some way. You tried to steal a man's wife."

He took a bite of his apple and laughed. She was full of a peasant's wisdom today, though hopefully, for the silversmith's sake, not a peasant's violence. "That's not quite how it happened, but I'm grateful all the same for the food." The cheese was excellent, a variety made of sheep's milk, he guessed. "But although you found good food, it would seem I'm the wiser for our visit."

"All you've learned is Marcus never came here and might be missing. Or, according to a man who thinks he's a bat, he might have been to the port because he thought The Turk had Calendula's body on his boat."

"Then what have you learned, my wise little friend?" he asked, tossing the apple core into the overflowing gutter.

"I've learned something you might not want to believe." She looked around quickly, as if to make sure there were no eavesdroppers, but no one seemed interested in them. "It is Imperia. The cook said she and Calendula were always fighting and that it started when Calendula first saw the finished painting. The cook said *The Marigold Madonna* was bad luck. It made Calendula go strange, and she screamed at Imperia that she was a liar and she hated her. They had some fearful fights about that ring too."

"What about the ring?"

"The cook says whenever one of the girls gets a gift, they have to share it with Imperia. Usually Imperia takes the gift to a certain Jew near the Campo dei Fiori. She gives some of the money back to the girl and keeps the rest for herself. Sometimes the girls use the money toward a dowry or to help their families. Only Calendula wouldn't agree to sell that ring. The night she got killed, they had a big fight, and Imperia told her she was too much trouble and ordered her out of the house. Calendula told her she didn't care, since she was going to be a lady again." Susanna threw her apple core to a pig rooting in the street. "No wonder she was murdered," she said as they continued on. "Out at night by herself with that ring."

Francesco was stunned. Why had Imperia not told him she had ordered Calendula from the house? He thought back to the night when Marcus kept asking who Calendula had left with. But she hadn't left with anyone—she had left alone. Was some of the grief Imperia now felt really guilt for having put Calendula in the murderer's path? Or a lament that she'd never received her share of the ring? *No.* She may have wanted her share, but he didn't believe her to be that cold.

"I told you I'd learn more than you," Susanna concluded triumphantly.

He was about to commend her, but the reappearance of the dead cow at the Cestio Bridge diverted their attention. "Look, it's been waiting for us," Susanna said with a laugh. Still on its back, with its legs sticking up absurdly, the cow seemed somehow a suitable companion on this mission. A couple of boys aimed stones at it from the bank, cheering every time they hit their target. They all kept pace with the carcass to the port, where it became snagged in the lines of a barge and bobbed there like a giant buoy, immediately attracting the attention of the seagulls that circled overhead.

"If we hang around here, you'll get to know what the Devil playing his pipes sounds like," Francesco said as the boys scrambled aboard the barge for a closer look.

The flooding had thrown the port into a frantic state. Crews stood by, not knowing whether to load or unload. Some men tied lines, then untied and retied them again, while others pulled small craft from the water and then put them in again. Yet more men rowed boats to one side of the river and back again for no apparent purpose. No one seemed to know whether the worst of the flooding was over and they could get back to normal, or whether the worst was yet to come and, if so, what they should do about it. Men stood in groups, passing around jugs of wine, ignoring the brazen prostitutes who worked the wharf. As the men argued, they pointed upstream, then downstream, then back again to the sky, every bit as gray and heavy as the last time they'd pointed at it.

Conturbatio super conturbationem veniet, et auditus super auditum . . . Calamity will come upon calamity, and rumor shall follow upon rumor. A promise of destruction by God so great no man would fail to know who is The Lord God. The words from the book of

Ezekiel came to Francesco as he listened to the men. Washed-out bridges, flooded roads, boats stranded on sandbars that hadn't been there before, drowned horses, cattle, sheep. And omens, omens everywhere. A dead cat on a windowsill, a gathering of crows over St. Peter's Square, a three-eyed fish, and, of course, the wolves, the starving wolves. Dozens of them, hundreds of them, a wolf to pick off every Roman fleeing for the hills. And at their head a white wolf, bigger than any other, that was said to walk on its hind legs and talk in a strange language no one had heard for thousands of years.

"It's like the market," Susanna said close to his ear, as a water snake slipped off the dock into the river. "You just have to listen." But no one mentioned Marcus, The Turk's ship, or the important shipment The Turk had alluded to.

Francesco swore as a clawlike hand encrusted with sores and dirt emerged from what appeared to be nothing but a mound of filthy sacking and grabbed at his leg. Sickened, he shook it off and yanked Susanna away. "Oh, how horrible!" she exclaimed, recoiling further as the moaning mound began to crawl slowly toward them on all fours. Like some sort of monster, its face was wrapped in rags, and only two lidless, staring eyes were visible.

Of course, it wasn't a monster. Francesco knew it was a woman, or had been before disease had eaten away even her eyelids. *Et qui in civitate, pestilentia et fame devorabuntur . . . And here in the city, pestilence and hunger shall devour them.* Francesco had heard tell of this, a new and disfiguring disease spreading through the port's prostitutes. It had made its way here from Naples, spread, some said, by French sailors. Covered with oozing sores that in the final stages of death ate the very flesh from their faces, its victims had been shunned by even the most undiscriminating sailors. Now, like this woman, they were reduced to begging along the docks, their faces bound in rags to hide the rotting flesh. Hardly recognizable as human, they evoked so much revulsion they were likelier to be clubbed and pushed into the river than helped. As he and Susanna retreated along the docks, Francesco couldn't help but think this was the merciful thing to do, though he wouldn't be the one to do it.

Susanna begged him to leave, but Francesco reminded her they were here to find Marcus and did his best to distract her with a story about the time he and his sisters filled his maestro's desk with dozens of lizards from the garden. It worked, and by the time they stopped to watch the unloading of a ship, she was laughing.

"You think that's the one?" Susanna asked. It was by far the largest ship in the port, a seagoing vessel, and Francesco was amazed it had managed to navigate the Tiber, so notorious for trapping much smaller boats than this in its shifting sands. A sole dockworker kept watch over bolts of cloth and bales of spices that did their best to compete with the smell of the river. If not a large cargo, it certainly seemed to be the most valuable they'd seen. They did their best to seem casually curious, sniffing at the sacks of spices, fingering the cloth, until the man asked what they wanted.

"I want to buy some cardamom," Francesco said. "Who's the owner of the ship?" The man shrugged, saying he was damned if he knew, but if they gave him the money, he'd make sure it got to him. Tall, thin, unshaven, already hunched from carrying too many heavy loads, he was one of those weedy-looking dockworkers who unloaded ships for enough to buy their next meal.

Had Francesco actually wanted cardamom and not the ship own-er's name, he would have given the dockworker the money and not cared if he pocketed it for himself, but the cardamom on its own was useless to him, so he told the man he'd changed his mind. He would have liked to buy the bolt of blue cloth Susanna was eyeing longingly, but he had only enough money for the day's wine and bread.

The next ship was a heavily guarded barge loaded with wooden poles. "Speculators," Susanna said. "They know the poles will be worth even more after the floods."

Francesco was ready to give up, buy some food, and call it a day. Marcus clearly wasn't here. But suddenly there was a commotion on the wharf, much bowing and removing of hats. All eyes were on the stone arch that marked the entrance to the port. Catching Susanna's sleeve, Francesco quickly looked around for a hiding place and pulled her inside the open door of a shed. Satisfied that they were alone, Francesco shut the door, leaving a gap just wide enough to give them a clear view.

"We're standing in horseshit," Susanna complained, hiking her already filthy hems over her ankles. "I'll scream if I see a rat."

"No, you won't. Your house is full of rats. They reenact the storming of Northern Italy by Hannibal every night under your bed. And over it too, believing it to be the Alps. We're only lucky they're not riding elephants."

"Then I'll scream if I see another woman like that one out there."

"I will too if that happens," he said, taking her hand as much to comfort himself as her.

She squeezed his hand and kissed his cheek. "Silly boy. I was only teasing. But don't worry. I'll protect you."

"Be quiet," he said, holding on to her hand. "I don't want The Turk to think I'm spying on him."

"Well, you are," Susanna said. "Except I don't think that's The Turk. They're acting like it's His Holiness himself."

She was right. It wasn't The Turk, but it wasn't Pope Julius, either. It was Cardinal Asino and Paride di Grassi in their scarlet robes, just as they'd looked when he'd met them at The Turk's the day before. They must have arrived by carriage, since the hems of their robes were unsullied.

They stopped at the ship where Francesco and Susanna had inquired about the cardamom, but they didn't seem interested in the cloth and spices on the wharf. Instead, the boat's captain came out on deck, and after Asino and di Grassi cast glances around, they went up the plank to meet him.

"I bet they wish they weren't so conspicuous," Francesco whispered, though there was no chance of them being overheard.

"No point in becoming a cardinal if no one knows it," Susanna said with more of her peasant wisdom.

Still, di Grassi and Asino didn't stay long on the ship's deck. They exchanged a few words with the captain before disappearing below. The dockworker they'd spoken to earlier stood guard on the deck, while on the wharf the cloth and spices sat unattended. An urchin dragging his club foot behind him attempted to carry one of the sacks away, but the dockworker saw him before he got far and aimed a wine jug at him. It shattered on the wharf next to the boy, shards of pottery flying in all directions. The boy dropped the sack and limped off, looking more startled than hurt, though surely he'd been struck.

Di Grassi and Asino didn't linger below deck any longer than they'd lingered above, and they were soon back on the wharf, walking away without so much as a backward glance.

"Well, that's a relief. I was worried we'd be here all day," said Susanna. They waited until di Grassi and Asino were out of sight before returning to the ship.

"I think I'll take some of that cardamom after all," Francesco said to the dockworker, pulling a coin from his pouch. He held it up, already grieving the wine he would no longer be able to afford, and nodded in the direction of the port entrance. "What did they want?" he asked, thinking such a question could hardly sound suspicious. Surely everyone was curious.

The man looked up, scanning the ship's decks. "Damned if I know," he said. "Got slaves, mostly. You're not the first person poking around here."

"Who else?" Francesco held up another coin. There went his bread.

The dockworker shrugged. "Haven't a clue. Wasn't here. They said he was prowling around last night, yelling bloody murder." He looked around him before handing Francesco a sack the size of a loaf of bread. "Take some fucking cardamom," he said in a voice edged with contempt, though for what or whom wasn't clear. "And that bolt of blue cloth your lady's been eyeing. If you still want to know, the ship belongs to The Turk. But you didn't hear it from me. Now hurry along and keep your money."

"He called me 'your lady,'" Susanna said, pressing one cheek against the precious cloth as they walked back in the direction of the port gates.

"That's a very valuable gift you just got. It would make a good dowry. Hell, even I would take it."

"Truly?"

At that moment, Francesco saw Michelangelo's assistant Bastiano just ahead of them in the crowd. He was sure Bastiano had seen him, but when he called to him, the apprentice turned tail and pushed his way toward the gate. How was it that Bastiano seemed to be everywhere Francesco was these days but was able to avoid him with such diligence? Annoyed, Francesco was about to run after him when a call went up.

"Got a floater here!"

"A floater . . . a floater . . ." rippled through the crowd. Bastiano forgotten, Francesco wheeled around and saw the same dockworker who had just given them the cloth and cardamom.

"Let's go see," Francesco said to Susanna. "But first, let me hide that cloth under my cloak before a cry of thief goes up too."

Reluctantly, she handed over the bolt, and he put it under his cloak before taking her by the hand and running back along the dock, where already a crowd was gathering. Seagulls circled overhead, adding their screams to the mayhem.

It was a floater, all right. It couldn't have been anything but a dead body, shrouded in seaweed and tangled in the mooring lines of The Turk's ship. Francesco and Susanna watched silently as a group of men pulled the body onto the dock. One eye open and staring, the other swollen shut. *Quoniam terra plena est iudicio sanguinum, et civitas plena iniquitate . . . The land is full of bloody crimes, and the city is full of violence.* And for the second time in three days, Francesco knew the victim's name. Marcus.

CHAPTER FIVE

THEY LAID MARCUS'S BODY OUT ON THE WHARF, AND THIS TIME Francesco had the courage to step forward and close the corpse's remaining open eye. He closed it as he'd seen the priest close his mother's, placing his palm over the eyelid. But he didn't know what to do about the poor man's mouth, still open as if in a scream, dirty water dribbling from one corner.

"You know him?" asked one of the dockworkers, and Francesco thought how he'd been asked the same thing about Calendula.

He had denied it then, but saw no reason to now. There were no police around, only curious dockworkers, children, and prostitutes. "Yes," he said, without elaborating. This time, however, he wasn't going to let the body out of his sight and risk it being claimed at the mortuary by another mysterious fat man. He looked around the growing crowd of curiosity seekers and called over a rag-and-bone man leading his donkey and cart.

Thinking how he was simply not destined to buy food that day, Francesco offered to pay the rag-and-bone man if he'd cart the body to Imperia's. The man agreed, enlisting the help of a couple of boys who, tired now of poking at the bloated cow, were eager for new fun. They grabbed Marcus by the feet and hauled his body over the rags and bones that lined the cart. An old woman stepped forward with a piece of torn sail and covered the body, jumping clear as the cart started with a jolt. Francesco decided it would be better not to involve the police, and no one on the docks seemed inclined to fetch them anyway.

Like mourners in a funeral procession, Francesco and Susanna followed behind, occasionally giving the cart a push when it became bogged in a muddy rut. By the time they reached the silversmith's, dusk was falling, and while it wasn't raining, the sky was still heavy with clouds. Francesco handed Susanna the bolt of cloth and promised to see her later. For once speechless, she held it tightly and nodded wearily at him. Francesco, thinking this was perhaps the most vulnerable he'd ever seen her, kissed her on the cheek.

The scene at Imperia's was much as he expected, in some ways a repeat of the night he'd told them of Calendula's death. Imperia even wore the same regal purple dress, and although this time she didn't faint, she went very pale upon hearing the news. She summoned the guards to bring the body inside, and they laid it, still wrapped in the dirty sail, along a bench brought from the kitchen.

It might have been too soon for the body to putrefy, but it stank all the same of rotting fish and filthy water. With Imperia's giant bodyguards towering over them, her girls huddled in the doorway, lace handkerchiefs pressed over their noses. Since it was still early, Imperia and her girls had very few guests, most of them familiar faces. Sodoma, Raphael, a couple of his apprentices, and Colombo were already settled in front of the fire with a pitcher of wine. Having taken his midday meal with Imperia, Chigi had been on his way to meet with the Vatican chamberlain, but instead had met Marcus's corpse at the door. He now looked torn between comforting Imperia and making his evening appointment. Two strangers, tall, thin men who looked enough alike to be twins, had glanced briefly through the door to see what the excitement was about, but they were quickly herded back to the music room by a couple of the girls. Imperia told Francesco the men were in the city on business with the Vatican and had arrived in Rome only that morning from Bologna.

And, of course, there was Dante. He was crouched on a chair in one of the corners, his cloak pulled over his head, sobbing quietly. *Dante,* Francesco thought, *may have been the last person—barring the killer—to see Marcus alive.* He tried to recall everything Dante had said that morning. A lot of nonsense about The Turk being a Greek, and Calendula not being the Madonna, or was it the Madonna not being Calendula? And something about making a fool of Marcus with her golden hair. *Stop! Stop! Or I'll kill you! I'll kill you!* he'd said. Francesco had thought Marcus was threatening Dante, but now he wasn't so certain. Had Dante overheard or even seen Marcus's killer?

According to Dante, Marcus had been convinced Calendula's body was on The Turk's ship. Why? Who or what led him to believe this? Surely not The Turk? Or had The Turk mentioned his "important shipment" and Marcus jumped to conclusions? Had Marcus attempted to board The Turk's ship and been killed for his efforts?

Francesco lifted a corner of Dante's cloak, revealing one frightened eye. Darting around in its socket, it seemed to be looking everywhere at once while not seeing anything at all.

"Dante," he said gently. "Who else did you see at the docks with Marcus?"

"No! No!" Dante shouted, his eye darting ever faster until the iris disappeared into his skull, leaving only the white showing. "I didn't see him! I didn't see him!"

"I know, I know," Francesco cooed. "Marcus told you not to tell anyone you saw him, but was anyone else there? Bastiano?" Francesco still didn't know what Bastiano was doing there, but he sure was in a hurry to leave when the dockworker's cry went up.

"No! No! Nobody!"

"Not even The Turk?"

"No, not The Turk! Not The Turk!" he screamed, and then Imperia was screaming too.

"Please, Francesco, I beg you! Make him stop!"

Francesco sighed and dropped the corner of the cloak back over Dante's eye, patting him on the head as he would a child until the screaming abated and Dante resumed his quiet sobbing. Across the room, Imperia held her head in her hands, quietly rocking back and forth. Chigi made soothing sounds to her not unlike the ones Francesco had been making for Dante. She took down her hands and asked for someone to fetch one of the houseboys, which was unnecessary since the houseboys had heard every word, and they emerged instantly from behind the skirts of the girls still gathered in the doorway. Like Raphael's houseboy, Alfeo, they were probably not older than eight or nine, though of sturdier stock. It suddenly occurred to Francesco that they'd probably been born here, the sons of whores with no claim to a father. "I want you to find Marcus's father," Imperia said. "Tell him to come for the body. It cannot stay here, and I don't know what else to do. We certainly can't let it go to the mortuary. God knows who might take it. Break the news kindly. He lives in the Arenula and has a workshop there. You've delivered messages for Marcus there before."

"Yes, ma'am, but the Arenula is flooded. Higher than my head," the taller of the two answered. He stood on his toes and held up one hand as high as he could. "Like that," he said, wiggling his fingers toward the ceiling.

"It's true," Francesco said. "I met a man in the street this morning who told me as much. He said many had left for the surrounding hills. It may be impossible to locate Marcus's father."

Imperia sagged even further in her seat. "Oh, God in Heaven, what is to be done?"

Her plea went unanswered by God and the entire room. Everyone stared at the canvas-covered body as if perhaps it could tell them.

Finally Raphael put forth a plan. "I believe Francesco did the right thing in not telling the police, given what happened to Calendula's body. Have Marcus moved to the empty storeroom on the ground floor of my palazzo. It is cold there, and the body will be safe until morning, when we will either seek out Marcus's father or have the body interred. We must send for a priest too."

Everyone nodded, and Imperia, looking visibly relieved, sent one of the houseboys to summon the bodyguards. They came promptly, their bulk seeming to fill the entire salon. Effortlessly they picked up the morbid bundle and, with Marcus's gray hands trailing from under the sail like the frayed ends of a mooring line, carried the body away. Raphael, donning his black beret, followed them out, then led the way across the square to his apartments.

Though her voice was shaky, Imperia called for wine, bread, and cheese. Chigi kissed both her cheeks and said he would return after his dinner with the chamberlain. Raphael would be back soon, and Francesco would keep her company in the meanwhile.

A maid brought in the wine and food, and Sodoma and Colombo pulled their chairs closer to the fire. Francesco caught enough of their exchange to know that, while they weren't surprised the hot-headed Marcus had found himself in more trouble than he could handle, they weren't particularly saddened by his death, either.

Francesco poured both himself and Imperia some wine and took the banker's place next to her on the settee.

"Do you really believe Marcus was murdered because he found Calendula's body?" Imperia asked.

"It certainly seems possible."

"And it was The Turk's ship?"

He nodded again.

"So The Turk must have taken her body after all. Why?"

"That I don't know," Francesco said softly. He certainly wasn't going to share his absurd theory about The Turk wanting to preserve Calendula as he'd preserved his crocodile.

"Well, at least I know where she is now," Imperia said sadly.

He held her hand, gladly relinquishing his seat when Raphael reappeared. He wondered if he should confront Imperia about what the cook had told Susanna, but it didn't seem like the right time. Instead, he helped himself to more of the refreshments before going to the bookcase. He looked at the volume by Erasmus and wondered if he would ever have the opportunity to sit and read it. He'd been here reading a volume of Petrarch's letters the day before Calendula was pulled from the river and still had several volumes to go, though it was true he'd read them before and had committed many passages to memory. *It is in the very nature of ignorance to mock what it cannot comprehend, and to yearn to keep others from reaching what it cannot attain. Hence the false judgments upon matters of which we know nothing, by which we manifest our envy quite as clearly as our stupidity* was all he recalled before Imperia let out a small scream. Francesco wheeled around to see none other than The Turk standing in the doorway, wet from the rain, the eagle-topped walking stick in his hand. He was breathing heavily, as if he'd run all the way from his villa.

"Oh, my dear, my dear, it is only I, your friend Silvio, and I came as soon as I heard the terrible news about Marcus! That poor, stupid man! I *must* apologize!"

His exclamations were met with blank stares. Not everyone knew he was a suspect in both Marcus's and Calendula's deaths, but even to the uninformed in the room, it was obvious The Turk knew something about the day's events.

"What is it, Imperia?" he said, dropping heavily to one knee in front of her and taking her hand to kiss it. "You're looking at me as if I'm a monster. Will you at least hear me out?"

Imperia tried to speak but managed only to nod rather numbly at him before signaling one of the houseboys to take The Turk's fur-trimmed cloak. Rising with the help of his cane, The Turk surrendered the cloak with a flourish, dropping it over the boy, who, after struggling out from under its weight, lugged it away.

If at all possible, The Turk was dressed even more regally than the day before. His doublet was of purple silk embroidered with gold thread, while, as before, deep layers of Venetian lace encircled his wrists. He raised his hand to his forehead to wipe his brow, revealing the amethyst ring. *Why?* Francesco wondered. How could he defend himself with that ring on his finger? He and Raphael exchanged a quick glance—there was no doubt Raphael had seen it too.

The Turk sat in a chair, the delicate piece of furniture looking as if it were about to collapse under his weight. He took Imperia's hands in his own. "They told me his body was brought here, and I knew you would be upset, so I came to explain."

With his bald head and numerous chins, The Turk suddenly looked to Francesco like a bullfrog with a lace collar. When he and his sisters were still in the nursery, his mother had told them the story of a princess who kissed a frog. It was out of pity for him, but her kiss freed him from a witch's spell and changed him into a handsome prince. If this had been the case with The Turk, Francesco thought absurdly, the transformation had been only partially successful.

"I'm afraid it's all a tragic mistake," The Turk continued. "Marcus came to me yesterday, wanting to buy back the painting of Calendula. But perhaps you know this already? I see the boy you sent is here," he said, and for a moment Francesco felt every eye in the room upon him.

"Yes, I know some things." Imperia's voice was barely a whisper.

"Then you may know Marcus flew into a rage all of a sudden, and I had my men throw him out."

Imperia nodded, and everyone leaned forward in their chairs, as if afraid to miss a single syllable.

"He didn't receive a beating, if that's what you think happened."

"I . . . I don't know what happened," Imperia stammered.

"Well, it seems the foolish boy had it in his head that Calendula's body was on my boat . . . I cannot think why. Oh, my dear, your hands do tremble terribly! It's not true, I swear! I don't know what happened to the lovely Calendula, nor did I discuss the whereabouts of her body with Marcus. I didn't even know it was unaccounted for until this boy here came to my house," he said, bobbing his head in Francesco's direction. "I only said I had very important cargo on board, but I didn't for one moment think he'd conclude I'd hidden her on the boat." He shifted in his chair, and it let out a groan of protest.

"But last night, he went there. He must have thought he could sneak on board and find her, but he was caught by my guards. They swear they intended no violence, they only meant for him to leave, but when they denied there were any dead bodies on board, he drew his dagger."

"I'll kill you! I'll kill you!" Dante screamed as he jumped to his feet, his chair wobbling beneath him. Spreading his cape like giant wings, he swooped down on The Turk, for a moment truly becoming the bat he believed himself to be. Raphael was the first to react, catching Dante around the waist and pulling him back, sending them both crashing into Sodoma's lap.

Seeing the strange man flying through the air toward him, The Turk lurched in his seat. This proved too much for the chair. The legs snapped, and The Turk plummeted to the floor.

Imperia leaped up and, with both hands pressed to her cheeks, stood over The Turk, unsure what to do. It was Francesco who held out a hand, flinching as the amethyst ring bit into his palm. "What in hell?" The Turk sputtered as he struggled heavily to his feet.

"I'm sorry," Francesco began. "He is not . . . well. And I think he saw Marcus at the docks. I think he saw what happened."

While the splinters of The Turk's chair were swept away and a sturdier chair was brought to replace it, Raphael pressed a cup of wine into Dante's hand. "We will take care of it now," he told Dante. "Be a man for us tonight and keep your peace." Raphael looked to the others. "Could you please take Dante to the music room and keep him amused? I am sure you understand." The other men did as they were told, but their reluctance was evident. They didn't want to miss out on the evening's entertainment. Taking Dante by the hand, Sodoma defiantly scooped up one of the wine pitchers. When the door closed behind them, only Francesco, Raphael, Imperia, and The Turk remained.

"Shall I continue?" The Turk asked, settling cautiously into the new chair.

"Please do," Raphael said, pouring wine for The Turk. The Turk took the cup, displaying the ring yet again without the slightest sign of embarrassment.

Drinking his wine in a single gulp, he held the cup out to be refilled, and Raphael obliged. "As I was saying," The Turk went on, "he became agitated and there was no option. It was not a very Christian burial, very expedient on my men's part. Had I but known his intentions, I could have prevented this tragedy. Can you forgive me, my dear Imperia?" He took her hands again in his.

A bell tolled the hour, and from the music room emanated the sound of laughter and the sweet murmurings of Colombo's lute, but the salon was quiet as they waited for her reply.

"But . . . but Silvio," Imperia finally stuttered. "You are wearing her ring!"

"Ring? Whose ring? Calendula's?" He stared down at his large hands, which still held Imperia's small ones. "I don't understand. Every one of these rings is mine."

"That one!" She pulled her hands from The Turk's and touched the amethyst as quickly as if it were burning hot. "That one! It was Calendula's! She was wearing it the night she was killed. It was cut from her finger. I mean, her finger was cut off, and the ring was taken, and now you are wearing it. Oh, Silvio! What am I to think?"

The Turk looked so taken aback Francesco could not believe for even one second he was acting. "Her finger was cut off?" The Turk asked weakly.

Imperia burst into tears. Raphael tried to intercede, but she waved him away, producing one of her lacy handkerchiefs to blot her cheeks.

"Oh, I cannot imagine my little girl's finger cut off," said The Turk. "It's just *too* horrible."

Imperia twisted the handkerchief in her lap. "I was very angry with Calendula about the ring. I asked her to sell it and give me my share. It's our business arrangement, the arrangement I have with all my girls. If I'd known what was to happen, though, I would never . . ."

Francesco thought this must be the fight the cook had been referring to. He tried to catch Raphael's eye, but he was too intent on the scene unfolding before them, his normally serene brow puckered with lines.

Imperia took a breath. "The night before Calendula was killed, she was wearing that ring. She refused to sell it, she was so proud of it." Imperia looked at Francesco. "I know I didn't tell you this part. I was embarrassed—it seemed so cold under the circumstances. But I swear I was only thinking of her. With the sale of the ring, even after giving me my portion, she would have had enough money to marry Marcus." She turned back to The Turk, who was now twisting the ring on his finger. "Still, she refused. She said she didn't need to sell it, that she was going to be a lady. Marcus was not only jealous but also heartbroken. I'm sure he believed the only thing standing between him and Calendula becoming man and wife was a dowry. And she goaded him too, telling him the ring was from a man far richer than himself. Marcus was so angry he struck her. And then, when her body was found . . ." Here Imperia started to cry, the words coming out in sobs, "Someone had cut off her finger and taken the ring . . . and here you are, Silvio . . . wearing the ring! And I swear to you on all that is holy and good: it is the same ring!"

The Turk closed his eyes for a moment, as if to let it all sink in. When he spoke, he sounded incredulous. "And so you think, all of you, that after I gave her the ring, I killed her and cut off her finger to get the ring back. I then threw the poor girl in the river . . ." As he spoke, he became increasingly indignant. "And then, after agreeing with you that you should collect the body from the mortuary, I took it after all and hid it on my boat? Why, why, why? Why do you believe I would do such things?"

Raphael, always the peacemaker, was about to interject, but Imperia interrupted him. "I know, it sounds so terrible. I didn't want to believe it. But why do you have her ring?"

"This is not her ring, Imperia. It cannot be. It was given to me by the Holy Roman Emperor Maximilian himself. The stone was set by Maximilian's own goldsmith. There's no other ring like it. You see the chain of my initials, SG, around the band. Silvio il Greco. That's my real name," he said, with a glance at Francesco and Raphael. "I like to say 'The Greek' was the name I was born with, and 'The Turk' is the name I earned. I'm afraid you are all terribly mistaken. It might have been an amethyst, but it was not this ring. It is impossible! But one thing *does* make sense now. I know why Marcus went mad yesterday. He saw the ring." He pointed a finger—this one bedecked in an emerald—at Francesco. "And you. You must have seen it too!"

"Yes, I did."

"And do you think it's the same ring?"

Francesco nodded. He hadn't known that the intricate chain etched in the band was a string of *S*'s and *G*'s, but it was most certainly the ring Calendula had held in front of his eyes, long enough for him to memorize every detail, every curlicue in the band's design, the intensity of the purple stone. Is that what she had wanted? He would have to think about that possibility later, though, as Raphael was now asking The Turk if Calendula could have "borrowed" his ring.

"And returned it before she was killed? She would have had to 'borrow' it, as you so nicely put it, and then return it sometime between showing it off and getting herself murdered. And if she returned it, why would her killer have cut off her finger if not to get the ring?"

"One of the servants then?" Imperia ventured.

"He borrowed the ring, gave it to Calendula, telling her he was going to make her a lady, then killed her and took it back?" The Turk's skepticism was evident. *If he is guilty,* Francesco thought, *wouldn't he go along with any theory that didn't point to him?* For that matter, why not just say there were many rings like his own belonging to all sorts of murderous types? "And I suppose you think the servant took her body too," The Turk volunteered sarcastically.

"I don't know," Imperia cried. "But where is her body? Where can it be?"

"I wish I knew the answer to that. I'll make some inquiries. But one thing I can assure you: Calendula's body is not on my ship!"

Francesco decided now would be the time to ask about something else that was bothering him. "What were Cardinal Asino and Paride di Grassi doing on your ship today?"

"What? You think they had something to do with Calendula? And how do *you* know they were on my ship today?" Francesco started to say he was there looking for Marcus, but The Turk interrupted him with an impatient wave of his bejeweled hand. "Let me answer before you think they had something to do with Calendula. Quite the contrary. They were there to buy slaves. Boys. No girls. Just boys. They like them very young and very pretty, if you catch my meaning." He lowered his voice and chuckled a little malevolently. "Just like His Holiness himself likes them."

"His Holiness? Pope Julius?" Francesco echoed, feeling ill. Christ, was he the only one not to have figured that out? That golden-haired boy he took everywhere. What an irony—the Christ Child in

The Marigold Madonna. What had Michelangelo said to him? *Rome would be wise to remember the fate of Sodom and Gomorrah ...*

Francesco looked at The Turk. "And you sell ..."

"A man's got to make a living, and better they get buggered by Christians than by heathens. Not that anyone will be making me a saint." He laughed. "Anyhow, they didn't take them. Too old, they said, though the eldest is ten. Now I have twenty pretty young boys with no higher prospects than breaking rocks in the quarries. Unless you have need of one?"

Francesco shook his head vigorously.

"You have a lot to learn, boy. But you can see that Asino and di Grassi would have no interest in Calendula."

Francesco cast a sideways glance at Raphael and was satisfied to see that he, too, looked taken aback by The Turk's cheerful confession.

Imperia, on the other hand, did not seem shocked. No doubt she'd been aware of this all along. "Please, please," she begged. "I don't want to talk of your business. I want to know where Calendula is."

"I promise I'll give this my full attention first thing tomorrow," The Turk answered. "It might help to know what exactly you were told at the mortuary."

Imperia took a deep breath. "That a fat man had already been there and paid handsomely for the privilege of taking a dead whore off their hands. The policeman asked him if he'd like another for the same price. He thought himself very amusing."

The Turk, who seemed to find almost everything amusing, looked like he wanted to laugh. "Are you sure I'm the only fat man Calendula fancied?"

Imperia was stony-faced. "I could think of no one else."

"I'll pay a visit to the mortuary tomorrow and see if a bigger bribe will elicit further details."

"I thank you, but I doubt the fat man would have left his name."

"It is very possible too," Raphael suggested, "that the fat man was working for someone else."

"Yes," The Turk said, nodding and sending his chins dancing. "Indeed, the man we really need to find could be tall and thin, sending the fat man only to distract us. Did Calendula know any tall, thin men?" The Turk now seemed to be enjoying himself, as if this were a puzzle or game rather than the death of someone he professed to care about.

"I'm beginning to believe we'll never know what happened," Imperia said with a sigh.

"Don't despair, my dear. A substantial bribe may work wonders. But perhaps tonight you might introduce me to the girl I saw on the way in. The one with the red hair. Such an unusual shade and such lovely curls." He bowed to Raphael and Francesco. "I trust, gentlemen, we will meet again."

They bowed in return. Imperia took The Turk's arm, but as she led him toward the music room, The Turk stopped to address Francesco. "You must come back to my villa, boy. I'll show you my collection of ancient and medieval weaponry. The largest in all of Italy. I have Mark Antony's breastplate, the one he was wearing in Egypt when he plunged his sword through his own heart. If you look closely enough, it still bears traces of his blood and, I like to think, Cleopatra's kisses." They could hear his laughter even after the door had closed behind him.

"And there goes the most cheerfully evil man I hope I ever meet," Raphael said.

"Do you think he's telling the truth?" Francesco asked.

"Absolutely. Though why do I think he is in the music room right now charming his next victim?"

"The one with red curls. He does like women with unusual hair."

"And he does like to own things no one else has."

"I wondered if he'd had Calendula's body preserved, to add to his collection."

"I would laugh if I did not believe it possible. I would believe almost anything of that old toad."

"I was thinking he looked like a bullfrog. Did you know about the Pope's boy?"

"No. I thought His Holiness was being kind to an orphan. I certainly did not believe what The Turk suggests. Perhaps it is to our credit that we do not think of such things?"

"Perhaps it's only because we have recently arrived in Rome and are, as the French say, naive. And yet I feel little better that those boys on the ship will be breaking rocks in a quarry. How many years will they live? One or two, before beatings or falling rocks end their lives?"

"I doubt even that long. I know I will be kinder to Alfeo tomorrow."

"Nonsense. I fear I now speak with experience on this matter. No boy could have a better or more generous master."

"I had hoped," said Raphael, "this evening would be spent with a fine cup of wine and the new volume by Erasmus. I now only want to close my eyes and sleep."

Francesco looked at the glass case. "Erasmus will wait for us. That is one of the marvelous things about books." He had a brief fantasy of being home again, sitting by the fire and reading Erasmus aloud to Calendula . . . No, not Calendula! It was Juliet he meant. Juliet. He imagined what it would be like to sit with *Juliet*. He shook his head; he, too, must be tired.

"Will you come to my apartments tomorrow?" Raphael said, interrupting his thoughts.

"Thank you. Perhaps then you can tell me how Marc Antony plunged his sword into his heart while still wearing his breastplate."

Raphael laughed. "You will have to ask The Turk. I am sure he would be happy to explain."

Raphael went to bid Imperia a good night, and one of the giants provided Francesco with a torch. Halfway across the square, he realized someone was behind him and turned to see Dante. "What are you doing, Dante?

"It's dark out," he said sadly as he shielded his eyes against the torch's light. "Bats go out at night."

Francesco put his arm around the man's shoulders and turned him back in the direction of the brothel. What spirits haunted and tortured this poor soul? "Not tonight, Dante," he said. "You need to rest. Go back to Imperia's for the night. Have some wine and something to eat." Dante started to protest, but Francesco remained firm. "No, man. Not tonight. Do as I say and go back to Imperia's." Finally Dante agreed and started back across the square.

Francesco waited until the door had closed behind Dante before resuming his own path home. The moon, still close to full, struggled to find a break in the heavy cloud cover. And while it had not rained all day, it started to spit now, a drop sizzling in the flame of his torch.

From beyond St. Peter's, past the port and The Turk's, he heard the wolves. Were there more of them now? The other night, their calls had seemed lonesome, single wolves calling out to each other. But now they called and answered each other as a chorus, dozens at a time. He thought of the refugees from the flood huddled up on the hills, listening to the wolves growing in number and wondering just how big a fire one needed to keep the hungry animals at bay. If emboldened by hunger, would the wolves raid the camps as they had the farmers' barns, swooping in and tearing apart the closest man, woman, or child before running back through the city walls?

His horrible imaginings made him walk faster, and he reached Susanna's gate in no time. Grateful the scarf was no longer there, he went in, only to find her already asleep, her arms around the prized bolt of cloth, holding it as tenderly as a mother holds a child.

He was turning to leave when the torchlight revealed a piece of paper on the table. Susanna couldn't read, but she had taken to bringing home notices she found nailed up in the squares. Whether they were announcing a new law or simply a festival, it impressed her enormously that Francesco could decipher what to her were mean-ingless scrawls. He would read the notice for her in the morning, he thought as he closed her door quietly behind him.

Inside Michelangelo's house, the wolves' cries were faint and distant. Michelangelo snored serenely while the chicken watched over him like a guardian angel from its perch on the headboard. Through what used to be the front door, the soap-maker and his wife's nightly quarrel was hushed and sleepy. Francesco held the pil-low to the light of the dying fire and was pleased to find it clean. He took off his boots, pulled the blankets up under his chin, and closed his eyes. He heard the soap-maker's wife giggle.

Sometimes it was good enough in life just to have a warm bed. But when his thoughts turned to those young boys huddled together on the ship, he felt guilty. He imagined them frightened and cold, not knowing they had escaped one terrible fate only to suffer another. The Turk must have bought them in a slave market in the East. Should Francesco attempt to free them? He could not overpower the guards, but could Raphael provide the means to bribe them? But what then? He imagined them running from the ship through the icy rain, their dark skin never having known anything but the sun, up over the hills to where the wolves waited in the shadows of the trees. A wolf for every boy. And if they were so lucky as to survive the ones with four legs, there were still plenty of the two-legged variety with evil on their minds.

CHAPTER SIX

My Dearest and Only Brother—

Let me begin by saying this letter comes with a thousand kisses. How long it has been since we have been parted, and how I yearn for the days when we played together! This past Tuesday marked the anniversary of Mother's death. How I do miss her. I can only believe you feel the same way.

Father has written to me of your troubles—you are to be punished for your sin of arrogance, he said. If Father is being unduly harsh with you, he is also harsh with himself, feeling he is being punished for his own sins. I will tell him you acted if not wisely, then of your own free will, the consequences of which were the predictable results of your actions and not brought about by a divine being in order to punish him. Did he not teach us to think so?

Oh, dear Brother, how difficult this time must be for you! To be denied everything you hold dear: your books, the conversation of the court, and Florence itself, with the hills we both cherish so much.

And does it still give you pain to be away from the source of your troubles, Juliet?

As there is no gentle way to tell the truth, I shall speak frankly and boldly, dear Brother, as I can with no other man. If I should cause you further pain now, it is only of your ultimate happiness I think when relating this.

I know you, Brother. For all your learning, you have a trusting heart. And what man would not have been tempted by her beauty? Perhaps that was Father's sin: not fully preparing us for the outside world. For I fear that, for all her outward sweetness, Juliet is capable of treachery.

While you were at the university in Padua and I was a maid in the court of Guido del Mare, Juliet and I often sat at the embroidery frame together. It is no secret that Guido often takes his pleasure among her maids, and it was only his respect for our father that saved me from his bed, if not from his glances. Juliet knew this and asked me who visited his bed at night, chastising me when I feigned not to know. But soon she saw my reticence as an asset, and she confessed to me her hatred for her husband. She found him distasteful, which is perhaps not surprising given he is more than thirty years her elder.

Before long I became her chaperone on her weekly rides. On these excursions she fulfilled her charitable duties as a rich noblewoman, delivering food to poor nobles, widows mostly, who live in the countryside. Her guards would wait outside, and I would enter with her. We would be greeted by the lady of the house and offered refreshment. It was the same at all houses but one, the cottage of a blind widow. Always her son would be there. He was a musician at court. Whenever he and Juliet were at court together, not so much as a glance passed between them. But for that hour at the cottage, I would sit with the widow and Juliet would be drawn into another room.

As you know, while the Church might look away for men, it does not for their wives. Men marry for money, connections, legitimate heirs, taking their pleasure whenever they please. But women, too, have desires. And so if that were all, I would have kept it in my confidence, as I had promised my lady that autumn.

But in winter, Guido's sister arrived at court, and that same musician fell in love with her and she with him. Juliet was jealous and confided in me that she'd told Guido of his sister's indiscretions.

I do not know if Juliet realized how heavy the price would be for her revelation, for Guido refused his sister and the musician permission to marry. When they would not obey him, he had the young musician killed. His sister was to be sent to a convent, but she instead threw herself from her tower window into the stone courtyard.

Juliet confined herself to her room and dismissed me. You arrived home in Florence just as I was leaving for England, and thus you and I were parted.

Had I known you were to fall in love with Juliet, I would have told you this before, though I do not know if it would have prevented your downfall. Reason is indeed weak in the face of love. I am sorry, my Brother.

I know you will want to learn of my life here, and I shall send news soon. But be assured I am well and my maidenhood safe from the young Henry, Duke of York, soon to be King Henry VIII. His father, the elder Henry, is not well and coughs up blood. I have received word from Adriana in Holland, who is also well and sends her love to you.

I ask you, Brother, for our safety, to burn this letter without delay. I also ask your forgiveness if its contents have brought you more pain. I will continue to petition our father on your behalf and hope he will soon find in his heart the ability to forgive you, if only for the love of our dear mother.

Your ever-loving sister, Angelina

He didn't know who had delivered the letter from his sister, only that it was there when he awakened. On going to bed, his fever had returned, and after a fitful night of tossing and turning, he had slept well into the morning.

Angelina had written in French, perhaps for additional safety, and he read the letter once again to commit it to memory before laying it on the fire as she requested. *Je suis desolée, mon frère...* she'd written. *For taking away the reason you live* she might just as well have added. He watched the edges curl and blacken and, after wondering if this was becoming a metaphor for his love for Juliet, gave the letter a vicious jab with the poker. A plume of ash and smoke evaded the chimney and poured into the room.

Eyes stinging, he threw the poker back onto the hearth. The chicken, observing him impassively from the table, gave one of its funny hops, coming to rest on top of Michelangelo's drawings, still surprisingly untainted.

"You shit on my pillow yet leave his drawings alone." Francesco pushed the chicken aside and flipped through pages densely packed with muscular figures, but there was no sign of the bird's likeness. Francesco pictured Michelangelo at work on the ceiling, a giant portrait of a three-legged chicken holding the place of honor in the center of the vault.

Wrapping himself in a blanket from the bed, he poured what was left of the drinking water into what was left of the wine. After gulping it down, he sat at the table and tried to think. There was no reason to doubt his sister. He knew the whole story except for this part about Juliet's involvement. Surely Juliet had known Guido would react with violence. Guido was loyal to his friends but ruthless with his enemies and those who betrayed him. And Guido had intended a far more lucrative match for his sister than a simple musician.

Francesco realized now he had his father's learning but not his wisdom. After completing his studies in Padua, Francesco had arrived at the del Mare court with his head full of Petrarch. Law, math, and languages too, but Petrarch especially. *Juliet will be my Laura,* he thought the moment he laid eyes on Guido's wife. Her golden hair, her downcast blue eyes. And he would be Petrarch, in love with a married woman who could never love him in return.

And so it was for over two years, until she came to him, cornering him in his offices one afternoon this past spring. *You're a lawyer,* Juliet had said. *You must help me get away from Guido. Help me obtain an annulment, for then I will be free and Guido will have to return my dowry.*

I'm so sorry, he'd replied. *It would be impossible to obtain an annulment.* Until that moment, he'd almost forgotten his Petrarchan infatuation, so thoroughly had he enjoyed the pleasure of the court's many willing young maidens—although he had often imagined Juliet's face in those darkened bed chambers.

I'll say the marriage was never consummated. They'll believe me—he is so old and ugly! Oh, I wish I were home in Milan! How could my family have been so unkind to me!

My lady, you cannot do that. None of your children may have lived past infancy, but they still prove you consummated the marriage. What would you say—they were someone else's? Then he would just kill you. I'm sorry. Guido will never let you win.

But I cannot live any longer with his cruelty. Oh, I wish I were dead! I'll kill myself if I have to!

He'd bidden her not to think of such a solution and promised he would find a way to help her.

What if Guido died? she'd then asked.

Then, yes, you would have not only your dowry but his property as well. And in time that will happen, for Guido is not young.

He will never die—he is so strong and hale! I'm trapped. I'll kill myself, I swear to you! She looked up at him, her eyes filled with tears.

He made her promise she would not kill herself, and she agreed on the condition that he continue to think of ways to help her. His better judgment was no match for her blue eyes, and so he met her again. And again. And again. Soon Francesco had all but stopped visiting the bedrooms of his favorite maidens, only going when the stretches between his meetings with Juliet became intolerable. Why Guido sought out other girls baffled him. If Juliet had been his, he would have been content to forsake all others. But she wasn't then, and she wasn't now, and here he was in Rome, spending his nights with a gypsy girl with a blackened tooth.

Francesco put his head on the table, remembering the day that stood out in his memory as the beginning of the end. Guido had formed a hunting party, and Francesco had gone out to wish him good luck. The sun was rising, but already the dew was being burned off the grass. Guido sat high on his favorite stallion. Pollo Grosso came closer as Francesco approached on foot, glaring down at him from his horse as if he already knew what Francesco was thinking. He brought his horse dangerously close, and Francesco, feeling the horse's breath on his face, jumped away from the stamping hooves. Francesco had already learned that Pollo Grosso guarded Guido zealously, instinctively distrusting everyone Guido knew. Furthermore, he watched Juliet like a dog in heat. When Francesco pointed out the latter, Guido had laughed. *I'm not worried. I throw him one of the local girls every once in a while to keep him happy. And I know he'd kill any man who dared think of touching my wife.* Francesco remembered that as Pollo Grosso continued to glare down at him, looking ready to tear him apart with his teeth.

Guido never hunted alone. Ten nobles accompanied him, and for every one of them ten servants. Everywhere carts were loaded with tents and food, and baying among them were greyhounds and mastiffs, tails quivering in anticipation of fresh blood. It was a party large enough to scare off every stag in the country, but Francesco knew Guido's huntsmen already had the prey cornered between the hills and the river.

I wish you would come, Francesco, Guido had said. His falcon sat steadily on his arm, and Francesco thought how, in profile, Guido and his bird looked much the same. *I was hoping to continue our discussion from last night about Castiglione. You maintain he thinks knowledge of the humanities is the most important quality for a courtier, while I believe the warrior spirit is the most important. Who is right—me or Castiglione?*

Yes, but the rents . . . Francesco said feebly, as though this wasn't a duty he could pawn off on one of the lesser secretaries.

You are a good man, Francesco. I am fortunate to have you watching out for me. You my purse and matters of the mind, and Pollo Grosso my back. He smiled, giving Francesco an affectionate flick on the arm with his whip. Francesco avoided Pollo Grosso's hateful eye.

Guido nodded toward three pretty girls giggling as they piled into a cart, their arms laden with flowers. They looked to be sisters, the youngest maybe twelve, the eldest sixteen. *I shall miss your conversation, but I will have them to console me tonight. I am sure you can understand why I married so late, with so many beautiful girls.*

Unfortunately, though, I may have waited too long, as I cannot seem to produce an heir.

I'm sure Juliet will give you a son soon, Francesco said, thinking he very well could be on his way to fathering Guido's heir for him.

One of the girls glanced at Francesco before covering her face coquettishly with her flowers. *You want that one?* Guido asked. *Since you are missing the hunt, I should not be so greedy. Although I know many young maids are vying for your affections.*

Francesco agreed weakly, suddenly justifying to himself the meeting he was about to have with his patron's wife. Why should Juliet have to live without pleasure when Guido had so much? Still, he couldn't help but feel disloyal. He knew too how angry this would make his father if he ever found out. And Pollo Grosso scared him to death. But he could not stop himself.

To Francesco's relief, the hunting horn sounded. *Enjoy the hunt,* he said. *We'll see you a few days hence.*

Yes, we will continue our conversation then, Guido replied, *although I must warn you, I shall win our next chess match or I will set Pollo Grosso on you.*

Laughing companionably, Guido bade him farewell, and Francesco waited until the last of the hunting party had crested the hill. Then, instead of returning to his offices in Guido's castle, he turned and ran beyond the gardens to the grove of monkey puzzle trees, where she waited for him. *Juliet.*

She ran to him, and he remembered the sun on her golden hair, her eyes so blue, her rose perfume. And when he picked her up, her yellow dress had swirled around her . . . No! Not yellow. Blue! It had been blue, like her eyes.

It was no good. He just couldn't recapture the excitement and passion for which he'd risked death and disgrace. Now that he had the yellow dress in his head, it wasn't even Juliet he was remembering. It was Calendula.

But what did it matter anyway? Here he was learning from his sister that he wasn't Juliet's first lover. And since his failure to free her from Guido, perhaps she had found someone else. Maybe he was just one in a long list, maybe the only one to have escaped Guido's sword—at least so far.

Susanna was right—he was a child. As if to prove it, he picked up the wine jug and threw it at the wall, where it bounced off and clattered to the floor unharmed.

Michelangelo had left some wine-soaked bread crumbs in a saucer for the chicken's breakfast, but there was no other food to be found. Francesco cursed himself for not filling his pockets with bread and cheese before leaving Imperia's. He still had the bag of cardamom he'd been given by the dockworker, but he couldn't eat that on its own. He'd give it to Susanna later. Maybe she could barter it in the market for some bread or, better still, one of those cakes soaked in honey and studded with almonds and currants.

How was he supposed to figure anything out when all he could think about was food? He hoped it wasn't too soon to go to Raphael's. Perhaps there'd even be more cheese from Alfeo's family. He didn't have to worry about taking food to Michelangelo at the chapel, as Susanna had completely taken over this task for him. He smiled at the thought of her pocketing a few of Michelangelo's coins for her troubles.

He began to wonder where she was. Had she looked in on him that morning and left after finding him still asleep? Every other such time, she'd woken him. She was probably at the market.

He got up from the table and went to the back door. Another gray day, soon to be dark, but it wasn't raining, and with any luck the waters had started to recede on the other side of the river so the area's inhabitants could return. Those who were still lucky enough to have a home would be shoveling the mud out for days. The rest would be digging soggy timber out of the sludge and struggling to rebuild.

He heard a small thump through the wall. Assuming Susanna was back, he decided to take over the cardamom. She'd probably have both bread and gossip from the market, and he could tell her what had transpired at Imperia's.

He entered the silversmith's without knocking and was about to call out hello when the greeting froze on his lips. Someone's behind was poking out from under the bed, one that did not belong to Susanna. It was a man's rear end, clothed in green hose, but it wasn't the silversmith's, unless the man had added a considerable amount of weight. The silversmith was every bit as thin as The Turk was fat, and this behind was somewhere in between. And what was it doing under the bed? He thought of Susanna's nest egg of small pilferings and wondered if this man was in search of it.

Grabbing the broom from beside the door and deciding that an element of surprise would be in his favor, he rushed over, the handle raised over his head.

"Who are you? And what is your business here?" he said in what he hoped was a threatening tone.

The man jumped, his head striking the wooden frame of the bed with a loud smack as he attempted to wiggle his way back out. Francesco ordered him not to move. "Stay down where you are and identify yourself!"

"I am unarmed!" came a man's muffled voice. Francesco couldn't quite place it, but it sounded familiar.

"Well, I am armed!" Francesco shot back, hoping the tone of his voice made his broom sound more lethal, silently cursing himself for leaving his dagger next door. "Now tell me who you are and what you're doing here!"

"Is that you, Francesco?"

Francesco recognized him now, and he resisted an urge to give the green-clad rear a good kick with his boot. "What the hell are you doing, Bastiano?"

"I'll tell you. Just let me come out."

"No. Not until you tell me why you have your head under that bed."

"I was looking for something."

"What? Rat shit?"

"No . . ."

"Spit it out, man, if you ever want to sit on your ass again."

"I was looking for money."

"What makes you think there'd be money here?"

There was a long pause. "Because I overheard you and Susanna talking, and she said she had money hidden away."

"And so you came to steal money from a poor girl saving for her dowry? What a despicable worm you are." Suddenly Francesco remembered when she'd told him about the hidden money. They'd been in bed, and she'd just told him about the miller being kicked by a horse. "You little shit! You were watching us in bed!"

"No!" Bastiano exclaimed, his head striking the underside of the bed again. "No. I mean, I was waiting outside, and I could hear you talking . . ."

"Yes, with your face pressed to the window, you pervert."

More silence, and then a weak, "Yes . . . I need money to buy bread . . . You know how Michelangelo is . . ."

"I know very well what a cheap bastard Michelangelo is, but that doesn't justify stealing from a poor girl!"

"Sounded to me as if she'd stolen it herself." Bastiano was indignant now. "And surely you don't believe that story about the miller being killed by a horse."

Francesco kicked him. "If you repeat that to anyone, so help me God, I will kill you," he said, meaning every word of it. "Have you been spying on me? Because it seems whenever I turn around, you're there."

"No. Not spying. Just . . . following you a little."

"Just following me a little? How about when I saw you at the docks? Were you just following me a little then?"

"It wasn't my idea, I swear."

"And the night I saw you at Imperia's? When Calendula died?" The night he'd heard footsteps behind him. "You followed me home then too, didn't you?"

"If you let me out, I'll tell you."

"You can tell me just as well from there. Who hired you?"

"Michelangelo. He told me to keep an eye on you and report back."

Francesco couldn't believe it. "That bastard!" he exclaimed, punctuating his verdict with another swift kick to Bastiano's ass. He'd kick Michelangelo's too, the first chance he got.

"Stop!" Bastiano cried. "That hurts! I don't want to do it, I swear. But I don't have a choice. He'll send me back to Florence, and my father will beat me blue."

"When I'm finished with you, you'll be wishing you were with your father. But first tell me why Michelangelo is having me followed."

"I don't know. He just told me to report where you go and who you see."

"So he knows I go to Imperia's? Is that why you were there the other night?"

There was silence, and Francesco imagined Bastiano nodding his head against the floorboards. What a shit that Michelangelo was. And just when he was starting to like him—or at least to find him a source of amusement. It shouldn't have come as a surprise that his distrust of all humans extended to his houseboy.

Francesco kicked Bastiano again. "Well, speak up, man! What have you told him?"

"Only that you go to Imperia's to see Raphael. And that you went to The Turk's and the port, although he already knew about The Turk's. He said you told him yourself the other night."

"Get out from under that bed! I'm tired of looking at your ass."

"You won't hurt me?"

"No more than if you stay."

Slowly Bastiano backed out and stood up, the front of his clothing coated in a mix of cobwebs, dust, and rat turds. Francesco lifted his broom, and Bastiano flinched, looking relieved if somewhat mortified when Francesco used it to sweep his clothes. Still, he gave Bastiano's beard a rough going over with it, finishing the job with a swat to the head hard enough to send the man stumbling against the table. "Stop it!"

"Why should I?" Francesco asked, although he already regretted hitting him on the head. Beating a man with a broom was hardly the most honorable way to fight.

"Because maybe I have some information you might want."

"I doubt it, but out with it quick. I want you out of here before Susanna gets back from the market."

"She's not at the market. That's what I was going to tell you."

Francesco felt a little knot of fear. This wasn't the safest city for a girl, even one as clever as Susanna. "Then where is she?"

Bastiano pulled himself up to his full height. "Went off with a man this morning. She was waiting for him right outside. Tall man."

"It was the silversmith, you ignoramus. He lives here."

"No, not Benvenuto. I know what he looks like. This man was younger. He had a fine black horse and a nice cape. She went with him the other night. The silversmith wasn't here then. You believed her story pretty easily for someone who's said to be so smart."

It was true—he had bought the story easily, even though there had never been any evidence beyond the scarf and Susanna's word. *You'd think I'd have heard them at it by now. He usually has a good go at her the minute he comes home,* Michelangelo had said. He probably knew all along where she was and who she was with.

"Get the hell out of here," Francesco yelled, "before I beat you to death with this broom! And don't forget—if you ever repeat any of what she said or what you told me now, I'll find you and kill you!" Bastiano covered his head with his arms and dove past Francesco for the door. Francesco threw the broom like a spear, and it glanced off the back of the door as it swung shut.

The room seemed suddenly quiet, and Francesco felt its damp gloominess pervade his entire body. The notice he'd seen on the table the night before was still there, and he could just make out the words in the dim light. *Repent! The End of the World is at Hand! Devils in the Guise of Wolves Eat our Children! It is Rome's Priests and the Pope who bring Armageddon upon us, while the Whores and Witches infect Righteous Men with Oozing Sores!*

Francesco read no further. He picked it up and, tearing at it angrily, tossed it on the cold grate.

✛　✛　✛

IT was Raphael, not Alfeo, who opened the door for Francesco. "It has been busy. Marcus's father came for the body, the poor man, and Alfeo has gone to share his good news with his family. I expected his return this morning, but perhaps he has decided to stay another day to celebrate."

"I'm sorry for Marcus's father. Pray tell, though, what is Alfeo's good news?" Francesco could use a little, even if it belonged to someone else.

"It turns out our Alfeo not only has the face of an angel but the voice of one as well. I took him to see Imperia's father, who arranged for him to sing for the choirmaster. As much as I hate to lose an excellent houseboy, I am pleased for him. He will sing the Christmas Mass. Imperia's father has taken a liking to the boy, and I have his word he will watch out for him and keep him safe from our more lecherous and immoral clergy." Raphael held out his hand for Francesco's cloak. "You may also be pleased to know the boys on The Turk's ship seem to have escaped, although no one knows how."

"I wondered if such a thing were possible, before concluding they were better off taking their chances where they were. Perhaps one or two will be lucky and find some safety. And I am pleased to hear Alfeo has a protector. Though do we have clergy who are *not* lecherous and immoral? If there are such men, they are rarer than an honest Frenchman and keep themselves as well hidden. Then perhaps I'm letting this wretched city poison my opinions. My own father is a member of the clergy and a man of great integrity." Francesco wrested off his boots, tossing them onto the hearth to dry before throwing himself facedown on the settee. "I won't be here to hear him sing, though," he said, his voice muffled by the tapestry cushions.

"Truly?" said Raphael, setting a jug of wine and a plate of bread and cheese on a low table. "And where will you be?"

"Home," he said, sitting up and nearly lunging for the food. "There's no reason to stay here. We'll never learn who killed Calendula, and no one will care even if we do. It could be anyone. I would even suspect *you* if I didn't know you so well. Of course, it depends on whether my father will have me. You should come for Christmas with me. That could be a point in my favor. My father is a great admirer of yours." The bread and cheese and thoughts of home were already restoring some of his humor. "It's a shame my sisters won't be there. They are too clever for most men, but I think you would enjoy a match of wits."

"I am sure I would." Raphael poured them both wine. "But tell me, why this new urgency to leave Rome?"

"This morning I went to Susanna's, and who should I find instead but Bastiano. I thought it was funny he kept showing up wherever I went."

Raphael raised one eyebrow quizzically. "And?"

"Michelangelo ordered him to follow me and report on my whereabouts."

"So he knows you keep company with me?"

Francesco nodded as he helped himself to more bread and cheese. There was a very fine mustard as well, which he spread copiously over the cheese.

"Yet he has said nothing to you?"

"Nothing, and on my way here, something struck me as very strange. Michelangelo is convinced that you would steal his ideas, given the opportunity. And yet, knowing I keep company with you, he leaves his drawings spread about for me to see."

"I suspect he is very torn. He is afraid to have his ideas stolen but cannot bear it if no one is admiring his work. Perhaps he has Bastiano follow you to be sure you are spreading word of his genius among his rivals." He laughed. "I cannot believe he has any evil intent, although he could use a lesson in manners. This morning, as I was walking with a group of students, I met him in St. Peter's Square. *There you go with your band,* he said, *like one of the Pope's merry little men.*"

"It sounds like something he would say. And what did you say in return?"

"*And there you go alone, my poor friend, like the Grim Reaper himself.*"

Francesco laughed. "I wish I could have seen his face!"

"He did not look amused. The students thought it very funny and laughed so much I came close to apologizing."

"Well, I'm pleased you only came close. Remember, this is the man who is having me followed and only God knows what else. I'm sure this is not what my father intended when he sent me here."

"But are there not other matters keeping you here as well? A woman, I think? One who looks a little like our poor Calendula, if I recall correctly?"

Francesco poured himself more wine. It wasn't easy telling another man, especially one he so admired, that he'd acted like a child, but somehow he felt he owed Raphael an explanation. "Her name was Juliet, and she was the wife of Guido del Mare."

"You fell in love with Guido's wife?"

Francesco went on, finding it a relief to tell Raphael. He hadn't been to confession for years (he doubted the very efficacy of the enterprise), but he was finding value in putting into words what weighed on his mind. "She wanted an annulment from Guido, and so I promised her I would find a solution." Francesco suddenly felt this was someone else's story, not his at all. "But by the end of the summer, I still could not think of a way out, short of killing Guido."

He could not tell Raphael about the time she had grown impatient and suggested just that. But he remembered it well. *Guido is my father's patron,* he had replied angrily to her suggestion. *We owe him everything. You must never again speak such vile treason.*

She'd started to cry. *I'm sorry. I didn't mean it; I was just desperate.*

He held her then. *I know you didn't mean it, Juliet. I will find a solution. I swear on my very life that I will.* But he knew his voice had held little hope.

"But Guido became suspicious," Raphael offered.

"I don't know how he found out. I swear Juliet and I never so much as exchanged a glance in the presence of others. Yet someone must have had suspicions, a servant, perhaps. One day, when I was walking in the courtyard, Guido came charging toward me. He was so angry I was sure he was going to kill me right then and there. I didn't have time to think. I struck out wildly and slashed open his face with my dagger. He must have a terrible scar now.

"If I'd been a soldier and not a scholar, I would have taken advantage of his shock and killed him, but I didn't. I couldn't. He's my family's patron after all, and has been so good to us. So I ran home to my father like the scared boy I was and begged him to help me.

"One thing I know for sure. If Guido had sent his bodyguard Pollo Grosso after me, I wouldn't be alive today. That's who Guido usually gets to do his killing, but I suppose this was a question of honor. He'd been betrayed by a trusted friend, so this was a score he had to settle himself." Francesco picked up his wine and looked at Raphael, who was listening patiently with the sort of sympathy he would have liked from his own father. "You can see why I hesitated to tell you all this."

"You must not be so hard on yourself. Can there not yet be a happy outcome?"

"I certainly dreamed of one. But today, in a letter from my sister, I learned I was not Juliet's only lover."

And now suddenly he wasn't thinking of Juliet, but of Susanna. Who was this man Susanna went off with? Bastiano had implied a lover. And while here he was unburdening his heart about Juliet, the woman he was supposed to be in love with, it drove him insane to think what Susanna might be doing right now with another man.

"Never mind," he said resignedly to Raphael. "I've told you everything now. I should leave you to find better company."

Raphael passed him the plate of bread and cheese. "Of course not. I enjoy your company, and I am honored you have taken me into your confidence at last. What you need now is a diversion. I may be short a houseboy, but I can have some food sent from Imperia's. Maybe a quiet evening would be of service to us both. A trip to the baths and some cards, perhaps, to take our minds away from women?"

"Our minds? Yours too? And who troubles yours? Imperia?" he asked half-teasingly.

"No," Raphael answered seriously. "Not in the manner in which you speak. You know, she is with child, and I worry for her."

"No, I didn't know. Is it impertinent to ask if she knows the father?"

"Chigi, of course. Men may pay for her company, but they do not share her bed. That is for Chigi only."

Except she had invited Francesco into her bed the day she told him Calendula was her cousin. He was certain he hadn't misunderstood her.

"And she shares her bed only with Chigi because . . ."

"Because she longs for the same thing all women long for," Raphael said firmly. "Love. A home. Security for her children."

"But why not you, Raphael? It's Rome's worst-kept secret that Imperia fell in love with you the moment you arrived here and now only settles for Chigi. Is it because of who she is?"

Raphael shook his head. "Her profession does not matter to me. It is not easy to explain. As much as I care for her, I feel I am seeking something else . . . something I cannot put into words. I love many beautiful women, and their beauty touches me, but . . . never mind. I cannot explain it. For now, I have my work. It is easier this way." He put down his cup and smiled. "Let me send for a great joint of venison, and we will eat, drink, and forget our cares for an evening."

✢ ✢ ✢

IT was Francesco who suggested they visit the Sistine Chapel. After many cups of wine, he was still angry with Michelangelo. But he was sure Bastiano would not be spying on him again, and if ever there were a good opportunity to show Raphael the ceiling, it was now.

The cold night air half-sobered them, though not enough to call off their mission. With jugs of wine and freshly lit torches, they set out, making the short journey to the Vatican longer by taking a wrong turn and ending up at a dead end.

When they finally arrived, the lone guard at the chapel door was slumped against the doorframe. "He's either asleep or as drunk as we are," Francesco whispered. "Our bribe may be wasted on him. You think we can sneak by him?"

"Not wise, I should think. If he does awaken, he is likely to go at us with that spear."

Raphael was right, for at the sound of their voices the guard awoke. "Halt! Halt! Who goes there?" He raised the spear, but his fumbled attempt to aim it in their direction sent it clattering to the floor. He dove to retrieve it, but Francesco planted his foot on it.

"Quiet, man. It is I, Francesco, houseboy to Michelangelo," he said with a drunken swagger. "We're not here to make mischief. Will you allow us in and keep your peace?"

"Who's he?" he said with a surly nod at Raphael.

"Only a wisp in your dreams. Take this wine, and let us agree you neither granted us entrance nor fell asleep at your post."

"That's a fair trade," he said, sampling the wine. He handed a large brass key to Francesco, who turned it in the lock.

"Good," said Francesco, handing him back the key. "We will need you to let us out again, so don't fall back asleep."

Their torches made only a small dent in the black cavern of the chapel. If at all possible, the air in here was even colder and damper than outside.

"It is not the first time I have been here," Raphael said as he removed his beret, his voice echoing in the vast room. He held his torch high and moved along the wall, the luminous colors of the frescoes flashing by. Francesco was about to ask if he was seeking a particular painting when Raphael paused. "Here. The work of Perugino, my old master, Christ giving the keys to Heaven to St. Peter, just as we were given the key to the chapel. See, this is him. He painted himself into the fresco, standing next to St. Peter. He joked it was so St. Peter would remember him when he appeared before the real Gates of Heaven. He loves to paint drapery, and no one can work more folds into a robe than he. It is the grace of his figures that makes him so popular, but what I truly admire are the settings. This landscape is more than just a backdrop. It has a story all its own.

Perugino laughed when I asked him what was beyond those hills and trees, saying, *Whatever you want, my boy.*"

Raphael studied the fresco wistfully a moment longer, then lowered his torch. "It is good to look on his face again. It has been a long time, and only God knows if I will see him again. I came to see this fresco when I first arrived in Rome, but Michelangelo was furious and told me to get out and stay out." Raphael laughed. "His Holiness said it is better to comply with Michelangelo's wishes for the sake of peace. I think His Holiness is a little afraid of him."

"And for good reason," Francesco said. "Once, His Holiness dared to say work was not progressing as he hoped. As he was leaving, a plank fell from the scaffold. It fell nowhere near him, but I don't doubt he took it as a warning. If he'd not gone to such lengths to convince Michelangelo to accept the commission, I'm sure the man would be sitting in a dungeon in Castel Sant'Angelo as we speak. It makes me almost laugh to think the Pope, who makes whole kingdoms quake in fear, is afraid of a painter."

Francesco then showed Raphael where generations of choir-boys had carved their names into the wall. "Look. *Josquin.* He was a choirboy here once, and now they sing his Masses. Tell Alfeo to carve his name beside his when he comes here. For luck. If you believe in such things."

Francesco led the way up the scaffolding, somehow managing to hold on to the side of the ladder with one hand while juggling the lit torch and their remaining jug of wine with the other. They emerged at the top, their laughter echoing through the vast chamber.

They picked their way across the spans to where Michelangelo had been working. Francesco took both torches and planted them in a pail beneath the painting of *The Flood.*

"This is it," Raphael said in wonderment. They lay on their

backs in order to see it better. The fresco was enormous, although they agreed it would appear very small from the chapel floor.

Francesco had to remind himself it was only three days ago he'd been up here and seen the colored chunks of plaster in the pail. Everything they now admired had been painted since then, and Michelangelo had worked largely, if not entirely, on his own. Bastiano had been spying on Francesco, and for all he knew Michelangelo had given his other assistants similar missions.

"It is extraordinary," Raphael said. "Not just the imagination that brings the story to life, with all its horror and fear. It is the figures themselves. Michelangelo is the true heir of ancient Rome. The rest of us had to struggle out of the darkness that was left when Rome fell. It has been a slow evolution from the infantile decorations of the early Church. Perugino made great strides, and I believe now we have found the light again. But with Michelangelo's work, you would think the intervening thousand years had never happened. It is as if the greatest Roman artists laid down their tools in the evening, only to have Michelangelo pick them up the very next morning and resume where they had left off."

"*My destiny is to live among diverse and bewildering storms,*" Francesco said, quoting from Petrarch. "*But for you perhaps there will follow a better era. This slumber of forgetfulness will not endure forever. When the darkness has lifted, our children's children can live again in the light.* I have often thought Petrarch was speaking to me when he wrote that. Deluded, perhaps, but I do think we are witnessing Rome's rebirth."

"*What else can history be but the praise of Rome?*" Raphael returned. "We certainly share a love of Petrarch. Have you ever wondered how different the world would be if Rome had not fallen? Imagine if we had spent the past thousand years building upon that greatness. Instead, we have had to pull ourselves out from under the weight of superstition that filled the void. Think of the poetry, the art, the music, the wisdom, the knowledge . . . Perhaps we would have chariots that could take us to the stars. But I do know there will never be anything greater than what we are looking at tonight. Imagine this whole ceiling when it is completed . . ."

"He still has a long way to go," Francesco returned bluntly. "And for all we know, he'll tear it down again and never be finished. He threatens as much." He broke off, realizing his own prejudice toward his master was clouding his reason, before continuing. "And while you commend him perhaps a little more than I feel is deserved, it humbles me nonetheless to see you give so much praise to this man's work. You call his work superior to your own and show no jealousy. I can assure you he says nothing in kind about your work. He calls it the work of a woman: all pretty faces and effeminate gestures."

Raphael's laughter rang heartily through the chapel. "He is angry that what he judges as inferior gets any recognition. The glory should all be his. It is a shame he cannot enjoy it."

Seldom do great virtue and great beauty dwell in one person, Petrarch had written, but then, he didn't know Raphael. If anyone was incapable of treachery, it was Raphael. "Even if my father doesn't allow me to go home this Christmas," Francesco said, "you should go, Raphael, and see it in winter. It's so peaceful. Steam rises from the hot spring and freezes on the branches of the trees. I enjoyed many a cold day with a cup of mulled wine, reading before a roaring fire. You really must go. I only hope I have the chance again."

"You will," Raphael said. "And I thank you for the invitation, but I shall decline until you can go as well." He paused for a moment. "I am not sure how to broach this, but when you told me your story,

I could not help but wonder if it were Juliet herself who told Guido of your indiscretions."

"What?" Francesco had not expected this turn in the conversation. "Why would she do such a thing?"

"Perhaps I am being too cynical. But she had to know that if she told Guido, he would try to kill you. She had to know, too, that you would defend yourself. What man would not? Had you been successful in killing Guido, she would have been free to do as she pleased."

"But what if he had killed me? She couldn't possibly have thought I would win in a duel. He's a renowned soldier, while words have always been my weapon."

"Do you think this was a chance she was willing to take?"

Francesco looked at him in stunned silence.

"I apologize. Perhaps the wine and this scene over our heads have made my imagination take a violent turn," Raphael said.

"I think in this matter you're wrong. I cannot believe Juliet capable of such deviousness."

Raphael didn't respond, and Francesco wondered if he *could* believe this of Juliet, given his sister's letter. She had betrayed her previous lover to Guido. Maybe she had never loved Francesco at all but was only using him as a means to an end.

Suddenly all pleasure taken in their clandestine visit to the chapel vanished. He noticed for the first time how the chapel was not without its own sounds. The squeak of a board, the scurrying of mice and rats over the stone floor, the whistle of a rising wind through the cracks in the windows—every small creak and groan echoed back like some moribund chorus. The boards under his back were hard, and the thought of the climb down the ladder was daunting. He shivered and wondered if his fever was returning. "I know a great deal, Raphael," he said, not knowing even what motivated his words, "but I don't always think."

"We should go. These torches will not last forever," was all Raphael said, and Francesco knew Raphael believed he'd judged Juliet's character correctly.

A few minutes later, the guard was opening the door for them. Raphael slipped him a few coins just in case the wine hadn't been enough to seal his lips, and the man told them to return any time they wished.

Francesco and Raphael parted on the steps; while they both resided but a short distance from St. Peter's, Raphael's path lay northward, while Francesco's was to the east. "Tomorrow, my friend," Raphael said, and although he attempted cheer, his farewell was as tired as Francesco's own.

Pulling his cloak tighter, Francesco watched as the light from Raphael's torch disappeared into the tangle of streets. Now Francesco's torch was the only light in the square. There wasn't even a glimmer from the papal apartments.

But it wasn't completely dark. The moon had struggled out from behind the clouds for the first time in days. Almost full, a small sliver carved out of one side, it cast enough light for Francesco to see a shadow moving toward him. Strange, until then he hadn't even heard the wolves. Already their howls had become part of the familiar noises of this wretched city. But he noticed them now, harmonizing with a new cold wind sweeping down from the north.

He felt no fear when he saw it. He knew, too, that he would never tell anyone, because he didn't know if he was dreaming. Not even when it walked to the bottom of the steps and stared up at him as if it knew him. It was white, pure white, as the rumors had said. Thick white fur, with a long tail and green eyes. *It will gaze at the moon and it will howl,* thought Francesco. *It will howl because it must.*

But it didn't. It only turned and walked away into the darkness, leaving Francesco to wonder if the wolf really knew him or not.

CHAPTER SEVEN

FRANCESCO COULD TELL SOMETHING WAS AMISS THE MOMENT HE entered the Piazza Rusticucci. It was normally deserted at this hour, but tonight a small knot of people was gathered around a smoldering fire in the middle of the square, the smoky light lending their faces an eerie cast. He recognized the soap-maker by his scabby, lye-burned face. The wood seller Michelangelo had so recently swindled was also there, standing next to a woman with matching stooped shoulders, no doubt his wife. The pair of them looked to be sixty but were more likely closer to thirty, a ripe old age, given their work-worn lives. Running circles around the fire were a handful of dirty boys who could have been anyone's or no one's at all.

"What happened here?" Francesco asked, holding his torch aloft. The fire, he observed, smelled more like burning rancid sausage than wood.

"Fancy man on a horse threw a torch into our shop," the soap-maker explained. "The walls were so saturated with grease it went up like a torch. Whoosh!" he exclaimed, throwing his hands up over his head.

The boys thought this amusing and were now throwing their hands up in the air too. "Whoosh! Whoosh! Whoo-oosh!"

Oh no! Susanna's house adjoined his own. If his house had burned . . . Hopefully she hadn't come home yet. "It was just the shop, right?" Francesco asked over the whooshing. He held his torch high, only to discover its circle of light and that of the fire did not quite reach the row of houses across the square. Still, he thought he could make out something different, an altered silhouette of their facades.

"Just the shop," the soap-maker said conclusively. "Torch went through the door just as the rain came down. Good thing too, or it would have burned down the whole row." He turned to the boys. "Shut up, you little shits!" The whooshing stopped. Satisfied, the soap-maker continued. "Not just the row. The whole city, maybe, though probably not now, since it's so bloody wet. But if it had been summer . . ." He let the possibility hang in the air. "Anyway, wife and I were putting wood on the fire. Faster than the Pope can screw an ass, the whole shop had gone up with a whoosh," he said, leveling a warning glance at the boys, "and the wife was over there knocking the walls down with a log. All in flames those walls were. But we got them down and dragged them out here. So much grease in them, they kept right on burning, even in the rain. Wife burned her hands. No blisters, though. You burn your hands as many times as me and the wife, you don't get blisters. Skin too hard." He held up his scarred, leathery hands and showed them proudly, as if his soap-making had been but a means to creating such a marvel.

"No one hurt then, other than your wife burning her hands?" Francesco asked, looking for further reassurance.

"No. Thanks to me and the wife."

Francesco relaxed. "That's good, but I'm sorry about your shop."

"We're alright. We got a place to go. The wife's at her sister's now." One of the boys had scooped up a rat and now threw it on the fire, provoking a shower of sparks and earning him a solid kick in the behind from the soap-maker. "Reckon we'll set up shop there," he continued as the boy let out an exaggerated howl of pain, drowning out the rat's real one. "Michelangelo has too many enemies. Makes it dangerous."

"Michelangelo? You think the fire was meant for him?"

"Only repeating what he said himself. Meant to burn him in his bed, he said. But it's got to be true. Can't think why they'd send a fancy man on a horse to kill a soap-maker."

"You got a look at him then?" It was the second time that day Francesco had heard tell of a man on a horse.

"Best I could. Big man on a horse with a torch. Never seen him before, but if I see him again, he'll wish he'd never been born."

"Why did you call him a fancy man?"

The soap-maker shrugged, the scarred palms he was so proud of held at his sides. "Don't know. Got a velvet cape on. Good horse. Not like Romeo here, with his hunchback and starving donkey." Romeo, whom Francesco had already recognized as the wood seller, grinned toothlessly from the other side of the smoldering fire. Now here was someone who had sufficient reason to burn Michelangelo in his bed, but Francesco suspected the wood seller was too feeble-minded to know he'd been cheated.

"You got a front door now, that's one good thing," the soap-maker continued. "You don't need to go down the alley no more."

Francesco liked that idea. "It opens then?"

"Michelangelo already came out of it. Running out like *his* house was on fire!" The soap-maker laughed at his joke until a bellow from across the square stopped him so short he started to cough.

"Francesco!" came the bellowing voice again. Michelangelo's, of course. It echoed around the square, and Francesco swore it made the wolves in the hills pause. "That you?"

"Yes," Francesco called back wearily. The crowd around the fire sniggered.

"Then stop gossiping like an old woman and get in here!"

Francesco bid the group good night and crossed the square to where Michelangelo, chicken tucked under one arm, waited for him in their new doorway. Dressed only in his nightshirt and boots, his filthy hair sticking out in all directions, Michelangelo looked even more deranged than usual.

The chicken blinked at Francesco, and Francesco couldn't help thinking it disapproved of him. "Are you drunk?" It was Michelangelo, not the chicken, who asked, but Francesco felt as if he were speaking for both of them.

"I *was*," Francesco said, refusing to look at either. He lifted his torch and regarded the transformation of the house. Beyond being a little charred, a few remaining bits of the shop clinging like barnacles to the facade, there was little evidence it had ever hosted a soap-maker's shop. "Very drunk and most pleasantly so," he elaborated, "but I see that, even with a front door, I still live in a shit hole. Only now someone is trying to murder me."

"Murder *you*? It was *me* they were after!"

"I live here too! It could have been me burned in my bed."

Michelangelo stomped his foot and let out an unintelligible gasp of frustration. "Get in here. This door lets in the cold."

"Funny door, letting in the cold when it's open," Francesco muttered as he stepped past him. Still, it did feel strange gaining entrance to the house this way. It was if he'd acquired a magic power, a sudden ability to pass like a ghost through walls. He turned and looked out on the square from this new perspective. The soap-maker and his party were still gathered around the greasy fire, smoke curling up into the darkness. He caught a flurried movement, a rapid beating of wings, so close he felt a breeze on his cheeks. Bats. Shuddering, he closed the door.

"So you think they were after you?" Francesco asked, turning his attention back to Michelangelo. "Who did you piss off now? Not the Pope again, I hope."

Michelangelo dropped the chicken onto the table, where it commenced pecking at a plate of wine-soaked bread crumbs. "We'll see soon enough. I won't go back there. Di Grassi and Asino must have been up on the scaffold before I arrived today. They were waiting for me at the chapel door. You should have heard them. *Blasphemy! Blasphemy! You spend our money on blasphemy!* Their faces were bright purple, spit flying everywhere. I want you to write to your sister in England right away. Tell her to get me a letter of introduction. That young Henry has respect for artists, and it sounds as if he'll be king soon."

"You read my letter!" Francesco exclaimed. "First you have me followed by that dunce Bastiano and then you read my letters!"

"I did *not* read your letter. I could see it was from your sister in the English court. That's all. And as for having you followed, someone has to keep an eye on you. You tell me your father pays me well for the trouble, but what am I to tell him? That you're a useless houseboy? Where was my bread today? Nowhere. You didn't even send Susanna to do your work for you. You do no work and laze around with the likes of Raphael, cavorting with whores and heathens. Do you think The Turk would hesitate to kill you if you interfere with his business? Or Asino and di Grassi? You're getting a reputation, Francesco. The reputation of someone who puts his nose into places where it does not belong. Maybe that fire *was* meant for you, and if they killed a blasphemous artist at the same time, it would make everyone happy."

It was quite a rant, even for someone as practiced as Michelangelo, but that didn't stop Francesco from teasing him. "My dear Michelangelo. It's kind of you to worry about me and my safety. I think you've grown fond of me. Like a son." The chicken flew up to the shelf above the window as if to improve its vantage point or else to stay clear in case objects started flying about the room.

"If you were my son, I'd whip you thoroughly and teach you to respect your elders."

"And you respect your elders? The man who tried to run away from the Pope just so you wouldn't have to paint his ceiling?"

"I was *not* running away from the Pope. And I should *not* be painting that ceiling. I'm a sculptor, and the best there is."

"We won't split hairs on that one. But I want you to call off Bastiano. I won't have that idiot following me. And where the hell is Susanna?"

"I don't know. Out casting spells with all the other gypsies and witches?"

"Stop it. I am very serious. Bastiano said she went off with a tall man on a horse this morning. The same man she went off with the other night when she said she was with the silversmith."

"But she *was* with the silversmith."

"That's what she told me. But Bastiano said it was the same man, and you said yourself it was too quiet. It seems like you were right, and the silversmith was never here."

"I never thought I'd hear you say I was right, but in this one instance your faith in me is misguided. The silversmith was here. I spoke with him myself." Michelangelo picked up one of the wine-soaked cubes of bread the chicken had left behind and put it in his mouth. "He was staying the night before going on to Ostia. I was just trying to get your goat—"

"And have a good laugh with Bastiano at my expense." Francesco finished the thought for him. Michelangelo didn't answer, only ate some more of the chicken's dinner while Francesco poured some water from the pitcher into the cleaner-looking of the two pewter cups on the table. All the wine he'd drank with Raphael had left his throat parched and launched a dull headache. Even if the silversmith was there the other night, Bastiano had said Susanna went with a tall man this morning. "But," Francesco continued, "there's one other thing. The soap-maker said a big, fancy man on a horse threw the torch into their shop. Could this big, fancy man and the tall man be the same?"

"Well, that solves it then. Susanna has hired a big, tall, fancy man on a horse to kill us. Probably had enough of doing your work."

"Be serious. Do you think it could be the same man?"

"I told you, it's Asino and di Grassi's doing. They hired someone to do their dirty work. I don't know who carried Susanna off this morning. Probably Bastiano was just trying to escape a beating by turning you against her."

"Well, she must be somewhere."

"Probably floating in the Tiber like your last whore."

Francesco slammed the door on his way out. Not the new front door, but the familiar back door. He kicked open the gate to Susanna's and picked his way through the dark yard. But inside the house, it was as he expected: complete darkness and as cold and damp as a tomb. She had not been back, and now he was worried. Since he'd been in Rome, she'd never been away for the night. Where was she, and who was the man Bastiano saw her with? That is, if there had been a man at all. But he didn't think Bastiano was lying on this point. He had waited until she was gone to search her house for the money. He must have been confident she wouldn't be back any time soon to interrupt him. Was it possible Bastiano had arranged for her to be abducted so he could search the house for her money in peace?

Francesco wasn't tempted to stay in her bed for the night, not even to avoid Michelangelo's snores. He didn't want to be found there by God-knows-who in the morning, and it was too cold anyway. Except whereas before he had been angered by her disappearance, he now just felt a knot of dread. *Probably floating in the Tiber like your last whore.* Not that Calendula was his whore . . . And it was true he'd probably been viewed as taking too much of an interest in her disappearance. But by whom? Not Di Grassi and Asino. What would they care of his interest, unless it had taken him a little too close to The Turk's boat, with its cargo of young boys. Except their secret didn't seem well kept and, like Imperia's brothel, appeared well tolerated if not completely sanctioned by the Pope himself.

But there were no answers to be found here, especially in the dark. Francesco decided to ask the soap-maker if he'd seen Susanna leave that morning, only when he went out her front door, the square was empty.

Still, knowing sleep would be elusive at best, he crossed the square and stood by the still-smoldering pile of timber. He picked up a charred board and gave the coals a poke, encouraging them back to life. He was rewarded with a small flame, and he stood close to it, holding his hands out to warm them. Somewhere a rooster crowed.

It had been good to see Raphael. The distraction—the wine, the excellent dinner, the drunken trip to the chapel—had been welcome, but now it somehow seemed as though he'd betrayed Susanna. Should he have been looking for her instead of enjoying himself? Of course, at the time, he'd been convinced she was taking pleasure in another man's bed, but now he couldn't shake Michelangelo's words from his mind. *Floating in the Tiber like your last whore. Floating in the Tiber. In the Tiber. The Tiber. The Tiber . . .*

Francesco pictured Calendula's body turning on an eddy of filthy water, the yellow dress pulling her body under as if she were being dragged down to Hell by an invisible hand, her beautiful hair all muddied and matted with seaweed and blood. But as he stood over the fire, picturing this in his mind's eye, her hair turned from gold to black. Black gypsy hair. Susanna's hair . . .

A *tall* man on a horse had taken her away. A *big* man on a horse had thrown a torch at his house. And a *fat* man had taken Calendula's body. Could all three be the same man?

✛   ✛   ✛

IT wasn't until the Pope and his boy entered through their new front door a few hours later that Francesco remembered the wolf outside St. Peter's. It was His Holiness's cape of white fur that brought back the memory, and for a moment he even wondered if the same wolf was now adorning the Pope. But of course that was impossible, and besides, the fur was shorter and softer, perhaps that of a winter hare. Lined with red velvet, the cape was slung over a long white robe, while the cap covering the Pope's thick white hair was made of the same fabrics but reversed, with the fur on the inside. The hem of his white robes was splattered with the muck of the street, and Francesco realized His Holiness had not taken a carriage or a litter but had walked here himself. It was a good thing they now had a front door. He could not envision the Pope picking his way through the alley. Susanna would have said the appearance of the new front door had not been a coincidence. Surely, she'd say, a divine force had guided the man with the torch to open the door just in time for His Holiness's visit.

With his head grazing the low beams, Pope Julius filled Michelangelo's house. Francesco had only seen the Pope from afar, and he was overwhelmed by the man's powerful presence. He might be a white-haired old man of sixty-five, but he didn't look it, and Francesco could well believe the stories that he still fought alongside his men in battle.

Nicknamed *Il Papa Terribile*, the man christened Giuliano della Rovere had waited a long time to become Pope and had been bribing, slandering, and perhaps even poisoning his rivals for decades. Now that the position was his, he was making up for time he saw as lost. He had taken the name of Julius after Caesar himself, and it was his goal to see Rome restored to an empire worthy of his namesake.

Following Michelangelo's lead and bearing in mind rumors of the disease that was said to riddle the Pope's feet with sores, Francesco kissed the air above them. Feeling weak and nauseated from a sleepless night of worry, he fought against the rising bile in his throat. Did the Pope share the same disease as the port's prostitutes? Would this be the man's undoing? Would it eat away at him until he, too, was forced to wrap his face in rags?

The boy stood serenely next to Pope Julius, one dimpled hand stroking the fur of his cape as if it were a pet. If anything, he was even more beautiful than Marcus's portrayal of him in *The Marigold*

Madonna. His golden hair, washed and combed in soft curls, shone in the dim room as if it contained its own source of light. And when he looked up, his eyes were of the softest blue.

"Why aren't you at the chapel today?" the Pope demanded in a booming voice. "Your assistants tell me you had a fire, and yet I see you are unharmed." Pope Julius tugged at his long white beard as he spoke, each finger on his large hands adorned with an enormous ring. He seemed to have a special liking for rubies, perhaps because they matched the lining of his cape. *They match his nose too,* Francesco thought, *the red nose of a mean, gouty old man.*

"I beg your forgiveness, Your Holiness," Michelangelo said in a servile tone Francesco knew must have nearly killed him with humiliation. "But I cannot enter the chapel when my life is being threatened."

"By whom? Tell me and I'll have the bastard whipped."

Francesco could see this invitation was giving Michelangelo pause. He told Francesco to put more wood on the fire, and Francesco obliged, knowing his master was just buying time. The thought of Di Grassi and Asino getting a good whipping would be a delectable notion to Michelangelo, but the artist was not unaware that these men outranked him. To openly accuse them could be dangerous. Still, if he could carefully lead the Pope to draw his own conclusions, victory would be his . . .

While Michelangelo was not to be dissuaded from his theories, a sleepless night had only further convinced Francesco of his own. At dawn, he had gone down to the bridge where he'd seen Calendula's body. He'd found nothing unusual, but it didn't make him feel any less afraid for Susanna. After crossing the bridge three times, he'd come home. He didn't know where else to look, but his inaction was driving him insane.

Francesco lifted the chicken from the topmost log and held it under one arm as he took advantage of His Holiness's presence to add not one but three pieces of wood to the fire. It might do his own aching head some good, and besides, he couldn't risk the Pope catching a chill, could he?

"There have been complaints about my work being blasphemous," Michelangelo began cautiously, casting a warning glance at Francesco.

"Your work blasphemous? Jesus Christ Almighty! Who is saying my chapel is blasphemous? It isn't that ass Asino, is it? I always thought him very deserving of his name. He has the face of an ass too, and not the four-legged kind."

"You know him better than myself, Your Holiness, but some-one has been spreading vile and baseless rumors, and I fear they're the reason for the attack on my house last night. Would Your Holiness like to sit? I shall pour some wine. I'm sorry I have nothing more to offer. It is but a humble room."

Francesco listened to this as he poked at the fire, relishing the unaccustomed warmth. He would hear about this later. Busy as Michelangelo was at manipulating the Pope's views of his most trusted servants, Francesco knew that glance he'd cast was a warning against wasting firewood.

"I like your chicken." Francesco turned to see the boy behind him. "Why does it have three legs?" he asked quietly. "Is it bad?"

"It is but an accident of nature," Francesco replied gently. "And makes him neither good nor bad."

Behind the boy, the Pope had taken the chair, and he and Michelangelo were now in earnest discussion, talking in lowered but still intelligible voices, heads close together in a study of ugliness: the Pope with his swollen red nose and beady eyes, and Michelangelo with his sallow, squashed face that had probably not met with a bar of soap since August's Feast of the Assumption. In contrast, here was this boy with his golden curls, long blond lashes over blue cornflower eyes, clean cheeks with a wholesome flush, and a tiny, girlish mouth. It sickened Francesco to think The Turk might be right about the Pope and this child.

"There is a parrot in a cage in the Vatican," the boy was saying. "It has blue and red feathers and can talk. That's better than having three legs. It can say my name."

"And what is your name?" Francesco asked as he looked over the boy's head to the men, who were now poring over Michelangelo's sketches for the ceiling medallions. They seemed to have forgotten they weren't alone.

"Agnello," the boy answered.

Agnello di Dio, Francesco thought. *Lamb of God.* Or perhaps, more appropriately, *I will bring them down like lambs to the slaughter.* "What else does the parrot say?"

"Words I am not allowed to say."

"I see," Francesco said. Words the Pope was very free with and whose meanings the boy was probably well acquainted with. "I won't ask you to repeat them. Do you want to pet the chicken?"

Agnello nodded and lightly stroked the bird. It blinked at the boy.

"I have seen your likeness in a painting," Francesco said.

The boy blinked up at him, not unlike the chicken. "I look like a little baby in the picture."

"Only because it's supposed to be the baby Jesus. How old are you, Agnello?"

"Six." Old enough to be apprenticed out to a tradesman. Old enough to be a houseboy. But when would the Pope decide the boy was too old to be his "companion"? When he was as old as the boys on The Turk's boat? How old were they anyway? Ten, The Turk had said. And what would happen to Agnello then? Where would he go? Would he be made a member of the court or be pushed out the door to fend for himself? Francesco was still haunted by those boys on the boat. Freed or stolen, had they perished in the cold, been eaten by wolves, or been taken by their "rescuers" to be sold into bondage elsewhere? He couldn't save them, and he stood even less of a chance of saving this one.

He looked over at the Pope and the artist, who were too engrossed in their own conversation to care what he and the boy were talking about. "There will be no more visitors to the scaffolding. Your assistants, myself, and no one else," Pope Julius was saying. "This is my legacy, and I will not have it jeopardized by a couple of jackasses. Five hundred years from now, people will see that ceiling and thank me . . ."

"Where is your mother, Agnello?" Francesco asked the boy quietly as the Pope continued to eulogize himself.

"In Hell, sir." It was as easily answered as if his mother had gone to market or been doing her needlework by the window.

"You cannot think that of your mother."

"His Holiness says she is in Hell because she was a whore."

"Do you know her name?" Francesco realized they were whispering now, the chicken under his arm looking from one face to the other as if following the conversation with interest.

"My mother was the Virgin Mary, sir. She was in the painting with me. Before she went to Hell."

Francesco saw nothing but innocence in Agnello's eyes, and it saddened him to realize that this boy, never knowing his own mother, had decided, because of this painting, that it was Calendula.

"I shall put di Grassi and Asino in charge of your safety," Pope Julius was saying. His chair scraped over the floorboards as he rose. "There will be no more trouble."

"You think it wise, Your Holiness?" Michelangelo asked. Francesco could imagine his nervousness, even as he sensed victory.

"Sometimes it is wise to let the fox guard the henhouse," Pope Julius said. "You'll see, Michelangelo. There will be no more problems, for it will be on their heads if there is. And it saves me the trouble of pointing a finger at them."

Francesco could see this meeting was swiftly coming to a close. His Holiness would leave, take the boy with him, and Michelangelo would return to the chapel. Just another day. If only Susanna were home.

And then he heard it. Another scrape, a muted thud. Footsteps even? All from the other side of the wall. He strained to hear. *Please let it be Susanna.* If he were to go over there only to find Bastiano again, or another intruder, he would kill him.

He no longer regretted not having more time to talk with the boy. He only wanted them to leave, but Michelangelo was holding up the Pope with almost slavish thanks and grandiose promises for the ceiling's swift completion.

The boy went and stood next to the Pope, holding his cloak again, stroking the soft white cape with his clean, dimpled hands. He did not look at Francesco again. *I will bring them down like lambs to the slaughter.*

✦ ✦ ✦

MICHELANGELO was triumphant on the Pope's departure. "At last I am free of that pair of papal leeches," he said to Francesco once the door had closed. Francesco thought Michelangelo might break out into a jig, he looked so happy.

"Who was that boy with Julius?" Francesco didn't think he could use the title "His Holiness" ever again. From now on, he'd just be Julius.

"A nephew, maybe? The boy seems to do well by him."

Francesco didn't enlighten him, but he was certain he could add "willfully blind" to Michelangelo's many character flaws. But for all the things Michelangelo was—a petty, obstinate, obsessive, proud, stingy, moody hypochondriac, for a start—Francesco knew he didn't have one drop of the Pope's evil in him.

He left Michelangelo in probably the best mood he'd ever seen him, happier even than the night he'd swindled the wood seller. No doubt he felt he'd one-upped Julius, along with Asino and di Grassi, and was now free to finish the ceiling without interference. Francesco would never tell Michelangelo, but he felt the artist's talents were wasted on this city.

✛　✛　✛

AS anxious as Francesco was to investigate the commotion next door, he opened the door with trepidation. Not wanting to alert a possible intruder, he opted to enter without knocking, and the door swung slowly inward on its leather hinges.

"There you are!" Susanna said. She stood scrubbing down the table while behind her a small fire burned in the grate. He could see she had rescued the notice he had angrily placed there—*Devils in the Guise of Wolves Eat our Children!* "I was just about to come looking for you. Did you miss me? I brought some good bread for you. Olives and cheese too."

The flippancy in her tone angered him most. After he had spent a sleepless night worrying about her safety, how could she stand there and so lightly ask: *Did you miss me?*

"Where were you?" he demanded. "I was ready to have the Tiber dragged for your body."

"Whatever for? I was only gone for a day."

"Who were you with?" Now that he knew she was safe, his jealousy returned.

"No one."

"No one? That's not what I heard."

"And what did you hear?" she asked with seemingly genuine puzzlement.

"That you left with a tall man on a horse." He was still irate, but her bafflement and his recollection that the information had come from Bastiano, not the most trustworthy of sources, tempered his tone.

She laughed. "Are you jealous?" she asked, putting down the scrub brush and wiping her hands on her apron. "I like it when you're jealous. You pay attention to me then, instead of pretending I'm that other woman."

He held up his hand for her to stop, realizing as he did so that there was truth in her words. He *was* jealous. Still, he wasn't quite ready to forgive her. "Is it true? Did you go with a tall man on a horse?"

Susanna gave a snort of exasperation. "Yes, I went with a tall man on a horse. A messenger. He delivered a letter to your house

173

and was heading on to Ostia. I went with him to see my father. I wasn't going to see Benvenuto, if that's what you're thinking."

He wasn't. He was trying to reconcile the tall man on the horse who'd delivered his letter and taken Susanna with his tall man, big man, fat man theory. Had he been wrong about everything? "Your father?" he asked, wondering now if he should tell her his ideas. "In the country?"

"Can't a girl visit her father? I've told you before he lives just outside of Ostia."

"And did you return with the same man just now?"

"Is that why you're angry? Because someone saw me with the messenger? I didn't share his bed, if that's what you're implying. He stayed at the inn in Ostia. I came back with him today only because he was returning to Rome too. I can't believe you're jealous. You're such a little boy."

"I am not jealous," he lied. "And so the same man brought you home today?"

"Yes. I just said that."

Francesco stared at her and decided she was probably telling the truth. It seemed very unlikely the man would have taken Susanna all the way to her father's, ridden back, thrown a lit torch into the soap-maker's shop, then returned to Ostia, picked up Susanna, and brought her back to Rome. But then he was no further ahead in learning the identity of either the man who lit the shop on fire or the man who'd taken Calendula's body. Unless the fire really was the doing of Asino and di Grassi, but he didn't believe that. "Did you come in by way of the square today?"

She shook her head. "I came by the alley. He left me by the port. Why are you asking me all these questions? At first I thought you were jealous, but now you're just being . . . strange."

Francesco went to the front door and signaled her to follow. They stepped out into the square, and Susanna gasped as Francesco pulled her back into the doorway and out of the way of a pig being chased by its owner, a scraggly man with an equally scraggly beard, bearing a heavy cudgel. The pig careened and skidded through the square, squealing like a demon, splattering mud, and sending chickens scurrying. A big black dog joined in pursuit and was rewarded with a blow to the head. The dog dropped to the ground with hardly a whimper, and Francesco was sure it must be dead, but moments later, it struggled to its feet and staggered off between two houses. But Susanna hardly noticed. She was staring aghast at the empty space where only yesterday the soap-maker's shop had leaned.

"There's been a fire! What happened?"

"The soap-maker told me a fancy man on a horse threw a torch into the shop, and someone else"—he omitted telling her it was Bastiano—"said you left with a tall man on a horse." Daylight revealed the full extent of the damage. The walls of Michelangelo's house were blackened, and it was clear that parts had indeed caught fire. Had it not been for the rain and the soap-maker's wife's calloused hands, the house would certainly have burned to the ground.

"I see," she said. She looked at him, arms crossed over her chest, her face scrunched into a comical picture of concentration. "You thought I left with a tall, fancy man on a horse and then he came back and burned down the soap-maker's shop?"

He nodded. "But obviously it wasn't the same man." He suddenly noticed that her hair was clean, shining despite the dullness of the day. She must have had a bath at her father's. Her brown dress seemed cleaner too, and she had a new white apron.

"Where are Rocco and Rocca?"

"Who?"

"The soap-maker and his wife, of course. I hope they weren't killed in the fire."

This was the first time Francesco had heard the pair's names. They'd always just been the soap-maker and his wife to him. It seemed fitting they shared the masculine and feminine versions of the same name. "No, they're fine. They're going to stay with her sister and set up shop there. It looks like they've already been back for the cauldron. I can't say I'll miss the stink."

"Why would anyone want to burn down their shop? It's such a mean thing to do."

"I'm not sure if it was intended to burn down the shop or Michelangelo's house."

"You think this was meant for Michelangelo?"

"Michelangelo does. And he thinks di Grassi and Asino are behind it. They're angry about the ceiling." The bells of Santa Caterina began to toll the midday hour.

"They would try to kill a man because they didn't like how he painted a ceiling?" Susanna asked over the clanging bells.

"I know, it sounds foolish. But they think it's blasphemous. All those muscular naked men, I guess. But I'm sure that's just an excuse. Julius has cut their allowances, and they think all their money's going to Michelangelo. Julius was just here, and he seemed to believe Michelangelo, or at least he was willing to humor his suspicions."

"Did you say Julius—*His Holiness*—was here? In your house?" The bells subsided with one last lopsided peal, and Susanna beckoned him back through the door. She offered him some bread and cheese, and he accepted with something very close to contentment. How good it was to have the jealousy removed and to know Susanna was safe. Maybe afterward they would lie on her bed . . .

He forced his thoughts back to the conversation at hand. "Julius wanted to know why Michelangelo wasn't at the chapel today."

"That's an honor for Michelangelo and should put di Grassi and Asino in their place."

"That's what Michelangelo is hoping. But I'm sure they had nothing to do with the fire."

"Well then, who did?"

"I don't know. But I wonder whether it could be the same man who stole Calendula's body."

"Why would he want to burn down the soap-maker's shop?"

"He might have been trying to kill me. Maybe he knows I've been asking The Turk questions. The Turk was supposed to go to the mortuary today to see what he could find out."

"Then why not burn down The Turk's house?"

"I don't know," Francesco said. Mention of The Turk reminded him of the boys who'd escaped from The Turk's ship. "You must be silent about this. But when we saw Asino and di Grassi at the port, they were there to buy boys. Very young boys for carnal pleasure." He had a sudden thought. "I don't want to upset you, but I think that's where Julius got that little boy from."

"I already know what he does with that boy."

"You do?" He remembered the night when they'd stood out in the rain talking, the first night they heard the wolves. "But I thought you said the Pope can't sin."

"He can't," she said with finality. She threw a couple of sticks on the fire and gave them a poke.

"Then what do you call what he does to that boy?"

She shrugged. "When I was small, the priest took me after Mass to this secret room. It had a fireplace, and there was a table with books and a human skull. He took it out . . . not the skull . . . you know . . ."

Francesco felt ill. "That's not sin?"

"He told me to do what he said and not to tell my father, or demons would take me to Hell and burn me forever with hot pokers. I didn't want to do it, but I didn't want to go to Hell and be burned, either. The priest took the poker from the fire and put it right there," she said, pushing her finger against her skirts to indicate the inside of her thigh. "He showed me how it would feel. And so I did what he wanted." She spoke matter-of-factly, busying herself with preparing the food she'd promised Francesco. "He got me pregnant. I couldn't tell my mother, so I went to the midwife to make me bleed. I bled so much I almost died, and then I never bled again . . ."

She hadn't answered his question, *That's not sin?* But he almost forgot he'd asked it. Sin didn't come close to describing what had transpired in that room. But he also knew her tormentor had made her think she was the sinner, such was his power. "You're not afraid anymore, are you?" he asked quietly.

"Not anymore," she said, pouring wine for them both, smiling bravely. "*È la vita, che ci vuoi fare?* That's life, what can you do about it?"

He started to object, but she told him to hush and handed him a plate with a generous chunk of cheese and a fat slice of bread. There were some olives as well, black and shiny with oil. He shouldn't be hearing these things and enjoying food at the same time. It felt wrong.

"And anyway," Susanna said firmly, "His Holiness's boy didn't come from Asino and di Grassi. He came from Imperia's."

"From Imperia's?" Francesco was astounded.

"Everybody knows that. That's why His Holiness lets her have her brothel. Because she gave him the boy."

"Why did you never tell me this?"

"You never asked me."

"But it could be . . ." He was going to say *important*, only as he didn't know whether it was, how could he expect her to know? He popped an olive in his mouth and chewed off the meat before spitting the pit out onto the plate. To a point, the boy's story did corroborate Susanna's. He did say his mother was a whore. But then he also said she was in Hell and that she was the Virgin Mary. "Well, who is the boy's mother? Imperia?"

"I don't think so. Just some whore's. There are enough of them." She said this last part with the usual haughtiness she employed when speaking of anyone connected with Imperia.

Francesco took a bite of cheese. Maybe Susanna should visit her father more often. She handed him his wine, and he was about to dip in his bread when he almost dropped it, cup and all. "Of course!" he exclaimed. How could he have missed it? The golden hair, the blue eyes. *His Holiness says she is in Hell because she was a whore.* "Calendula! It has to be Calendula."

"Why?" asked Susanna, seemingly unimpressed.

"Well, the blond hair and blue eyes, for a start. And Agnello told me: *My mother was the Virgin Mary, sir. She was in the painting with me. Before she went to Hell.*"

"But Calendula didn't have any children."

Francesco swore. "You're right. Imperia told me her husband had thrown her out because of her barrenness. Or at least I think that's what she said. Do you know how long Calendula was at Imperia's? Could she have had a child after her arrival? There are enough children in the house."

Susanna shrugged. "I don't know, but Imperia has only been there for two years, so Calendula could only have been there that long. How old is the boy?"

"Six," he said. "So if the boy was Calendula's, he would have been four when she came to Imperia's."

Susanna counted the years on her fingers. Or at least made a display of doing so, mouthing random numbers as she pointed at the fingers of one hand with those on the other. Francesco felt embarrassed for her. How did she not get cheated at the market? He was going to have to teach her to count, as well as read. She would never save for a dowry this way. "Yes!" she said quite triumphantly, as if she were Euclid and had just discovered geometry. "He couldn't have been born two years ago, because then he'd be two, not six." She picked up her cup of wine. "Sometimes I'm smarter than you."

"Sometimes it's not difficult," he said. "Still, I think I'll go and talk to Imperia." Obviously Imperia hadn't told him the whole story. For one, she hadn't told him she'd given the boy to Julius. Neither had she admitted, at first, to ordering Calendula from the house nor fighting with her over the ring. Perhaps there was even more she'd omitted.

"Not tonight, I hope. I want you to come with me later."

"Why?"

"There's to be a necromancer in the Colosseum. They say he can raise all kinds of spirits. Evil and good. I'll show you. I'm going there tonight. He wears a black hood like the hangman and speaks with the Devil's tongue."

"Who told you this nonsense?"

"It isn't nonsense, and I'm not lying. The messenger told me."

Francesco sighed. "I know you're not lying. You're silly enough to believe such things, but the messenger who told you this *is* lying."

"Well," she said defiantly, "I'm going even if you don't come."

"You are not to go. It's not safe for a man to go to that part of the city at night, let alone a woman." Although, after what she'd just told him, he supposed there were very few safe places for a woman. He put down the plate and pulled her onto the bed next to him. "Come here, and if you really want to go, I'll take you and you can see for yourself it's all tricks."

She laid her head on his shoulder. "When Benvenuto was home the other night, I put herbs in his wine so he would sleep and leave me alone."

"Is that why it was so quiet?"

She nodded.

"You lied. You told me the next morning you were all worn out!"

"That was just to make you jealous so you wouldn't think of that other woman. You're not thinking of her now, are you?"

"No, I'm not." Her freshly washed hair smelled of rain and rosemary. He kissed it and undressed her with more tenderness than he'd ever felt before, telling her about the hot spring near his house in the hills above Florence, how it had once been a Roman bath, and how it bubbled out of the ground, warmer and softer than any queen's bath, and how if she lived there, she could wash her hair every day.

È la vita, she'd said. It shouldn't be like this, with her afraid of predatory priests, of Hell, of demons, scrounging for a dowry to avoid a life of drudgery, and it shouldn't be about little boys caught between toiling in the mines and being slaves of lecherous old men.

He searched for the scar, and in the dim light he found it, high inside her thigh, a long, pink, smooth mark. How it must have hurt, bubbling up into a terrible blister she had to hide from her mother. Even if Susanna had confessed it all, her mother would likely have called her a witch for blaming the priest. Francesco knew that the bastard had burned her as close to that place as he'd dared, the place the priest wanted and feared and hated.

He'd threatened her with Hell, and she had failed to see how, in that room, she already was in Hell. How long had it gone on? Weeks, months, years? *I'll find the priest and kill him*, he thought as he kissed the rise of her belly.

He would find Guido too and appease him if it took everything he had. It was over between him and Juliet, he realized now, and maybe there had never been much to it at all. And while only days ago that knowledge would have torn out his heart, the memory of their affair was already becoming as illusory as the white wolf on the steps of St. Peter's. He drifted off to sleep, his cheek against Susanna's breast, and dreamed they were already home. He would finally read the new book by Erasmus, and she would make them sweet cakes with honey and almonds, and Raphael would come to visit, and they would talk into the night while breezes of a Florentine evening perfumed with flowers from his mother's garden wafted through the open windows.

CHAPTER EIGHT

FRANCESCO WOKE TO BELLS STRIKING THE HOUR. HIS SLEEP HAD been sound, and so he was surprised to see light still struggling through the room's only window. Susanna lay beside him on her back, lips parted, snoring softly.

He had plenty of time before he had to take Susanna to see the necromancer, so he rolled over in an attempt to go back to sleep. But he found himself instead staring up into the smoke-blackened beams, going over the day's events. There must be some link between Calendula and the Pope's boy that only Imperia could shed light on. And the sooner he went to see her, the sooner he would know that connection. If he learned something that could free the boy, all the better.

He gave Susanna a gentle shake, and she mumbled to leave her be. "I'm going to Imperia's," he said, flicking a flea from her cheek, "but I promise to be back by the time the bells ring for vespers, to take you to the Colosseum. Don't leave without me." Retrieving his hose from the foot of the bed, he slid out from under the covers.

✢ ✢ ✢

IT wasn't one of the bear-wrestling giants who opened the door for Francesco but instead a houseboy.

"Imperia's in her room, resting."

"Tell her it is Francesco. She'll see me."

The boy nodded and was about to go when, on a whim, Francesco called him back. "Who's your mother, boy?"

The boy looked at him as if he'd been asked if he were the queen of France. "Don't have one," was his answer in the end.

"So your mother doesn't live here with you?"

"Don't know. Just don't have one."

Not knowing how to respond, Francesco waved him on his way and went into the salon, where he found Sodoma sleeping in a chair by the fire, a cup of wine held loosely in one hand, threatening at any moment to spill onto the carpet. Francesco took the cup gently from him, though not quite gently enough. Sodoma woke with a start and leaped to his feet, his hand flying to the dagger sheathed in the folds of his turquoise dress. "State your business, man!"

Francesco jumped back, careening into the bookcase. "Calm yourself," he said with a laugh, not quite able to call Sodoma "man" in return. "It's only me. I was just trying to save Imperia's carpet from your wine."

Sodoma, now properly awake, laughed and dropped back into his chair, tossing his dagger onto the table. He plunged his hand back into the folds of his dress, this time pulling out a delicate fan. "Sorry, Francesco," he said, flipping it open and fanning himself daintily. "But you should be careful waking a dreaming man. I might have taken you for a murderous heathen."

"I think you did," Francesco said, handing him back his wine. "Speaking of murderous heathens, have you seen The Turk today?"

Sodoma shook his head. "I've only been here a couple of hours. Just me and the old man there." He nodded his head in the direction of the window, where the old man in question sat very still, his hands resting on the arms of the chair. He had long white hair and a wisp of white beard. His eyes were white too, the milky color of someone long blind. "No point asking him anything," Sodoma asked. "He just arrived this morning. He's Venetian and blind as my boots."

"Ah, but my boots see very well," said the old man in a strong, steady voice. "They saw me all the way from Venice to Rome."

"Nothing wrong with your ears, either," said Sodoma. "What are you doing here in Rome?"

"I've come to see His Holiness in the interest of peace between Venice and Rome."

"Peace between Venice and Rome? You waste your time. His Holiness will not be deprived of a chance to ride into battle on his favorite horse and have your whole city excommunicated. Just how old are you, old man?"

"I was born the same day Constantinople fell to the Venetians."

Francesco laughed. "That would make you about three hundred years old."

"Whatever you say, boy. Never did learn to count."

"If you live in Venice, how do you keep from falling into the canals, Old Venetian Blind Man?" Sodoma asked.

Old Venetian Blind Man took a draught of wine that Francesco offered him. "I didn't tell you the whole story. My boots don't just see well. With them, I can walk on water."

"I must get myself some boots like yours," Sodoma said. "I'll put wings on them, and then I'll be able to fly too." He looked to Francesco and mouthed the word "crazy" over his fan.

Francesco thought it more likely the old man was simply having a bit of fun. He would have liked to hear more, but the houseboy returned and told him Imperia would see him, so he followed the boy up the stairs and through the halls, remembering as he did to not look in any rooms, lest he receive a tempting invitation. This, of course, made him think of Susanna, probably still asleep, the memory of their lovemaking coming back to him in a flash vivid enough to make his breath catch in his chest.

The boy knocked at Imperia's door. When she called Francesco in, she was sitting on her settee, wearing a new dress of pale blue silk. Her dark hair, still crimped from having been recently released from a braid, fell loose around her shoulders. Her composure suddenly angered him and, skipping all greetings and inquiries about her health, he commenced immediately with the reason for his visit.

"Imperia, what do you know about the Pope's boy, Agnello?"

He could see he had taken her by surprise, and it was a moment before she could answer. "What do you mean?" she asked, as if already knowing she could not plead ignorance.

"The boy, Agnello. You gave him to the Pope, did you not?"

"Why you are asking me this?"

"Because you've been keeping some things to yourself. Is the boy Calendula's?"

Imperia shook her head slowly.

"Then who *is* his mother?"

Without answering, Imperia rose from the settee and went over to stand before the window, the pale blue dress replacing the darkening November sky with a cloudless June one. When she moved, the dress shimmered and the folds became waves on a tranquil sea, making him forget for a moment his anger and the reason for being there. His mind momentarily drifted to the shores of the Adriatic, where he'd once watched silver dolphins play.

Church bells tolling the hour returned him to the present. The next time they rang, it would be vespers, the promised time of his return to Susanna. How often had he heard his father recite vespers? *Oh God, come to my assistance. Oh Lord, make haste to help me. Gloria Patri, et Filio, et Spiritui Sancto . . .*

"Agnello's mother," Imperia said finally as the bells died away, "was a young woman who lived here only briefly. She brought him with her but died soon after from fever. His Holiness took a fancy to him, and so Agnello went to live at the Vatican."

"And in exchange, Julius sanctioned your brothel," Francesco said bluntly.

Imperia nodded slowly. She didn't sit down but rested her hands on the back of the settee, fussing with a loose thread in the silk upholstery. Behind her, the pewter sky had deepened to slate.

"You know what he does to that boy?" Francesco could barely contain his anger.

She didn't look at him. "His Holiness desired the boy, and what His Holiness desires, he takes. My choice was to give Agnello to him willingly in exchange for His Holiness's protection, or resist and earn his wrath." She met his eyes now. "You cannot imagine what he is capable of. So what was I to do? Either way, His Holiness would still have the boy. We all do what it takes to survive, you know that as well as anyone. Besides, Francesco, it was a better fate than befalls most orphans of prostitutes."

Francesco didn't answer. As much as he despised the fact of her complicity, she was right. What the Pope wanted, he indeed took. *When in Rome . . .* It was a reference to following local church customs, but Francesco didn't think St. Ambrose had the customs of Rome under Pope Julius II in mind when he wrote it.

Francesco went to the table and poured two cups of wine. He handed one to Imperia, and they both drank deeply. "I apologize," he said, sitting on the ottoman next to her. "Last night, a torch was thrown into the lean-to that adjoined our house and very nearly burned it to the ground. I am told the torch was thrown by a well-dressed man on a horse, and I've come to believe he was after me. And so I wonder if there could be any link between Agnello, Julius, and Calendula's murderer. This could be a matter of life and death, not just for me but for anyone who knows me."

"I don't follow you, Francesco."

"Julius told Agnello his mother was a whore who lived in Hell. Julius could have been referring to his real mother, who was a dead whore, but he also could have been referring to Calendula, who was, of course, the Virgin Mary in the painting. The boy's exact words were, *My mother was the Virgin Mary, sir. She was in the painting with me. Before she went to Hell.* So could Julius be involved in all this somehow?"

Imperia sighed. "What a cruel thing to say," she said, crossing herself. "Imagine telling a young boy his mother's in Hell. Please believe me that I want to know the answers too, that I meant everything I said about my love for Calendula." Leaning over, she took his hands in hers. "Tell me you believe me."

"I do," he said with a little more sincerity than he felt, but he'd been wrong to let his emotions get the better of him.

"I did not lie to you the other day, Francesco. Time after time, Calendula was with child, and time after time, she lost them. About five years ago, I stayed with her all one spring when she was with child. This particular time, she had carried the child for almost six months and was hopeful it would live, that she would finally give her husband the heir he wanted so desperately. But it was not to be, and she lost this child too. It was the night of the summer solstice. The smallest little boy. He came so quickly, there was no time to summon the midwife. He was no bigger than a newborn kitten and lived but a few hours, but I'll never forget his cry. So faint and unhappy, his tiny hands reaching out . . . And Calendula . . ." Imperia met Francesco's eyes briefly. "How she wept!"

Imperia was quiet for a moment, and when she continued, her voice was composed. "A few weeks later, my mother died and I returned to Rome. This very house had been my mother's, though everything else had been lost long before. My father was a chorister with a meager salary, and the house had fallen into disrepair. I won't tell you how it all came about, but I had my beauty and I found a way to keep us. One by one, they came to me, unwanted daughters and disgraced wives of poor nobles, and soon this house became what it is."

"And Calendula was one of them."

"Two years ago, she was abandoned by her husband after yet another stillbirth, and so she came to me. While she knew of Agnello, she'd never laid eyes on him. His Holiness doesn't come here, and she'd never been to the Vatican. It wasn't until Marcus completed *The Marigold Madonna* that she saw him, or at least his likeness. I curse the day Marcus decided to paint it."

"The Turk said from the moment she saw the portrait, she was never the same. He's of the belief she became aware of her own beauty, and it spoiled her."

"Calendula was always aware of her beauty," Imperia said wryly, "and used it to her advantage. All women must. Except beauty can only go so far. A nobleman can have his choice of mistresses, but to be his wife demands a dowry, and he will hold out for the highest bidder. You will do the same yourself."

Francesco didn't respond. Hadn't he just hours ago dreamed of taking Susanna as his wife, dowry be damned? Or was he more like Calendula? Resigned to this idea until a better offer was made? If he learned Juliet was free, what would he do then?

"How is it that Calendula and Agnello were in the painting together but never met?" he finally asked.

"They sat for him separately. She sat first. Marcus added Agnello later. Neither of them saw the painting until it was completed. It was the likeness of Agnello that affected her so strongly, not her own image. Marcus may have exaggerated their similarities, but they do indeed look very much like mother and son."

She released his hands and was quiet for a moment. What a strange tragedy, Francesco thought: Agnello looking for a mother and Calendula looking for a son, and both thought they had found each other in this painting.

Imperia again took up her cup before continuing. "Calendula became convinced he was hers, in fact the very child she had given birth to when I had been a guest in her home. He was about the right age and had the same hair and eyes. She screamed at me, 'How can he not be mine?' She was convinced the baby hadn't died after all but that I had stolen him, brought him back with me to Rome, and given him to His Holiness. I don't know whose tiny body she thought we buried, but she was beyond reason. She told me she hated me. She called me a liar and demanded I get Agnello back for her. Her life had been destroyed because she couldn't bear her husband a son, and here I had him all along."

This must be the fight the cook had told Susanna about. But there had to be more. "Did you throw her out the night she was murdered? And why didn't you tell me?"

Imperia sighed. "How could I tell you I'd done something so

terrible? Did she die because I threatened to throw her out? Because I didn't throw her out, I swear. I only threatened to, and then I left the room in exasperation. In the morning, she was gone. When I learned of her death, of course I blamed myself. But now I'm certain she already meant to leave. She'd decided to meet the man who gave her the ring. He's the man we must look for."

"So was Julius aware of Calendula's obsession with Agnello? Could he have seen her as making trouble?" Francesco had another thought. "Could the man who took her from the mortuary have taken his orders from the Pope himself?"

Imperia put her cup back down. "If His Holiness killed Calendula, why the ruse of the ring? And why is it in The Turk's possession?"

"True. But I still think it's possible Julius could be involved if he suspected Calendula was trying to get to the boy. And I still want to know when it was that Julius told Agnello his mother was in Hell."

Imperia looked thoughtful. "Do you think if you talked again with Agnello . . . ?"

"Maybe. And I also need to talk to The Turk. He was supposed to go to the mortuary to see if he could learn anything new. Have you seen him?"

Imperia shook her head.

"Perhaps he hasn't honored his word?" Francesco suggested.

"No. That's not like The Turk. He takes his word very seriously."

"Then I will speak with him in the morning. Tonight I've offered to help a friend."

"You're a good man, Francesco." She smiled. "When you leave, will you send me one of the girls? It's time for me to prepare for the evening."

He was about to leave when he noticed her rings scattered on a silver tray in the middle of her dressing table, six in total. It would be easy for somebody to slip away with one. He picked up a large ruby not unlike the ones the Pope wore and turned it over in his hand a few times before replacing it.

"What is it?" Imperia asked.

"I was thinking how easy it would be for someone to take these. Would you notice one missing? I'm thinking of The Turk's ring, of course."

"Perhaps not. I normally take them off at night and put them on again in the morning. But lately my fingers have been swollen. A sign I'm with child, I'm told, and so they sit here. You're right—they would be easy to steal. Do you think someone took The Turk's ring and returned it later?"

"Maybe. The Turk doesn't think so, but I'll ask him again tomorrow when I see him." It suddenly occurred to him there was something different about the room. "What happened to your little bird?"

"I decided to release it. Its song was sweet but unrelenting, I'm afraid. It's probably happier now."

Francesco didn't have the heart to tell her the bird had most likely perished in Rome's cold November rains. This made him think again of the boys on The Turk's ship, also released to the harsh elements. He wondered if any of them were still alive.

Neither of the giants was at the door when he left, and he helped himself to two freshly prepared torches by the door. He'd need them tonight for their journey to and from the Colosseum. He didn't relish this outing, but there would be no dissuading Susanna. And as much as he wanted to know what The Turk had learned, he didn't want Susanna going to the Colosseum by herself.

✢ ✢ ✢

AS Francesco entered the Piazza Rusticucci, the bells were signaling vespers. He found Susanna already wrapped in her cloak, impatiently awaiting his return. "I was beginning to think I'd be going on my own after all," she said crossly.

"I told you I'd be back. Why are you taking all the cardamom?"

"I have to take some sort of payment for the necromancer."

Francesco told her he'd hoped she'd trade it for honey cakes instead, and in the end she agreed that even half was still a generous offering. Francesco placed the lightened sack in the otherwise empty money bag on his belt, tucked the torches under his arm, and made sure his dagger was in easy reach.

To avoid the worst of the flooding, they took the route toward the port, crossing the river at the Cestio Bridge. Francesco had hoped the evening light would linger until they reached the Colosseum, but it scarcely lasted to the bridge. They stopped in the middle of the second span and looked up to where fires dotted the Palatine and Aventine hills to deter the wolves, who were already yapping.

At the other end of the bridge loomed the ruins of the Theater of Marcellus. Planned by Julius Caesar, who was murdered before the first stone was laid, it was a smaller version of the Colosseum, its remaining walls forming a semicircle, the other half having been pillaged to build the bridge they'd just crossed. Through the stone arches, they glimpsed fires, and Francesco assumed the theater had become a temporary shelter for those who'd lost their homes to the flooding. Two men stood guard at one of these arches, and Francesco asked them if he could light his torch. The men shrugged and nodded toward the nearest fire, where a group of filthy children sat huddled under an equally filthy blanket. By their sides were scattered their last few possessions: a couple of earthenware pots, a few pewter plates and spoons, and what appeared to be a small wooden casket. Behind them a wooden door was laid over two waist-high stones, creating a cave-like shelter. Inside, a woman sat on the ground, suckling a child. This scene was repeated with few discernible differences around the dark amphitheater.

Francesco expected to encounter the same desperation at the Colosseum and was relieved when they finally arrived to find the atmosphere almost festive. Here, too, the refugees had gathered, setting up their camps inside the nooks and crannies of the ruin, but tonight, no doubt in anticipation of the necromancer's visit, their fires burned brightly.

They found the necromancer at the southern end of the vast ruin, preparing for the rituals. He was a spindly man with a gaunt face, sunken eyes, and the scraggly beard of a goat—or, Francesco supposed, the Devil. He wore a long black robe with wide sleeves and carried under his arm a large black book. "Good evening, my pretty one." He leered at Susanna, his smile revealing yellow teeth filed to sharp points. His two assistants, an ugly pair who Francesco suspected would play more than one role that night, had already built a good-sized fire and were now scratching a pentagram into the packed earth with a stick. Francesco knew that, while these were forbidden rites, the Church was willing to look the other way so long as enough Biblical names were cited as part of the spectacle. It was conveniently agreed that these were not spells to encourage demons but prayers to vanquish them.

That said, the Church's position didn't satisfy everyone, and to one side of the display a robed monk, his cowl covering most of his face, was decrying the scene as blasphemy. He was ignored by the adults, but the children made a game of pelting him with stones, loudly cheering every hit, forcing the monk to shield his face further with his arm. Thirty or so men and women gathered around the necromancer, already speculating about his abilities to raise the dead. Francesco would normally have enjoyed dispelling their illusions, but tonight it seemed mean-spirited when their only alternative was to huddle in their makeshift shelters.

Francesco left Susanna with the crowd and went to look around. He had been here before, but only during the day. Tonight, lit by smoky fires, with the clouded sky as its roof, the arena felt different. He could see how over the centuries the lower levels of the Colosseum had filled with earth, burying a warren of foundations and stone pens that once held wild animals and human gladiators. An earthquake had brought down the southern stretch of wall, and loose stone had been carted off to build palaces and bridges, with more destined for the new St. Peter's. Trees had grown up in the interior, and in the northern end a religious order had built a piece-meal abbey out of the existing stone arcades and salvaged wood. Except for the one brave (or foolish) monk who was challenging the necromancer, there was no sign of the abbey's inhabitants tonight, though Francesco thought he could hear the sound of goat bells coming from inside.

Finally the necromancer was ready, and Francesco could hear him entreating the crowd to move back. "Farther, farther, my beautiful ladies," he kept repeating. "I implore you, it's not safe. The demons are difficult to control, and you don't want any of them to have their evil way with you." Nervous giggling could be heard from the "ladies" as they backed away.

Finding Susanna at the center of the group, Francesco took her by the arm and led her over to a large, flat rock where they would be safe, he assumed, from getting too close a look at the "demons." Opening his big book, the necromancer stepped inside the pentagram and positioned himself behind the fire, giving the impression of being engulfed by flames. The fire cast an eerie light on his face as he looked up to the sky. His eyes rolled back in his head as he began to chant in a low voice, too low for Francesco to make out, while from the sidelines the monk screamed, "Devil! Devil!" until someone told him to shut up before he cut his tongue out.

The necromancer appeared to notice none of this, and he droned on in this trancelike state for some time. But just when it seemed the audience might grow restless, his voice gained in intensity, rising in volume and pitch. His shouts were answered by the shrieks and screeches of invisible demons, and the echoes bounced off the ancient stones, swirling around the Colosseum like a scene from Judgment Day.

"What's he saying?" Susanna yelled into Francesco's ear as she gripped his sleeve. Her eyes were wide with excitement, while nearby a child started to cry and a woman screamed.

"Gibberish," Francesco answered. And it was. He caught a few words of Latin, some counting in German, a string of Biblical names, including those of the Magi, another scream, none of this seemingly originating from the book in the necromancer's hands. Indeed, the book seemed to have become too hot for him to hold, and he now dropped it onto the ground. Waving his hands over his head, he implored Beelzebub to appear to him.

And so Beelzebub did. The necromancer shook his hands over the fire and from the flames emanated a loud explosion, followed by black, belching clouds of smoke. The boom echoed around the walls of the Colosseum, and out of the smoke emerged a grotesque figure with a black face and horns, screaming as if it were being tortured by every pitchfork in Hell. "What is it, Francesco?" Susanna cried.

"Saltpeter, I suspect, for the explosion," Francesco said coolly. "Had it up his sleeves. And that demon is nothing but one of the necromancer's assistants with charcoal on his face."

"Oh, no, it can't be a man. It is too terrible. And look, he's flying!"

"He's standing on the wall. It's just that the smoke makes it look—"

The necromancer shook his hands over the fire again, and another boom went up into the night, the demon's unnatural screams nearly drowned out by those of the onlookers. Now the necromancer was demanding that the demon come down out of the air to talk to him. "Beelzebub, come down! I command you in the name of the baby Jesus!" Beelzebub waved his arms and shrieked some more before diving down out of the air (from Susanna's perspective) or from his perch on the wall (from Francesco's) and disappearing into the thick smoke. The necromancer raised a crucifix and commanded the spirit to leave Rome and take his Hellhounds with him, by which Francesco assumed he meant the wolves.

But the demon didn't seem to want to leave. The crowd gasped as he grabbed the crucifix and hurled it onto the fire before seizing the necromancer by the beard. The two wrestled furiously, the smoke and flames every bit as blistering as if they were truly in the midst of Hell. They threw each other this way and that. One moment the necromancer was in control, and the next the demon was hurling him about by his beard. The crowd loved it. No longer afraid, they cheered and threw their support behind the necromancer. Susanna, at Francesco's side, had let go of his sleeve and, with her hands over her face, peered out through her fingers.

Francesco was sure the crowd would have been happy to have this last all night, but finally the necromancer wrestled the demon to the ground. With one knee planted on the demon's chest, he dove for his book and opened it, incanting another apparent prayer. Francesco heard again a witch's brew of languages: "Whore of Babylon, one, two, three, I smash your baby's head against the rock... four, five, six . . ." With his knee still holding down the demon, the necromancer shook his hands at the fire. Francesco predicted that, under cover of the explosion and smoke, the demon would disappear and the necromancer would be named the winner in this struggle against evil.

But the conclusion wasn't quite as Francesco forecast, nor, presumably, as the necromancer had planned. The man shook his hands over the fire, conjuring the same loud boom and plume of smoke as before, but this time lighting his flowing sleeves on fire. As the smoke cleared, the thought-to-be-defeated demon was now wrestling the screaming necromancer to the ground, swatting at the flaming sleeves with a piece of sacking.

"What's happening?" Susanna cried as, along with the rest of the crowd, she jumped to her feet.

"Not to worry. I think the demon has things under control," Francesco answered, trying his hardest not to laugh.

His sleeves extinguished, the necromancer rose to his feet, and with his face contorted in pain, he swayed uncertainly, gazing down at his blistered arms. The demon, looking more confused than a demon probably should, glanced from the necromancer to the crowd and back, as if unsure what to do next. With no suggestions being offered by the necromancer, the demon settled for letting up a terrible wail. In what appeared a desperate attempt to salvage his evil persona, he stomped around the fire once again, shrieking louder and flailing his arms faster than ever.

He might have succeeded if the show had ended there. But all of a sudden, from out behind a large rock, came what Francesco assumed was the next act, a corpse rising from the dead. He was a gory sight, his face and tattered clothes smeared with blood, animal entrails hanging around his neck. He walked slowly around the fire, his arms straight out in front of him, hands bent down at the wrist, dragging one leg behind him, all the while making woeful wailing sounds. It was more than Francesco could take, and he started to laugh.

"What are you doing?" Susanna demanded.

But it wasn't just Francesco. One of the men in the crowd jumped up and joined in with the demon and the ghoulish corpse. "Woo, woo, woo," he wailed, waving his hands around. Now everyone was laughing as they flailed their arms and attempted to fill the Colosseum with the sound of dozens of wailing corpses. The children especially loved it. They ran to the fire and passed their hands over it in vain attempts to make it boom. Francesco was reminded of the children in the square imitating the soap-maker's whooshing sounds. The monk ran past Francesco and Susanna with his robe held up to keep from tripping and disappeared into the makeshift abbey.

Only Susanna seemed disappointed by this unexpected deviation from the ceremony. Plunking herself back down beside him on the rock, she looked at Francesco with bewilderment. "He isn't a real necromancer! It's just a joke. Why didn't you tell me?"

Francesco laughed. "I did!"

"I should slap you," she said, crossing her arms over her chest as a dozen or so "corpses" limped by, hands out, eyes rolled heavenward.

Men, women, children—all giggling as they made whatever sounds they imagined the walking dead to make.

"Woooo," Francesco said, joining in after attempting to tickle Susanna in the ribs. She snatched his hands and, to his great surprise, pulled him to his feet and into the line of shuffling corpses. A bearded young man who was inexplicably hopping on one foot passed him a wine jug, and Francesco took a deep draught before passing it on. "One, two, three, four," Francesco chanted, imitating the necromancer and letting out his best wolflike howl. He grabbed Susanna around the waist and twirled her around until, both dizzy, they collided with another pair of dancing corpses. It wasn't long before every man, woman, and child was parading around the walls of the Colosseum while from the sidelines the old, sick, and crippled watched and clapped.

The necromancer and his demons slipped out without anyone noticing, and it was past midnight when the celebrations came to a close. Women and children disappeared into the primitive shelters around the walls, and around the dying fires the men drank the last of their wine. Tomorrow there'd be no wine left for their breakfasts, no dry wood for their fires, but no one here would care, as this reprieve from the desperation would sustain them. Francesco had never felt warmer toward his city of exile.

"I never gave the cardamom to the necromancer," Susanna said as they carried their torches back over the Palatine Hill.

"Perhaps that's why everything went wrong for him tonight," Francesco said with a laugh. "But now you can take it all to the market and trade it for honey cakes."

"All of it?"

"All of it. Then we'll eat until our bellies hurt and we never want to eat again. And make sure you pick the cakes with the most almonds and raisins."

A wolf howled from the too-near distance.

"You hear that?" Susanna asked. "They're close."

Francesco wondered if he should tell Susanna about the white wolf he'd seen in St. Peter's Square but decided against it. She would believe him, but he wasn't sure he believed it himself.

"Not that close," Francesco said, doing his best to sound reassuring. "The wolves are afraid of fire," he elaborated. "They won't come near our torches." *Unlike bandits,* he didn't add. He'd been glad for the diversion of the evening, but he wasn't anxious to pay for it with a dagger in his ribs from some desperate man in search of a few coins.

At the Theater of Marcellus, Francesco began to relax. The guards at the entrance reported no mischief that night, and once they reached the other side of the river, they'd be in familiar territory.

He shuddered when a rat crossed their path at the foot of the bridge, and Susanna chided him for being cowardly.

"And who said at the docks that she'd scream if she saw one?" he asked.

"You know I was only teasing you, silly boy." She took his hand with a promise to protect him, but soon she gave his hand a tug and forced him to a halt.

"What is it?" he asked. He could see very little beyond the circle of torchlight. A few fires still burned on the hillsides, while over the river hung a thin fog. They'd stopped at the highest point on the bridge. He could hear the water as it ran beneath their feet. Something was bumping against one of the arches. *Not another body,* he hoped, but with the flooding, so many things had washed into the river it was quite possible. Susanna let go of his hand and gripped his arm. He felt for his dagger, only to realize it was on his other side. He switched the torch to his other hand and, shaking Susanna off his arm, reached for his weapon. "What is it?" he murmured, more urgently now. She took hold of him again, and he thought how stupidly useless he was with Susanna clutching his sleeve while he gripped a dagger he didn't know how to use well.

"There. At the end of the bridge. Just to the side," she whispered. "A man. He was standing still, and then he moved. I swear he did. What's he doing there?"

Francesco didn't know, but peering into the blackness, he could just make something out. Standing among the equally dark shapes at the foot of the bridge, it looked like nothing more than a line drawn in charcoal on an equally black canvas. *Or,* Francesco thought with relief, lowering the dagger to his side, *like any one of the hundreds of poles for mooring boats that lined the riverbanks.*

"It's just a pole," he said.

"But it moved."

"Your eyes must be playing tricks on you . . ." And on him, it would seem. He was sure he saw it wobble. Yet even if it was a man, Francesco reasoned quickly, it didn't necessarily mean he was out to harm them. The pole man could be someone like himself: scared of his own shadow and hoping whoever they might be wouldn't pull a dagger on him. "Who goes there?" Francesco asked in what he hoped was a commanding yet friendly voice.

No answer. Francesco's torch spat and fizzled, sending out a shower of sulfurous sparks. At first there was no movement at the foot of the bridge, but then the pole swayed again.

"Oh, Mother of Mary," Susanna said, and Francesco watched as the pole began to change shape, folding over and straightening again, while what appeared to be large wings unfurled at its sides.

"A demon . . . ," Susanna stuttered, letting go of Francesco's sleeve long enough to cross herself. "Hail Mary, full of grace . . . ," she said in a voice somewhere between a choke and a scream.

Francesco's grip tightened on his weapon as the figure started toward them with a strange loping gait, its footfalls echoing unevenly on the stone bridge, wings flapping at its side as if it were trying to fly.

Demon, my ass, Francesco thought. Still, as he put his dagger away, his hand was shaky. "Damn you, Dante! Are you trying to scare the shit out of us? Why didn't you answer me?"

"I am the bat man," Dante moaned, punctuating his words with a sad sigh. "And I must wait here in the dark like a bat."

"Here? Why here?"

"I followed you to the Colosseum and knew you'd return this way."

"Why didn't you . . . ?" He stopped. There was no point asking Dante why he hadn't talked to them then and had instead waited here all this time in the cold and darkness. He'd already answered. He was a bat, and bats wait in the dark. "What do you want then?" he said, a little more impatiently than usual. "It's late, and we're not bats, and we want to go home."

"The Pope's boy. You saw the Pope's boy. Imperia told me. But not the Pope's boy. The Madonna's boy. In the painting Marcus made. He painted the Madonna and the baby Jesus. Calendula the Madonna but not the Madonna. And the Pope's boy not the Pope's boy but the Madonna's. But not the Madonna's. A whore's."

Francesco took Susanna's hand and gave it a squeeze. She still hadn't recovered from the fright and was a bit shaky. He would have to remember not to tease her about this.

"His name is Agnello," Dante continued, his words no longer sad and slow but falling over each other as he tried to straighten out his thoughts. "Agnello. A lamb. Like the Lamb of God, only he is not the Lamb of God, he is the Pope's boy. Not the Pope's boy but the Madonna's. Calendula was the Madonna but not the Madonna. A whore. A whore. Making a fool of everyone with her golden hair." He stopped and stepped closer to Francesco. He was a full head shorter than Francesco, so he stood on his toes in an attempt to look straight into Francesco's eyes. "Are you Francesco or not Francesco?"

"Yes, Dante. I'm still Francesco. And the Pope's boy is not the Madonna's boy but the son of one of Imperia's whores. Don't you worry your head about it. Now, why don't you go home and get some sleep?"

"Bats don't sleep at night. Get the boy for the Madonna. Get him from the Pope. Get the boy for the Madonna."

"Dante, you go near that boy, you won't be a bat anymore. You'll be dead. You understand?" He said this as clearly and forcefully as he could.

"The Madonna wants the boy. You saw the boy."

"Dante, go home. We'll talk tomorrow."

They watched Dante slouch away. "He's always been like this, ever since I met him," he said to Susanna. "I'm told he's a wood-carver, but I've never seen him carve anything."

"Maybe he works alone in his workshop," Susanna said. "I bet he was in love with Calendula."

"You think so? I thought she just told him things because no one would listen if he repeated them. I'm sure she told him Calendula wasn't her real name. And it confused him. But you could be right about him being in love with her. I wonder if she told him about Agnello too. Do you think she told him to get her the boy, but she was killed before he could do it? Maybe in some way he feels responsible for her death."

"And now as punishment he must stay a bat forever," Susanna said sadly.

They had reached the alley now, but Susanna reminded him he could use his front door, "if you want to go to Michelangelo's?"

He didn't, and soon he was under Susanna's covers with the bolt of blue silk cloth as his pillow. He was still thinking about Dante and wondering whether the man was jealous of Calendula's other lovers. "Do you think Dante just pretends to be a bat and he's really quite sane?"

"If he was in love with Calendula, why would he pretend to be a bat?" She paused for a moment, then laughed.

"What are you laughing about? Dante?"

"No, not at Dante. At you. For a little bit, you thought Dante was a demon too, didn't you?" Not getting a response, she started to tickle him. "You did, didn't you?"

"Stop," he laughed, trying to push her away, but he was helpless against her tickling.

"You thought Dante was a real demon from Hell, didn't you? Confess, Francesco! You aren't always so smart."

"Alright, I'll confess! Just stop! Bless me, Susanna, for I have sinned," he gasped. "And this is my first confession in over a year!"

It worked, but not in the way he expected, as she slapped him instead.

"What are you doing?" he asked, catching her wrist.

"Don't talk blasphemy!"

"What do you mean?"

"You can't confess to me. And what do *I* mean? What do *you* mean you haven't confessed in over a year? What if you die? You won't go to Heaven!"

"Don't worry," he said, doing his best to sound serious. "If I die, you can get the necromancer to bring me back with his spells."

She was about to smack him again with her free hand, but he

managed to catch this one too and give it a playful bite. She squealed, and he remembered what Michelangelo had said the night the silversmith came home. *Can hear them right through the wall. Makes it hard for a man to sleep.* Francesco gave her another bite, just in case the first squeal hadn't fully shaken Michelangelo awake.

CHAPTER NINE

FRANCESCO HAD WOKEN BEFORE SUSANNA AND DECIDED HIS BEST hope of seeing The Turk was to go to his villa as early as possible, before business at the port called the man away. There was also the chance breakfast would still be on the table.

But when he reached St. Peter's Square, he changed his mind. Francesco watched as the multitude of workers parted like a human Red Sea for Raphael, the architect Bramante, and Pope Julius himself. Francesco knew Pope Julius frequently toured the work site, but today something struck him as odd. And then he realized Agnello wasn't with the Pope. Francesco looked up to the windows of the Vatican apartments and wondered if Agnello was there, perhaps alone with the parrot. It might be his only chance to talk to the boy.

Watching from behind a stack of marble blocks, Francesco waited until the three men were swallowed by the old St. Peter's and everyone in the square returned to their labors. How long did he have? Francesco knew from Raphael that Bramante could keep the

Pope for hours, expounding on his latest ideas for the basilica. But he also knew the Pope could become impatient.

Dodging workers and nearly colliding with an ox cart, Francesco ran back through the square, breathlessly explaining to the Swiss Guards at the palace door that he was there on Raphael's orders. The guards eyed him without interest and let him pass.

He had never set foot inside the palace before, but he knew Pope Julius's apartments were on the third floor, overlooking the courtyard Bramante was designing to link the Papal Palace with the Belvedere Palace. He didn't know how to reach them, though, and so for a few moments he stared into the vastness of the crowded entrance hall. On one side, stinking beggars waited for alms, while on the other side, clerks, bishops, priests, secretaries, and cardinals waited for favors—alms of a different sort. This latter group was a well-fed lot, and scanning their ranks Francesco thought how any one of them could easily be described as a "fat man." He was tempted to yell out Calendula's name just to see if any guilty faces turned his way.

Of course, he wasn't going to do this and was still wondering how to proceed when, by complete luck, he saw Sodoma, who was leaning against a pillar, watching two dwarfs wrestling on the hard marble floor for the amusement of the men waiting in the hall. Although he wasn't wearing a dress today (even Sodoma didn't have enough bravado to wear a dress in the Vatican), he was still in his finest velvet and lace. Francesco wondered what he was doing here in such finery—surely he didn't paint in those expensive clothes.

"What brings you here?" Sodoma asked, tossing a couple of coins to the dwarfs.

"I've come to see Raphael," Francesco said, without inquiring about Sodoma's business.

"Then you've missed him. He is out with Bramante and His Holiness, contemplating the dimensions of the columns in the new St. Peter's, or, as I call it, 'The Pope's Folly.'"

"Perhaps I can wait then," Francesco said. "Can you direct me to the rooms where he's at work?"

"I'd take you there myself, but I'm here awaiting a handsome new patron and do not dare leave my post. So if you follow this corridor here to the very end, take it to the right, then the second, or is it the third—" Sodoma broke off and grabbed a passing boy by the collar, nearly knocking him off his feet. "Give this one a coin and he'll take you."

Francesco snickered. "A coin? Have you forgotten who my master is?"

"Ah yes, the ever-amusing Michelangelo. He certainly has earned my admiration. I was in the chapel earlier this morning, and he was ordering that twit di Grassi around as if he were his house-boy—but that would be you, wouldn't it? I must sympathize with you. But it was still entertaining. Michelangelo insisted di Grassi jump up and down on each board of the scaffold to make sure it was secure. I just had to climb the ladder and take a peek. Di Grassi's robes were flapping around his hairy legs, and his face was as red as his hat. I was waiting for him to go straight through the scaffold and splatter all over the chapel floor like an overripe pomegranate."

"That's Michelangelo's goal, I'm sure." Francesco didn't know how long he had before the Pope returned, but Sodoma, who wasn't to be rushed when telling a story, was still gripping the boy's collar.

"A goal I wish him much success at. Every time I see di Grassi, he shakes his dirty little finger at me . . ." And here Sodoma waggled a finger from his free hand in Francesco's face. "And he tells me he will see me excommunicated or burned at the stake if he has to implore the Pope to his dying day. I don't doubt him, either. As a matter of fact, I am holding him to it. And I shall stick my tongue out at him every time I see him, just in case he forgets. He was complaining about one of the new choirboys too. Sings sweeter than the angels, His Holiness said, and the twit started grumbling that, if that were the case, the child must be possessed by the Devil. He actually suggested His Holiness bring in an exorcist!"

Alfeo, Francesco thought with alarm. "What did His Holiness say to that?"

"He called him a fucking idiot and told him to shut up." Sodoma made a rude sound with his lips, opened the pouch at his waist, and took out a couple of coins. "Here," he said to the boy, finally releasing his collar. "Take him to His Holiness's library, the room where Raphael's working." The other coin he pressed into Francesco's hand. "And you buy yourself a sausage. I swear you look hungrier than those wolves that wake me up every night. If I had more with me, I'd send you to buy a new cloak too. What a stink," he said, producing a lace handkerchief and waving it in front of his nose.

Francesco thanked him and followed the boy. He lifted a corner of his cloak to his nose, catching the smell of wet, dirty sheep. Still, the Vatican palace was no sweetly perfumed meadow, and his nose was assailed at every turn in the long corridors by varying combinations of urine, sweat, incense, rancid tallow candles, and wood fires.

"Will you show me the room where they keep the parrot?" he asked, and the boy tossed him a look. Francesco knew it was going to cost him his sausage.

But the loss was worth it. Agnello was indeed there, having a conversation with a parrot tethered to its perch by a fine gold chain. *That is*, Francesco thought, *if talking to a bird that regularly interjects the words "Go fuck a monkey" can be called a conversation.* While the walls of the richly frescoed room were lined with chairs, the boy and parrot were alone, reenacting, to Francesco's amazement, the defense of Rome from the exiled king Lucius Tarquinius Superbus. Francesco quietly closed the doors behind him and watched for a moment. If Julius returned before he was gone, he'd just tell him he'd come to see Raphael and stopped to talk to the boy.

"You be Horatius Cocles. He had only one eye, so you have to pretend," Agnello said.

"*Go fuck a monkey,*" the parrot squawked.

"That's right," the boy returned as if he'd heard something completely different. "But you must pray to the Father Tiber River, because you must kill the Etruscans with your sword and swim to safety." He recounted much of this in Latin, and Francesco wondered at this strange boy's fate. Agnello looked up then and, seeing Francesco, picked up a doll made of sheepskin and cloth from a chair. Holding it to his chest as if for protection, he took a step closer. "You're the one with the chicken," he said. "Did you come to see the parrot?"

"I came here for one of the painters," Francesco lied. "But I see he's not here. So it's a good time to meet your parrot." He would have to enlighten Raphael later, so he could cover for him if necessary. "If that's all right with you?"

The boy nodded, and Francesco approached the parrot's stand. He put out a hand and the parrot grabbed his finger with his beak. "Ouch!" Francesco pulled his finger away.

"He bites," Agnello said matter-of-factly.

"*Go fuck a monkey,*" the parrot added.

"Does he ever say anything else?" Francesco asked, inspecting his finger.

"Sometimes," the boy said without elaborating.

"You like to play games with the parrot?" Francesco asked him in Latin, thinking it was a damn good thing Ovid had written a poem to a dead parrot or he'd never have known the word. *Psittacus.*

The boy shrugged. "Sometimes."

"Do you play with any of the boys here?"

Agnello shook his golden curls. Francesco now wondered why he'd come here. Could he really ask Agnello about Calendula? Wouldn't the boy tell Julius a man was here asking him questions about her? He decided to risk it. He needed to know whether Julius had told Agnello his mother had gone to Hell before or after Calendula died. Then he'd know which mother Julius was referring to. Francesco was still struggling with how to phrase his questions when Agnello raised the subject himself. "Did you know my mother?"

"No, I don't think so," Francesco said as truthfully and gently as he could while at the same time revising his defense: *I was here to see Raphael, and Agnello asked me if I knew his mother . . . no idea . . . funny parrot.* "Do you miss her?"

Agnello nodded. "I saw her in the painting. She was pretty. Did she go from the painting to Hell or is she still in the painting?"

"I don't think she's in Hell, Agnello. But I don't know where she is. And that's just her likeness in the painting, just like it's your likeness." There was no point in giving the boy false hope, but he didn't want to tell him the brutal truth, either. "I'm sure she misses you too."

"*Go fuck a monkey.*"

Francesco couldn't help but think the parrot was calling him out as a liar. Or at least a coward.

Agnello turned to the parrot. "We'll play soon," he said patiently.

Francesco glanced toward the doors nervously. "When did His Holiness tell you your mother had gone to Hell?" he asked carefully.

The boy shrugged. "I don't know."

"Was it a long time ago or just a few days ago?"

Agnello looked at Francesco blankly. "I don't know."

"Don't worry," Francesco said, his heart breaking for the boy. "It doesn't matter. But I have to go now. You can come again and see the chicken."

With "*Go fuck a monkey*" ringing in his ears, sure that every servant eyed him with suspicion, Francesco wound his way out of the palace, an endless dark labyrinth of marble halls full of dead ends and doors that led to more doors until he finally emerged near the entrance to the Sistine Chapel. He wouldn't go in. If Michelangelo saw him, he would send him on some silly errand.

But as he passed by, he heard the choir. Above all the other voices soared one clear line of melody sung in a voice beautiful enough to make the Devil himself weep. It had to be Alfeo. *Possessed by the Devil?* Honestly, someone should give that ass di Grassi a punch in the nose. He was glad Michelangelo was putting his new authority over him to good use. Francesco stopped and listened for a moment before peeking inside and confirming the source of the sound.

Standing next to Alfeo was an older man he assumed was Imperia's father, a man Raphael clearly trusted. But what protection could even the most upstanding man provide if Julius ever decided he wanted Alfeo as his new companion? *What the Pope desires, he takes,* Imperia had said. And would they castrate Alfeo to preserve that sweetness? Francesco had heard rumors of such practices. But surely they would need to seek permission from Alfeo's family. Or would they? Since Francesco had been in Rome, his legal training had failed him at every turn.

He slipped out of the chapel, unseen by Michelangelo, and into the square just as Bramante, Julius, and Raphael reappeared from inside the old basilica. He would tell Raphael that, for Alfeo's safety, he should be sent as far away from the Vatican as possible. Alfeo was lucky to have Raphael as a savior, but who would be Agnello's?

‡ ‡ ‡

LUCK was still with Francesco when he arrived at The Turk's. The Turk was, as he'd hoped, still at breakfast and more than willing to share. Francesco hadn't seen this much food in one place since the Christmas festivities at Guido del Mare's. And while that feast had served a hundred people or more, this spread seemed to be put on for the benefit of The Turk alone. Beside a brace of pheasants, so freshly killed their blood still drained onto the table, were platters of eel, fish, and mutton, loaves of bread, and bowls of olives and dates. Reigning over it all, on a massive carved throne, upholstered in scarlet velvet and dripping with gilt, was The Turk, with a monkey on his shoulder, while in the corner a white lion paced around a cage not much bigger than itself. The Turk handed the monkey a fig, and it took a bite before hurling it at the cage. The lion let out a low growl.

"Still got that hungry look in your eye, boy. Eat! Eat! Eat!" The Turk waved his amethyst-ringed hand at a small dark girl, commanding her to pour them wine. She did as she was told, sloshing some over the table when the lion let out a ferocious roar. The Turk laughed indulgently. "Not to worry, my dear, you're hardly worth his consideration." He picked up one of the bloody pheasants and threw it toward the cage. It landed a foot short, and the lion lunged against the bars, rocking the whole cage. Now it was Francesco's turn to jump. The Turk laughed even louder. "You're as skittish as that little girl," he bellowed. "A beauty, isn't he? Just arrived yesterday, all the way from the south of Africa. Extremely rare, these white beasts. When I heard one had been captured, I had to have it." He rose with the help of the eagle-topped cane that had aroused Francesco's suspicion on his last visit. With the monkey clinging to his collar, The Turk snagged the pheasant with the cane and pushed it through the bars.

Francesco watched the lion tear into the bird before turning to the girl, who still held the jug of wine, her whole body tensed as though ready to flee. "What's your name?" he asked. With her dark eyes and skin, she probably came from a place where lions roamed wild.

"Mosa," she said without taking her eyes from the cage. The lion had the pheasant between its paws and was rending it with an appetite The Turk clearly admired. Francesco watched the cage quake and wondered how long it would be before it was shaken apart.

The Turk resumed his throne, and it groaned beneath him. "Don't be shy, boy. Eat what you will," he boomed, dotting his bald scalp with a delicate lace handkerchief not unlike the ones Imperia and Sodoma favored. "But what brings you here today? Did you come to see Mark Antony's armor, or am I under suspicion again?" He waved his hand at the girl, whose full attention was still on the cage. "Come on, girl, get the boy some mutton. Make sure it has lots of fat. That lion isn't the only one here who's hungry."

She did as she was told in quick, nervous gestures, and Francesco decided if this were to be his last meal, he should make sure it was a good one, and so he bit off a large hunk, chewing as he talked. "No, though I'd like to see your armor some other day. I've come to hear what you learned from the mortuary."

"Oh yes, of course," he said with that galling nonchalance. "I think you'll find this most interesting and not interesting at all, which is why it must have slipped my mind. I have learned less than nothing."

"What do you mean?" Francesco asked, quaffing his wine. The monkey ran across the table and snatched a piece of meat from Francesco's plate, then ran back and resumed his perch on The Turk's shoulder.

"Well, it would seem our fat man may not have been fat at all," he laughed, the throne trembling beneath him. "So, you see, the only thing we thought we knew about our mysterious kidnapper of bodies may not be true."

"So he wasn't fat?"

"Let us say my offer of a ducat to find out about our fat man drew very little more than an argument between the two clerks as to what 'fat' meant. They concluded he was not nearly as fat as myself, but larger than either of the two of them—which isn't saying much. He may have had a square head or he may have had a big round head. It was agreed that he wore a hat and had a very nice cape, although not as nice as my own. They said his friend called him fat, and so they called him fat."

"What friend?" Francesco asked, wiping the grease from his plate with a chunk of white bread.

"He was with another man, who waited outside on his horse."

"Not another man on a horse!" Francesco exclaimed.

"Yes," The Turk said. "The one clerk said he was a thin man, so maybe that's why he called his friend fat, but the other clerk said he thought it was the man's name, something *Grasso,* which means 'fat.' I asked him if the man's name might have been *Basso,* which means 'short,' and the clerk thought that must be it, and they soon agreed that the man was indeed short. So you see why it was a waste of a ducat."

"And all this time we've been squandering our time looking for a fat man," Francesco said. "Did they say how much the man paid for the body?" He didn't want to say that *Grasso* was very close to *di Grassi.* Paride di Grassi would certainly have the money to pay for the body. Would he have gone in disguise? Surely the men would have identified him had he been wearing his red robes.

"Imperia said they bragged that the man had paid well, but it would seem it was, in the end, less than I paid for nothing," The Turk said. "And don't look so glum," he ordered, waving a bone at him. "This is Rome, boy. Dead bodies come cheap here, and the truth is greasier than that mutton. Eat up, and I'll show you my armor."

Francesco nodded. He'd fit in another piece of meat and see The Turk's armor, and by the time he returned home, Susanna would be back from the market with their honey cakes. Later, he'd go see Imperia and tell her what The Turk had learned, but there seemed little urgency. *How do you find a fat man who's not fat?* he thought. Unless it was di Grassi. But what could he do if it was? It was pointless to keep pursuing this. And in case anyone else thought they'd burn down his house to keep him from learning the truth . . . well, they could save themselves the trouble. He was giving up.

Francesco was about to take another bite when, from out in the hall, a great deal of shouting erupted. Dante? It sounded like him, and whoever it was called Francesco's name. Moments later, Dante was escorted inside by one of The Turk's guards. "I beg your forgiveness," the servant said, keeping a firm hold on Dante's arm.

Dante was clearly distraught. His eyes rolled around like he was having a fit. His face was streaked with mud, his clothes were filthy, and he smelled of garbage and sweat. "Francesco! Francesco! Oh, it's true! She's dead!"

"Calm yourself, man," Francesco demanded, rising from his chair. Mosa took this as her chance to escape and fled the room. The lion roared, and Dante screamed even louder.

"Oh, what is that?" Dante cried. "All around us murdering beasts!"

"Not to worry, Dante. It's a lion, but it's in a strong cage," Francesco said, sounding more confident than he felt. "Now calm yourself, and tell me who's dead!"

"Susanna, Susanna . . ."

Francesco looked at him, stunned. "Susanna?" he repeated weakly. "Oh my God, not Susanna!"

"No! No! Not Susanna! Susanna told me you'd be here. Oh, Francesco, she really is dead!"

"Who, Dante?" Francesco shouted.

Behind him the lion roared again, and again Dante screamed, throwing himself into Francesco's arms. The man was ice-cold and shaking violently. "Here!" He shoved something into Francesco's hand.

"What . . . ?" he started to ask as he stared down at a dirty piece of cloth, but he stopped there. He didn't need to ask. Wet and mildewed, crusted with mud and quite possibly blood, it was barely recognizable, but that particular yellow hue could only have belonged to one person.

"What is it?" The Turk asked, lumbering over to them.

"A piece of Calendula's dress," Francesco said.

The Turk held out his hand—the one bearing the amethyst ring—and took the cloth. "Where did you find this?" he asked Dante, not unkindly.

"Up, up, up . . . over there . . . across the river . . . by the tomb of Remus," Dante stuttered, still shaking uncontrollably.

"You mean the Pyramid of Cestius," The Turk said before turning to one of the guards. "Where did that girl go? Get this man some wine before he dies on my carpet."

The guard did as he was told, and Francesco held out the chair he'd just vacated and pressed the goblet into Dante's hand, but Dante's hand shook so hard Francesco had to raise it to his lips for him. "Come on, drink. It'll do you good."

Dante obeyed and swallowed the contents of the goblet.

"You found this by the Pyramid of Cestius, near the Porta San Paolo?" Francesco asked, already forgetting his pledge to let the matter rest. "Was her body there too?"

"No," Dante said. "The wolves. The wolves took her away in the night. From her grave."

"I'll go and look," Francesco said, handing Dante a piece of bread. "Can you tell me exactly where it was? Was it right beside the pyramid? Inside the gate?" He didn't want to take Dante with him. If the man hadn't been completely mad before, he was now.

"In front of the tomb . . . inside the gate," Dante stammered. "By the house where she lived."

Francesco turned to The Turk. "She lived there?"

"I have a villa there. Built it where I could see the pyramid. She was there once or twice, maybe. I rent it now. This house is much more to my taste. I'll get a guard. He can take you across the river. It will save some time."

The Turk was still holding the soiled piece of cloth, and Francesco was surprised to see him raise it to his elephantine cheek for a moment, the first indication he'd given that this discovery had affected him. Was it grief or guilt he felt?

Is that what Dante had been doing these past nights? Had he gone in search of her, still thinking he would find her miraculously alive? After all, it was only Francesco who'd witnessed her pulled from the river. Her body had disappeared from the mortuary before anyone else had seen her. Had Dante not believed Francesco? Or had he thought him mistaken? And why had he said she'd lived at The Turk's villa?

Francesco continued to ponder these questions for the better part of the journey. He and the guard crossed the river by the Emporium, where the guard agreed to wait. With the Aventine Hill and the ruins of the old Servian walls on his left, he followed the ancient road to the Porta San Paolo, one of the gates in the later Roman walls.

Even though he was still inside the city, it was countryside here. In summer, sheep and cattle would be grazing, and the grapes would be lush and green. Francesco saw no one along the route. The hovels of the farmers and shepherds were shut up tight against the damp and wolves, and no one worked in the soaked, freezing fields. Grapevines hung gray and dead-looking from their trellises, and the ground under the olive trees was slimy with olives that, rather than ripening, had rotted. Here and there, blackened circles in the earth marked recent fires built to deter the wolves.

He saw the pyramid long before he reached it, jutting out and over the red brick walls that had incorporated its bulk. Petrarch wrote that it held the body of Remus; according to legend, he and his brother Romulus were raised by wolves before founding Rome. Francesco left the road and started walking along the wall. He passed through a small grove of fruit trees. *Apples*, he thought. The branches were bare now, but in spring they would be covered in white blossoms and later in sweet red fruit.

He had a good view from the wall, and looking out over the

gray fields, it wasn't difficult to ascertain which dwelling was The Turk's old villa. While there were a few grander houses here, summer homes for some of Rome's wealthy clergy, The Turk's stood out as the most ostentatious. With its sloped pinkish stone walls, its front door guarded by sphinxes, he supposed it was meant to be Egyptian like the pyramid, but it was as if the architect hadn't known where to stop, and so the house bristled with minarets, domes, columns, obelisks, statues, and towers, appearing to Francesco every bit as ridiculous as a horse with an elephant's nose and the tail of a peacock.

He found Calendula's grave, just as Dante said he would, at the base of the pyramid, in a thicket of low, thorny shrubs. Whoever had buried her here had done so in a hurry, digging a trench that was little more than a hollow in the ground. Francesco imagined a faceless figure laying her stiffened corpse in the trench before taking up his shovel and covering her with dirt. The figure would have stamped on the dirt, packing it down with his boots but leaving a small mound all the same. *Gone for good,* he might have said as he walked away, while in the hills the wolves, catching the scent, had slunk down in the night and scratched back the soil, their yelps echoing off the walls as they fought over the rotting flesh.

The hollow was filled with water now, no doubt having collected the rain sliding off the sides of the pyramid. Around its edges, among the paw prints left by wolves, were a couple of boot prints. *Dante's,* Francesco thought.

Francesco broke off a branch from an olive tree and dragged it through the muddy water, pulling out a strip of yellow cloth. He held it over the grave, watching the water drip from the end of the stick. He shook it off and stirred the surface of the water once more, this time pulling out a clump of matted yellow hair still anchored to a piece of flesh. He dropped the stick with its clinging gore and backed away, nearly slipping in the mud in his haste. With one hand resting on the pyramid for support, he vomited into the thorny bushes at its base.

He was trembling, shivering with the cold that until now he hadn't felt. He leaned with his back against the damp stone and looked down the slope to The Turk's ugly villa. It had appeared empty before, but now he could see a horse tethered to one of the sphinxes. The door opened and closed, though no one went in or out.

Why was the body buried so close to The Turk's villa? Coincidence? The Turk's lover, The Turk's ring, and now the grave near The Turk's old villa? Everything pointed to The Turk, yet nothing added up.

Nothing added up, that is, until from around the side of the house came a man. Not a big man, or a fat man, or a short man. A man whose name almost sounded like di Grassi. Not *Grasso* as in "fat," but *Grosso* as in "big." A man with red hair sticking straight up like the comb of a chicken. A *big* chicken. *Pollo Grosso*. Francesco's mind started racing. If Pollo Grosso were here, it meant someone else was here too.

Francesco watched motionless as Pollo Grosso untied the horse and led it back around the corner. If he'd looked up the hill toward the grave, he would surely have recognized Francesco as easily as Francesco had recognized him. Heart pounding, Francesco ran along the wall in the direction of the river, where the guard waited for him. Francesco knew he wasn't mistaken, but he needed to hear it from The Turk himself. More than once, he looked back over his shoulder, surprised he wasn't being pursued.

When he arrived back at The Turk's house, it was his turn to burst inside, and to the guards he must have seemed every bit as crazed as Dante had earlier. "The Turk!" he shouted. "Where is he?"

A guard seized him by the arm, but Francesco shook him off and, running through the atrium with the guard in pursuit, almost collided with The Turk himself.

"What is it?" The Turk asked as he wiped his mouth with a cloth.

"Your villa!" Francesco cried breathlessly. "Who is renting your villa?"

"That is all?" The Turk asked. "My wife's cousin—"

"A name! A name!" Francesco demanded. "Tell me his name!"

"Why, Guido del Mare."

Francesco stumbled back, not sure he wasn't going to fall to the floor. Thoughts were flooding his mind so quickly he was almost incapable of making a single one take shape. *Could Guido have something to do with Calendula's death? But why?*

"He isn't there now," The Turk continued helpfully, tossing his cloth to the floor, where it was scooped up immediately by Mosa. "I received a message from his wife that he has gone on to Naples. What has you so excited?"

"His wife is here too—in Rome?" Francesco asked weakly. To think that all this past week Juliet had been in Rome. Why would Guido bring her here?

"Yes. I've never met her, but I hear she's quite a beauty. Guido always had an eye for beautiful women. He took quite a liking to Calendula's portrait."

"I'm sure he did," Francesco said, recovering his voice. After all, Calendula looked so much like his wife. Would he kill her for that? His heart was still pounding, but he willed some calmness into his words. "Why didn't you tell me he was here?"

"Why would it interest you? Ah, but you are from Florence too. You know, I could put in a good word for you. You could do well in his service."

I was in his service, Francesco wanted to scream. "When did he get here?"

"Last week. He said he was here on business. I offered him the villa. That was it."

"And you showed him Calendula's portrait?"

"I showed him around. I didn't want him to go away thinking I was the poor relation. I've met him on only a few occasions. Never really did like him. But he is family."

"He only came here once?"

The Turk paused. *Think!* Francesco silently urged him, sure now who had given Calendula the ring, if not why. "Yes. No! I saw him just once, but he came again. I wasn't here. I believe he waited a while and left."

Waited long enough to put the ring back where he'd found it, Francesco concluded triumphantly. "Now think carefully," he said. "What day was that?"

"I can't remember. No, I do. I didn't know about it until the next day, because he came while I was at Imperia's. It was the night she told me about Calendula's death. I was in shock. It wasn't until the next day I learned Guido had been here. He didn't leave a message for me, and when I sent word to him regretting that I wasn't here to receive him, his wife replied that he'd gone on to Naples. Wait! You suspect *my wife's cousin?* Why?"

Francesco questioned the wisdom of telling The Turk more. *He is family,* The Turk had said.

"Perhaps it's nothing," Francesco said finally. "But the grave was dug very close to the villa. Perhaps your cousin saw something. But I suppose there's no asking him now, if he's in Naples." That seemed to appease The Turk, and Francesco, pleased he'd found such an easy escape from scrutiny, now asked where Dante was.

Dante hadn't believed Calendula was dead. Well, maybe at first he had. But then he must have seen Juliet and thought it was Calendula. No wonder he'd taken the discovery of Calendula's grave so hard. He'd thought she was still alive, all his garbled nonsense an attempt to reconcile the death of Calendula with the very much alive Juliet.

"He insisted he had to leave," The Turk said. "Something crazy about bats not being out in the day."

With so many unanswered questions swirling around his head, Francesco felt as if he were going crazy too. He hurriedly made his excuses, promising to come again another day to see the armor. Once outside, he walked down the drive between the rows of potted cypresses and antique statues, piecing together the events that might have led to Calendula's death at Guido's hands. Because that must have been what happened. And in a strange way, had he not fingered the killer the moment her body was pulled from the river? When he told the policeman his name was Guido del Mare, had he not thought, *Find him if you have any further questions?*

What was Guido doing in Rome with Juliet? Had his father failed to soothe Guido's anger, and had Guido, on his way to Naples, decided to stop in Rome long enough to cut Francesco's throat? Maybe Guido had gone to ask his cousin The Turk if he knew where he could find Francesco, but before Guido could start asking questions, The Turk had showed him the portrait of Calendula, unaware that, in doing so, he was sealing Calendula's fate.

Francesco had little trouble imagining Guido's reaction to the painting. The Turk was right: Guido always did have an eye for beautiful women. And Calendula, with her rare golden hair, was so like his own wife but not his own wife. He imagined The Turk offering his villa for the length of his stay, and Guido, his eyes locked on Calendula's, agreeing, his desire for revenge subsumed at least temporarily by a more carnal desire.

Did he then, seeing The Turk's amethyst ring lying on a tray, pick it up with the idea of giving it to her? Did The Turk tell Guido where and how she lived? The Turk certainly did like to talk. Did he even tell him she was once noble and still longed for her old life? It would make sense. According to Calendula, the man who gave her the ring had promised to make her a lady. But if Guido had known she was a whore, would he have bothered with the pretense of the ring and the promises? Would he not have just paid for her services like other men? So perhaps The Turk had not told him this detail, and Guido had taken the ring and lured her into his bed with promises to make her his lady. It had been what Calendula had been waiting for.

But Guido tired of women quickly. Woo them with a trinket and a promise or two, sate his desire, and leave them in tears. But Calendula was not the twelve-year-old daughter of a tenant farmer. Not only had she seen him as the answer to her prayers, she had bragged to Imperia and probably the other girls at the brothel, that she would soon be married to a rich man. A lady again. Everything solved, until Guido had asked for the ring back.

Francesco could well imagine both her disappointment and her rage. *How dare you humiliate me!* How could she, after all the bragging and gloating, go back to Imperia's and be scorned by the other women? He imagined her flying at Guido, willing to scratch out his eyes if that would save her. But of course it wouldn't, and Guido, with a rage to match her own and the strength of a man, would not have hesitated to kill her for her insolence. Had he smashed her face in first? Had she still been alive when he took out his dagger and cut the finger with the ring from her hand? Had he thrown her body into the swollen river and watched it float downstream before going home to his wife, who looked so much like the woman he had just murdered?

Juliet. What did he, Francesco, feel now when he said that name? Pity, certainly. But love? "Juliet, my love," he said, testing the words aloud. She was so close. He could go to her right now. But Guido had left Pollo Grosso with his wife. How was Francesco going to see Juliet with Pollo Grosso guarding her? He did have to see her, didn't he?

Only the night before, he'd considered marrying Susanna—forsaking the dowry and taking her home to his father's. But didn't some honor bind him to Juliet, even if he was no longer sure he loved her? He had, after all, vowed to rescue her from Guido. Was it possible that, on seeing her again, his feelings of love would return?

He wondered if Juliet knew of Calendula's death. Did she watch Pollo Grosso and Guido—for surely Guido had been the man on the horse at the mortuary—dig a grave at the foot of the pyramid and bury a woman in a golden dress? *Not to worry, my love. Just a little trouble Pollo Grosso ran into with one of the local whores.*

Did Guido go to Naples and leave Pollo Grosso to kill off Francesco? Did Pollo Grosso throw the torch into the soap-maker's shop? But that seemed like such a halfhearted attempt. Why not just follow him one night and slit his throat? Was it still a question of Guido's honor? Was Guido going to come back from Naples and kill him? And why would Guido go to Naples anyway, leaving Juliet in the same city with Francesco? Francesco paused at the end of the rows of cypresses, his eyes locked on those of the stone lions that guarded the gate. What if Guido had come to Rome with no intention of harming Francesco until Francesco had decided to pursue Calendula's murderer?

That was an irony too great to grasp, and so his thoughts turned to what he now considered the most urgent problem: seeing Juliet.

✛ ✛ ✛

"THEN you will go to her," Susanna said.

Francesco was annoyed that she seemed to have heard nothing else he'd said. "Yes, but I don't know how to see her with Pollo Grosso guarding her. He's not exactly going to let me in, is he?"

"You should have known it was him." Her voice was accusatory. She took the baker's dozen of honey cakes from her basket and placed them in a pewter box on the table without offering him one.

"Why?" he asked, ignoring the slight. He was still digesting The Turk's mutton and for once wasn't at all hungry. He took off his cloak and threw it on the bed; his dagger he tossed on the table, where it rattled off the pewter box.

"The three-legged chicken. I told you he was an omen. But you didn't believe me."

"What do you mean?"

"He appeared on the day Calendula was killed. He was trying to tell you about Pollo Grosso. You aren't very smart for someone who reads books."

"Well, if you're so smart, why didn't you tell me then? It would have saved me some trouble, not to mention the soap-maker's shop."

"Well, you didn't tell me there was someone called Pollo Grosso," she said indignantly. "You only told me about that woman. Are you going to kill Guido?"

"I don't know," he said angrily. He didn't like the way she was looking at him, both accusing and sad. What did she expect him to do? He picked up a piece of wood and threw it into the cold fireplace. "When did you let the fire go out? I'll go over to Michelangelo's and get some live coals. I'm hoping he had the sense not to let his fire go out."

"I'll go," she said.

"Never mind. Pollo Grosso is sure to try to replicate the great fire of Ancient Rome any moment now, and we'll be warmer than we've ever been."

"Stop!" Susanna shouted. "Not Michelangelo's. I'm not talking about the fire. I meant I'd go to The Turk's villa and tell Juliet you want to meet with her."

"What?" Surely he hadn't heard her correctly.

"I said I'll go and tell her you want to meet with her. If that's what you want me to do."

There were a thousand reasons why this was a bad idea. But at that moment, he couldn't think of a single one. Instead, he decided it might even be a good idea. She would meet Juliet and know why it made sense that he couldn't be with a silversmith's housekeeper.

But they shouldn't rush into this. "Wait. I'm going to Michelangelo's to get embers to start the fire. I have to think about this. You can't just announce that you're there to arrange a meeting between the lady of the house and her lover." He didn't look at Susanna on his way out the door. The back door. The way he'd come so many times in the night to see her. This silly, superstitious girl, with her blackened tooth and dark gypsy eyes.

He hadn't even reached the gate when she called for him to stop. He turned and saw her standing in the doorway, wearing her cloak. "My money . . . ," she said, looking around as if someone might hear.

"What money?" he asked impatiently.

"My money is behind the first stone from the wall, over the mantle. For my dowry."

"Sure," he said, wondering why she was telling him this now. "Take off your cloak. I said I'd get us some embers." He slammed Michelangelo's door behind him. It closed with a satisfying bang that rattled the windows and sent the shelf crashing to the floor. He leaned back against the door. In front of him the fireplace was cold and dark. Of course it would be out, with no houseboy to take care of it. There were no live coals here to restart Susanna's fire.

The chicken perched on the table next to Michelangelo's drawings, the pile a little higher than before, as was the mound of candle stubs. It blinked at Francesco and shifted legs. "What the hell are you looking at?" Francesco asked, but still the bird didn't move. Francesco stuck his face close to the chicken's. "Get out of my sight, you stupid bird. There's been nothing but trouble since you arrived." *My God*, he thought, *I sound like Susanna.*

The chicken blinked again, and Francesco pushed it roughly off the table. The bird landed on its feet—all three of them—and flew up onto the headboard of the bed, where it continued to watch Francesco impassively. Francesco knew he'd acted cruelly, but he was too angry to care. "I am not apologizing to a chicken," he said. God, his head felt like it was about to split in two. He picked up the wine jug, and finding it empty, slammed it down and started flipping through the sheets of paper on the table. Juliet was here in Rome. Why wasn't he happy?

Second from the top was a drawing of two hands reaching out to each other. Francesco barely saw it, as something came back to him. *I am not sure how to broach this,* Raphael had said as they'd looked up at Michelangelo's depiction of the Flood, *but when you told me your story, I could not help but wonder if it were Juliet herself who told Guido of your indiscretions . . . She had to know that if she told Guido, he would try to kill you. She had to know, too, that you would defend yourself . . . Had you been successful in killing Guido, she would have been free to do as she pleased.*

Francesco sat down at the table and rested his head on his arms. His sister Angelina's letter had arrived that same morning. *I fear that, for all her outward sweetness, Juliet is capable of treachery . . . Je suis desolée, mon frère . . .* The story of the young musician Juliet had visited in his mother's cottage while Angelina had waited outside. But this same young musician had fallen in love with Guido's sister, and Juliet had told Guido, and Guido had killed the musician, and his sister had thrown herself from the tower.

I loved you, he thought. *I know I did. I won't believe these lies.*

His head still resting on his arms, he closed his eyes and tried to conjure up Juliet's face. He stayed that way for a long time but only succeeded in bringing up Calendula's, lying on the bank of the river, bashed and bloody. And then, this afternoon, the chunk of hair, hanging from the stick as he held it over her shallow grave.

"Oh my God!" he said aloud, his eyes wide open now. "How could I have been so stupid?"

The chicken blinked back at him.

The door slammed behind him, as did the gate in the silver-smith's yard. He pushed open the door and called Susanna's name, but she wasn't there. Nor was his dagger, which he'd left on the table. And something else was missing. The bolt of blue silk. She'd taken that too. And the money? He looked at the mantle. The first stone . . . No, she hadn't taken the money. She'd left it for him. He grabbed his cloak from the bed.

What the hell had he done?

231

CHAPTER TEN

HOW MUCH OF A HEAD START DID SUSANNA HAVE? A HALF-HOUR AT most? But even if he ran, could he really hope to catch her before she reached The Turk's old villa? Because that was where she'd gone. He was sure of it.

It had grown colder, his breath in the fading light of late afternoon coming out in white puffs. The drizzle of the morning had turned to sleet, coating everything with a malevolent layer of ice. He slipped on a patch of cobblestone, breaking his fall with a painful wrench to his wrist. Cursing, he picked himself up and ran out of the alley toward the bridge.

Of course Susanna wouldn't wait for his permission. She thought she was losing him, thought there'd be no more talk of his father's home in Florence or the hot springs. Not that he'd made any promises, but he knew he'd led her to believe it would happen. And while he might not have been sure of his feelings before, he was now. Susanna was not the kind of girl a man of his position fell in love with, but he had nonetheless. And he wanted nothing more than to be with her now, curled up in front of the great fireplace in his father's library, waiting for the Christmas snow.

It was only his confusion and anger that had made him impatient with her. But she couldn't have known that. And he'd been tempted by her offer to set up a meeting with Juliet. Instead, he should have told her in no uncertain terms she was not to go. Was Guido even in Naples? Or was he here in Rome, the Naples story only meant to mislead? What an evil, conniving pair they were. More so than all the wolves of Rome. And he had fed them Susanna. Now he knew there was no going back. Not now. Not ever.

He reached the Cestio Bridge. A shepherd was crossing with his flock, and Francesco yelled at them to "Move, move, move" as he shoved the docile animals out of his way. She had taken the bolt of blue cloth with her, the same one she wrapped her arms around at night. The one he'd teased her would make a good dowry. *Hell, even I would take it,* he'd told her, and she'd believed him and gone to trade him for a bolt of blue silk. No, Susanna was not the girl he was supposed to fall in love with, but she was better than he deserved.

He left the road, the frozen grass of the fields crunching under his feet like slivers of glass, the sleet in his face like needles. Running, running. He scared up a flock of grouse, their wings whirring around his head. A pain stabbed his side, and every breath felt like it could be his last. He was gaining on The Turk's old villa, the Pyramid of Cestius rising behind. Running, running . . .

Until he knew there was no point in running at all. He was too late.

Susanna lay on the grass, facedown, her brown cloak and dark hair fanned out around her. Beside her on the ground was Pollo

Grosso, a heavy club lying between them. And Dante, standing frozen over them, a big rock raised above his head.

Francesco stumbled toward Susanna, willing himself to reach her. Oh God, what had she done? What had *he* done? He put his hand to his side, forgetting that his dagger wasn't there, that she'd taken it. Already he knew he would be haunted forever by what-ifs. *No! No!* he wanted to scream.

"I tried to stop him," Dante said, lowering the rock and dropping it at his feet.

"I know, I know," Francesco murmured.

Pollo Grosso pressed his hand to his head. Blood was streaming through his fingers, but like a bull in an arena, unable to admit defeat, he struggled to get up again. Francesco kicked him in the head as hard as he could, knocking him back down to the ground.

Ignoring Pollo Grosso's bellow of pain and anger, Francesco knelt down beside Susanna. He lifted her head onto his lap, knowing as he did that her skull had been broken. Blood ran from her nose and the corner of her mouth. It flowed thick and warm over his hand and spilled onto his cloak.

He knew he didn't have much time. His heart was pounding in his chest, and fragments of words escaped his lips. Things he wanted to say yet had no words for. And so he just held her, cradling her broken head and stroking her hair, sticky with blood, while she lay still in his arms, looking past him to the sky with a calm intensity. He followed her gaze for a moment and saw nothing but the same gray clouds that had been hanging over Rome for weeks. He found a few words—*Remember the night I met you and you slapped me?*—but he wasn't sure he said them aloud. Was that only two months ago? He stroked her hair, shielding her face from the sleet. She did not breathe. A fox ran through the field, and somewhere a dog barked.

And then she was gone. Quietly, quietly the light went from her eyes, and the words he'd wanted to say no longer mattered.

He heard Dante crying and was aware of Pollo Grosso struggling to his feet, but he couldn't take his eyes from Susanna's. *Her soul has gone to Heaven, son—she is happy now,* his father had said as they'd sat at his mother's deathbed, but all Francesco knew was that one moment there is life and then there isn't. Thought, happiness, love, pain, and then nothing, and he would never feel the finality of it more than he did at this moment. He placed his hand over Susanna's eyes, those dark gypsy eyes he'd teased her about, and closed them gently.

When he looked up, he saw her coming across the field from the direction of the villa. She wore a veil, and the hood of her cloak covered her golden hair, but he knew it was her. *How could I have been so stupid?* He'd spoken the words aloud with only the chicken to hear, and then he'd run from the house—at that moment, he'd realized what had really happened and that Susanna was in danger. He gathered Susanna tighter in his arms, as if to keep her safe, and his hand struck something hard in the folds of her dress. His dagger. He pulled it from her pocket and set it on the icy grass beside him before looking up again at the woman walking toward him.

She skirted Pollo Grosso and came to a stop a couple of feet away from Francesco. "I'm sorry," she said, her voice steady and betraying no emotion. "I only wanted to speak with her, but as soon as she saw it was me, she ran away. I didn't mean for him to kill her. I wanted him to bring her back, but then I suppose he saw you coming and panicked. He was protecting me." She turned to him now, where he lay writhing on the grass. "Get up!" she commanded as if he were a dog. "Go to the house."

And as obediently as any dog, he did just that. Blood running from his scalp, he stumbled toward the villa, but Francesco had no doubt the man would live. He had taken far worse blows in Guido's service.

Dante followed behind Pollo Grosso, but after a dozen or so yards stopped and dropped down onto a rock under a bare thorn tree, burying his face in his hands.

She turned back toward Francesco, raising her veil, a thick lock of golden hair falling over her forehead. That golden hair. She lifted a ringless hand and unhurriedly brushed it away, a gesture he'd seen so many times, as if she were drawing attention to its wondrous color.

He had stood at the edge of the Tiber and watched her body pulled from the river. It had been a day like this. Like every day since he'd been in Rome. Gray and cold and hopeless. He had stood with the mud sucking at his boots and watched as the yellow dress, torn and muddied, pulled her under the water. Her skin the sickly green hue of a dead carp, her face smashed and broken, her golden hair entwined with weeds, her finger hacked from her hand. *Most likely just another whore*, he had said to the policeman before crossing over to the middle of the bridge. He had stopped there and, while overhead the gulls had circled, screeching for dead flesh, he'd watched as another policeman closed her eyes.

But they weren't Calendula's eyes. They were Juliet's eyes. Juliet dressed in Calendula's yellow dress. Juliet's finger removed as if it had worn an amethyst ring. Juliet's golden hair entangled with seaweed. Juliet's face disfigured beyond recognition. Juliet. Juliet. Juliet.

He had been so close, yet had failed to see the truth. And because of his failure, not only was Juliet dead but Susanna too.

Calendula looked at him, and he saw her face framed in a field of sun-kissed marigolds. *Hail Mary, full of grace. Blessed art thou among women . . .*

I could kill her, he thought. *I could pick up the dagger and kill her.*

But instead, he asked, "Why am I still alive?"

"You were both fooled," she said without answering his question. "You and Guido both. He didn't come to kill you. He wanted your legal advice. He wanted to know how to get out of his marriage without having to pay back her dowry. Don't feel sorry for Juliet. She was the one who told him you'd made advances on her. You were supposed to kill him. Then she'd be free, and everything would be hers."

Francesco remembered how Raphael had come to this conclusion the night they'd visited the Sistine Chapel. He wondered how Guido had become wise to this plan. Had she tried it again with another poor bastard, until even Guido had seen the pattern to her deceit? He didn't know if he cared. Not now, with Susanna growing cold in his arms. But Francesco was sure he knew how the rest of this story unfolded.

"Tell me if I'm right then," he said. "Guido went to The Turk and asked him where he could find me. But when The Turk showed him *The Marigold Madonna,* Guido saw a much simpler solution to his problem."

Calendula made no objection, so Francesco continued. "Guido took The Turk's ring, a little gift with which to woo you. Tell me if I'm right, Calendula. He offered you your own little palace. Maybe not too close, but a place where you could live and where he could occasionally parade you around in your veil to keep anyone from asking questions. A place where you could be a lady again. Or pretend to. Is that how it went?"

She nodded, adjusting the hood of her cloak, bringing it closer around her face. "He said he'd set me up in a house with a staff far from the castle, but if anyone saw me, they'd believe I was Juliet, exiling myself from society to pay for my sins against my husband. No one would object."

"And so you wore the amethyst ring," Francesco said. "You flaunted it in front of everyone. It would be easy enough to believe you'd been killed for it. And if The Turk was blamed—it was his ring after all—Guido wouldn't lose any sleep over it."

But Guido tried to be too clever, Francesco added to himself. Had Guido just buried Juliet in the first place, instead of trying to pass off her body as Calendula's, he might have succeeded. He'd be back in Florence now, and Calendula would be locked up with a couple of trustworthy servants while he enjoyed all of Juliet's money. And since her family lived in Milan, there was little chance they'd visit unexpectedly.

"He thought he was very clever," Calendula said, echoing his thoughts. "Until he learned that you'd seen the body pulled from the river and had told everyone at Imperia's. He started to panic. He worried that Pollo Grosso hadn't disfigured her well enough. And you were too smart, he said. You wouldn't let it go. You'd go to the mortuary and, once up close, you would see that it was Juliet. And then you'd come looking for him, with the aid of The Turk's men. The Turk wouldn't be happy to know Guido had stolen the ring to implicate him. That was why Guido and Pollo Grosso went to claim the body. Pollo Grosso buried her by the wall. I know the wolves dug her up, but there was no hope of her being recognized after that." Calendula's voice held no remorse. No pity for the woman whose life she'd helped take, just as there was no pity for the woman growing cold in his arms. Did she believe Juliet deserved to die for her treachery, or was Juliet's death simply a means to an end?

"Why didn't he kill me before I went to the mortuary?" Francesco asked.

"The damage was already done. You'd already told everyone. Besides, he liked you. He talked about getting you back into his service. He thought once you learned about Juliet's deceit . . ."

"He liked me?" He knew Guido had liked him before discovering his liaison with Juliet, but he was surprised to learn the man still did. Hadn't Guido tried to kill him? Then he suddenly realized that Calendula was speaking of Guido in the past tense: He *liked.* He *talked.* He *thought.*

"Where's Guido now?" he said, although he already knew the answer. "And don't tell me Naples."

"Dead," she said bluntly. "Pollo Grosso killed him. I wanted Agnello. I told Guido I'd go along with his plan if he let me take my son. He agreed. None of Juliet's babies had lived, so why wouldn't she take to a beautiful orphan boy and adopt him as her own? That was to be my story. I didn't care, so long as I could have Agnello back. Imperia took him from me and gave him to the Pope." Her eyes now filled with passion, and her cheeks flushed with indignation. "I must have him back!"

"When did you tell Guido that Agnello belongs to the Pope?"

"After he returned the ring to The Turk's. Guido wanted to leave for Florence, but I said we still had to rescue Agnello from the Pope. He flew into a rage and called me a madwoman, saying the Pope would have us murdered. We fought, but Pollo Grosso came to my defense and killed Guido. I tried to stop him, but it was too late. He left Guido's body for the wolves."

Big Stupid Chicken probably thought Calendula was Juliet. Juliet, whom he'd always watched like a dog in heat. Clearly, in the end, his loyalty to her was greater than to his master.

"Why did Pollo Grosso throw the torch into the soap-maker's shop?"

She looked at him, startled. "What are you talking about? He's been here with me the whole time."

Francesco knew she was telling the truth. Beyond the passion with which she'd spoken of Agnello, her surprise at his question was the first emotion she'd shown. But if she weren't lying, it could only mean one thing: Michelangelo was right. The attack had been intended for him. For all the reasons he thought. A desperate attempt by Asino and di Grassi to keep him from finishing the ceiling of the Sistine Chapel.

Francesco wiped the blood from the corner of Susanna's mouth with his cloak. Beads of sleet clung to her dark lashes like tears. He had to do something. He'd heard enough.

He started to rise, but Calendula put a hand on his shoulder to stop him. She dropped to her knees, her cloak a tent around the dead girl between them. Grasping his arms tightly, she looked into his eyes. "Come with me, Francesco," she whispered urgently. Francesco could smell her perfume. "We'll tell them Pollo Grosso killed Guido when he tried to harm me. Or something else . . . You're smart, you'll think of something. We can live in Florence. You, me, Agnello . . . You can help me. I'll live as Guido's grieving widow, and you can be a very rich man. Far richer than Guido would ever have made you."

She was animated now, inventing a fairy-tale ending to this gruesome story. It was as if she'd forgotten she was responsible for the death of the woman in his arms, forgotten she was Calendula, so ready was she to step into the role of Juliet, so deluded she thought he would do this for her.

She was still pleading with him, but now her voice had become seductive. "And you won't only be rich. I'll give you whatever you want. Anything at all. I know I remind you of her. I can be her for you. I just want Agnello. Please, Francesco." She started to cry. "You can get him for me. You know where he is." And now she was leaning in to him, seeking out his mouth with hers.

Why now, you bitch? he thought, reaching for his dagger. Supporting Susanna's body with one arm, he stuck the dagger in Calendula's face, pressing the point against her cheek, the skin denting beneath it. One sharp push and he could erase her beauty forever. She gasped, her blue eyes flickering with fear, but she held his gaze. *No,* he thought, *not just any whore to me.*

And without relinquishing his hold on the dagger, he wrapped his arm around her neck, pulling her toward him, Susanna's body now pressed between them, the blade still against Calendula's face now grazing his own. He kissed her with all the strength it had taken not to push his dagger through her cheek. He kissed her for Susanna, for Juliet, for everything he wanted back. His youth, his mother, his certainty. She grabbed his hair and kissed him back with the same violence, her mouth urgent and hard against his. Whatever she kissed him for, he knew it had nothing to do with seducing him. And when he finally broke away, the kiss—if that was what it was— ended as brutally as it had begun.

The only sound was the whisper of sleet and his own breathing. The expression on Calendula's face was inscrutable.

"Go help Dante find a shovel and meet me by the grove of apple trees near the wall," he said hoarsely.

Silently dropping the veil back over her face, Calendula obediently turned away and beckoned to Dante, who gave no sign he'd seen or comprehended what had just happened.

Francesco looked down at Susanna, as still in death as she'd been animated in life. It seemed impossible that she would no longer smile for him, her face lit up with childlike joy. He had ridiculed that joy, had seen it as proof of a simple mind, a mind unable to grasp the inevitable stupidity of human existence. But now it was the thing he would miss most about her.

He sheathed his dagger, lifted Susanna, and started up the slope toward the apple trees. Averting his gaze from Juliet's shallow grave, he walked along the wall until he came to the grove. The tree branches were bare, coated in ice, but in spring they would be lush with fragrant white blossoms, floating down like perfumed snow. It was the only thing he could do for her.

Holding her, he looked down the slope to the garish villa, watching as Dante and Calendula made their way toward him. Dante carried not one but two shovels, an axe, and a rod, while Calendula held Susanna's treasured bolt of silk. "I don't know why she brought this," Calendula said. She set it on the grass and started to unroll it.

"She brought this cloth because she thought you were Juliet and I was still in love with her," Francesco said. "She thought she could trade it for me. Like a dowry. And I was too blind to understand just how important I was to her." They spoke calmly to each other, now just two people with a task that needed to be done.

He laid Susanna gently on the blue silk, which was already dotted by sleet. Her dowry, now her shroud.

"There are sure to be rocks and tree roots," said Dante. "That's why I brought the axe and rod."

Francesco stared at him blankly, not sure at first what was wrong with him. But it wasn't what was *wrong* with Dante, Francesco suddenly realized, but what was *right* with him. The shock of what had just transpired must have shaken him out of his delusion. For Dante was no longer a bat man, but a wood-carver who made fine moldings, helping a friend dig a grave.

"Go home, Dante," Francesco said. "I can do this."

Ignoring him, Dante put the tip of a shovel to the ground and stepped down on it hard. "It should be deep enough so the wolves can't find her."

Knowing Dante had his own ghosts to bury, Francesco murmured his agreement as he, too, set his shovel against the hard ground.

They dug together in silence, down through the layers of Rome, piling the soil to one side while on the other side Susanna's body rested on the shimmering blue silk. Time and again, they dropped their shovels and picked up the rod to pry up a rock or the axe to chop through a tree root.

Deeper, deeper. He and Dante reached their knees, their waists. They were not deep enough yet when night settled around them. Calendula left and returned with two torches, planting them at either end of the grave.

He had never worked like this. Francesco Angeli did not labor; he carried the purses of important men, watched over their fortunes, their land, and their wives, and woe to him and everyone he loved if he should covet said wives. His arms ached, his back ached, but still he dug and chopped and pried, his tears and sweat mixing with the sleet that ran down his cheeks.

Some children came to investigate the torchlight and ran back down the hill to spread the news from farmhouse to hovel: *Susanna—you remember her—the silversmith's girl from the market.*

Soon, over the edge of the grave, Francesco could see lights making their way up the hill toward them. He was momentarily confused. Fireflies. Fireflies on a summer night in Florence. Chasing them with his sisters. No, not fireflies. Torches. Not many at first, a few lone torches from beyond the villa. No, from all directions. Men and women bearing torches, converging on the grave, lighting up the night. He put his shovel into the ground and lifted more wet earth.

They gathered around the grave. *Two, three, four, five, six, seven* . . . An English rhyme his mother knew . . . *All good children go to Heaven* . . . Another spade of earth, another torch at the graveside.

Someone passed a torch down to Dante, and he planted it in the ground between them. They were up to their shoulders now, every shovelful of dirt needing to be lifted higher. Francesco's arms screamed for mercy.

Above them in the torchlight, the ice on the tree branches glowed like fine crystal. And still they kept coming. He recognized some of them as the men and women who had danced and laughed in the Colosseum. *A time to be born. A time to die. A time to dance. A time to mourn.*

Beyond the walls the wolves howled, but no one flinched. The crowd stood silently, holding their torches high.

When it seemed he would dig ever deeper until it was his own grave, Calendula broke the silence. "It's deep enough."

"No," he said, speaking for the first time since his shovel had bit into the earth. "The wolves . . ."

"She's right, man," Dante said. "It's deep enough."

Francesco allowed Dante to take the shovel from his blistered hands. He ran his sleeve over his forehead and felt the grit and dirt, his hair slick with sleet and mud and sweat. Francesco reached up and an unknown hand took his arm and pulled him out of the grave and back to earth.

Around him, the crowd parted. Calendula was not among them. How many people were there? Twenty? No, thirty. Forty. Fifty. Simple folk, their clothes wet, but they didn't shiver. They didn't speak, either, only looked at him with the knowledge that one day this was their destiny too.

Susanna's hair and clothes were soaked through from the sleet, but it had washed the blood from her face. He folded the cloth over her body, her skin cold to his touch. After holding her close one last time, he carried her over to the grave and, kneeling on the ground, handed her down to Dante, careful not to snag the cloth on the rough sides of the hole.

Someone had gone for a priest, who now said the Mass for the Dead: *"Grant her eternal rest, O Lord, and let perpetual light shine upon her."* People silently crossed themselves. Francesco had not prayed for a long time, but he knew they did it out of respect and was grateful to them.

Dante set her down gently, taking a moment to smooth the blue silk. He removed the torch and handed it up to Francesco, who, with his muscles close to failing, pulled Dante back above ground.

Again they took up their shovels. Francesco tried to drop the first shovelful softly, but winced as the dirt hit the silk shroud. He had no sense of how long it took them to finish, only that it was so deep into the night that dawn could only be an hour or two away. They smoothed the last of the soil. Slowly, one by one, the men and women passed by the grave before making their way back down the hill, a fading trail of light like the tail of a passing comet.

There's nothing left now, he thought, *but to return to the house in the square.* Susanna's house or Michelangelo's—whichever he could face. He could feel exhaustion weighing him down, and he wondered for a moment if he would lie there on the mound of freshly turned earth, never to wake again. Where was that fever that had haunted him these past days? If only it would come back now and take him away.

"Come on, man," Dante said. "It's time for you to go home."

Dante handed him one of the remaining torches, and they walked together down the hill. He could just make out the hulk of the villa in the darkness when he heard Calendula calling from a window.

"Francesco, you will bring me Agnello?"

Dante came to a halt beside him, but Francesco gave him a push and kept walking.

"I know you'll bring him," continued the disembodied voice. "I'll wait here. And when I have my son, I will leave."

"I haven't been well," Dante said as if he'd heard nothing. "I don't know why. I remember so little. It's all so confused."

Francesco didn't know how to answer, and he lacked the strength to do so. But Dante didn't seem to need an answer, and as they walked toward the bridge, Francesco wondered if he should tell Dante to keep what he'd seen quiet.

"I loved her, but what would she want with a poor wood-carver?" Dante said, shaking his head. "I think I'll leave Rome and go back to my father's in Urbino. Will you go back to your father now?"

"No," Francesco said, telling the truth, although it had nothing to do with confronting his father and ending his exile. To return to Florence now was to follow Calendula. With Pollo Grosso's help, she might succeed in impersonating Juliet for a while, maybe a long while, but sooner or later she'd be found out, and he didn't want to be there when it happened.

They parted at the other side of the bridge just as the first light of dawn was forcing its way through the clouds. The sleet had stopped. Knowing this to be the last time they'd meet, they embraced each other. "Wash your face before you go," Francesco said, managing a faint smile. In the cold dawn air, his breath was like puffs of white smoke. "It's so dirty your mother won't recognize you."

"Nor yours you."

"Sadly, I have no mother to return to. You're fortunate, Dante."

Dante nodded, then asked, "Will you go to the authorities?"

"No. It won't change anything."

"But you'll take her the boy?" he asked quietly.

About that Francesco didn't know, but he gave Dante the answer he knew Dante wanted to hear, and after a final embrace they parted.

Francesco turned toward the Piazza Rusticucci, imagining Dante in his shop, gathering his few tools before finding his way back to Urbino, where rest and the good air would make him feel like a man again. He had less hope for himself.

He took the alley to the back gates. He knew it was irrational, but somehow he thought he might see Susanna waiting for him there, as she'd waited the morning Calendula—no, Juliet—had died. She'd been watching the three-legged chicken and wondering if it was there to bring them bad luck or good. But of course she wasn't there. Deciding that opening her gate was more than he could bear, he opened Michelangelo's instead. He stumbled around the blocks of marble and puddles before finally pushing open the door.

Michelangelo was already awake, rolling up one of the drawings on the table while the three-legged chicken watched from the back of the chair. The only light in the room was the weak dawn seeping through the dirty window, but even that was enough to reveal Francesco's face and hair caked with mud from Susanna's grave, his clothes soaked with her blood. *If Michelangelo makes some remark about her being just another whore,* Francesco thought, *I'll kill him.*

But that wasn't what happened. Michelangelo let go of the paper, and it slowly uncurled. "My God," he exclaimed, his voice filled with genuine concern. "What the hell happened to you?"

"Susanna is dead," Francesco said, choking on the words.

"Oh no," Michelangelo said gently. "I am so sorry. How?"

Francesco opened his mouth to speak, but no words came out. He stammered for a moment longer, and then he couldn't help it. He went to Michelangelo, laid his head on the man's shoulder, and started to cry. Cried like he hadn't cried since his mother had died and his father had held him in his arms and made all the pointless reassurances a father makes when comforting his son.

Just like Michelangelo was doing now.

CHAPTER ELEVEN

FRANCESCO WOKE WITH A START, CONVINCED HE'D BEEN ASLEEP for hours, but the bells in the square told him otherwise. It had only been an hour since Michelangelo had built him a fire, given him a soothing balm for his blistered hands, and left him to sleep.

He shifted in the bed, and every muscle, sinew, and bone in his body screamed out for him to lie still. Yet while this pain would pass, he wasn't so sure about the ache in his heart.

He turned his head. The fire wasn't dead, but it was far from roaring. He couldn't expect Michelangelo to break completely from his stingy ways. He knew, too, that when he saw Michelangelo next, the man would treat him more disdainfully than ever out of embarrassment for having shown a more generous side.

Francesco raised his hands and studied them in the room's dim light. Greasy with Michelangelo's balm, they looked as if the skin had been flayed from them. But as much as they hurt, he knew he'd still be digging that grave had Dante not taken away his shovel.

He forced himself into a sitting position, and the room swam in front of his eyes before going momentarily black. His head rolled forward onto his chest, then he recovered with a jerk, finding, to his surprise, that he was dressed only in his chemise. Gradually it came back to him that Michelangelo had insisted he remove his clothes before getting into bed, and he had meekly complied, handing over one blood- and mud-encrusted garment after another.

Even his chemise had not stayed clean, and he touched a dark, coin-sized stain he knew to be Susanna's blood. At the foot of the bed, Michelangelo had left out some of his own clothes: a shirt of dubious cleanliness, his extra hose and breeches, and the jacket of fine brocade Francesco had seen in Michelangelo's trunk the day he had searched for the missing letter.

Francesco's dirty clothes were soaking in one of the cauldrons they used to collect the rain that dripped through the ceiling. He threw in his chemise, knowing he wouldn't come back to wash or retrieve any of them. He imagined them sitting in there until Michelangelo needed the cauldron again, when they'd be thrown out into the yard and trampled into the mud.

He bade the chicken a final farewell. As he closed the door behind him, he couldn't help but think it looked sorry to see him go. He paused for a moment under the eaves, remembering how he'd stood here with Susanna and pointed out the autumn constellations, all the while wishing it was Juliet at his side. The memory gave him pause. How was it he'd given Juliet's death so little thought?

He left the shelter of the eaves, recalling as he unlocked the gate his disappointment at seeing Susanna's scarf wrapped around it. As he walked through the muddy yard to the door, Francesco wondered what the silversmith would think when he returned and found her gone. Would he miss her too?

Taking a deep breath, he pushed open the door, which creaked inward on its leather hinges. His mind was on her final words to him: *My money is behind the first stone from the wall, over the mantle.* Try as he might, he couldn't remember his last words to her. But he knew they'd been angry and impatient. And why had she told him about the money? She must have known she might not return.

Leaving the door open to let in more light, he heard the scrambling of little feet as a scruffy rat scooted across the floor and under the bed. The pewter box was still on the table, a rock weighing down the lid. He opened it. The honey cakes were still there. He put the lid back on. He knew he'd take them in the end. He would need them, but if he were to eat one now, he'd choke on it.

First stone from the wall, over the mantle. The hearth was still cold. He looked at the stones, seemingly secure in their mortar. He ran his finger around the one just above the mantle, but there was no indication it could be freed without a chisel. Surely she hadn't mortared it in? He imagined her pulling it out and adding a tiny coin, the kind of tiny coins that, in the days of working for Guido, he wouldn't have picked up in the street and, had they been in his purse, would have tossed to beggars.

He looked at the stone adjacent to it and the one above it before dragging the chair over to the wall. No wonder Bastiano hadn't found anything. It was, as she'd said, the first stone from the wall, but it was high enough it could be reached only with a chair. A small space on either side of the stone was the only indication it was loose. Francesco inserted a finger on either side and slid it toward him. It was a good eight inches square and felt quite heavy, especially given the state of his arms. Francesco set it down on the mantle before reaching into the dark hole.

His fingers touched something smooth, and he pulled it out. It was a pewter box not unlike the one on the table, but smaller. It sat easily in his hand. It didn't weigh much, and he gave it a shake, listening to the coins rattle against its sides. *Poor girl,* he thought. He set it down on the mantle and was about to step down from the chair when something made him reach into the hole again. Another box. As he slid this one out, he was shocked to find it weighed more than the last box—in fact, it was heavier than the stone behind which it was hidden. He felt something strange in the pit of his stomach as he set it down.

He carried both boxes over to the table. He started with the lighter of the two, and it contained, as he expected, a few dozen coins, though a few were gold and of a substantial size. Any one of them represented several months' wages to a housekeeper like Susanna.

He turned a couple of the coins over in his fingers before opening the other, much heavier box. Why did he feel such sadness?

It was completely full of coins. How could Susanna have amassed so much money? He poured the coins onto the table and started to pick through them. Coins in silver and gold from Rome, Florence, Venice, Milan, Naples, Sicily, France. He counted them, separating them into little stacks according to their value. He completed a stack that equaled the wages of a craftsman for a year, and then another that matched the amount Michelangelo had been advanced for the chapel. He kept making stacks. This was what he'd pay for a small villa in Florence, and this for a larger one.

She'd gone to her father's the other day, and he'd wondered if it was to ask him about the state of her dowry. Francesco had considered taking her home with the excuse that his father had done the same—lived with a woman who had brought not so much as a sheep into the family. Susanna would have been saving for a dowry suited to a farmer or a craftsman, and here she had a dowry The Turk wouldn't have scoffed at. Why, then, did she take the bolt of cloth to trade with Juliet? He remembered watching her count on her fingers and wondering how she didn't get cheated at the market. Yet she had all this. All this wealth that could have saved her a life of drudgery—and possibly saved her life—and she didn't know it. As for where it had come from, that was a mystery she had taken to the grave.

Angrily he scooped up the coins and dropped them, clanging, into the boxes. When they were full, he slammed on the lids and replaced the boxes in the chimney. Then, changing his mind, he removed them again and took out several ducats. He might need these. He would be back for the rest.

✛　✛　✛

FRANCESCO made his first stop Raphael's. His friend opened the door and expressed horror at his appearance. "What can I do for you first? Give you some breakfast or take you to the baths? You could use some clothes that fit too."

"I'm not hungry."

Raphael raised an eyebrow under his beret. "Then it is serious, indeed. And I am not making light of whatever it is that pains you." He led Francesco up the stairs to his studio, where the morning light filtered through the glass and lit the painting on the easel, a portrait of Julius in his fur-trimmed red robes. Francesco studied it as Raphael went in search of clean clothes.

"Everything I have is at your disposal," Raphael said emphatically when he returned with a cloak of black velvet and other garments. "Do you need money?"

Francesco took a deep breath, willing himself not to cry at his friend's kindness. "No. That's the least of my worries. But thank you. You are a good friend. I'm not quite sure where to start, but do you remember the other night when you asked me if it was possible Juliet was using me for her own gain?"

"I am sorry."

"No, you were right. Although, in the end, it's Calendula who got what Juliet wanted."

Raphael shook his head in bewilderment. And so Francesco told him everything. Calendula's plot, Susanna's death, everything but what was yet to come.

"There's more," he said. "I'll be leaving Rome shortly, and I think you'll soon know why. I don't know where I'm going, but even if I did, I wouldn't tell you. I don't want you hauled over a beam by the Pope's men in an attempt to extract my whereabouts."

"The Pope's men? You know what you are doing?"

"I think so," Francesco said with more confidence than he felt. In truth he had no plan. Or maybe he did. The kind of insane plan only someone who really didn't care whether he lived or died would concoct. As for leaving Rome, it could very well be facedown on the currents of the Tiber.

"You are not to worry about me," Raphael said. "His Holiness is as determined that I finish the rooms in the Vatican as he is that Michelangelo complete the ceiling of the Sistine Chapel. I think you need not worry on either of our accounts."

"I would rather err on the side of caution. And speaking of caution, I think it would be wise to send Alfeo back to his family in the country."

"Why? He is under the protection of Imperia's father."

"I don't think he is the most suitable guardian. Should the Pope or any of the wolves in his employ set their sights on him, no one could keep him safe."

Raphael nodded slowly. "This is connected, I am sure, to what you have not told me. I will take him home immediately. He will be disappointed, as he loves to sing, but perhaps I can be of some assistance in finding him a safer post."

"And now," Francesco said, willing some levity into his voice, "let me take you up on the offer of a trip to the baths. I don't know when I'll have the comfort of another."

Raphael gave him an encouraging smile. "If the revival of Roman culture has accomplished nothing other than making bathing fashionable again, it is enough for me," he said, putting on his cape. "Soap truly must be one of the greatest wonders of civilization."

"Did you know, under the right conditions in the grave, the human body can turn to soap?" It was a macabre fact to bring up at the best of times, let alone right after he'd buried the woman he loved.

Still, Raphael chuckled. "How do you know such things?"

"I don't know. And worse, I don't forget them."

"I know it seems impossible, my friend, but there will come a time when you can laugh again."

"I can tell you one thing for certain. I no longer feel like a boy. I feel like a tired old man."

✛ ✛ ✛

THE baths were housed in a cavernous stone building with a vaulted ceiling, massive stone pillars, and high arched windows that filtered the light through milky glass. In the center of the room was a round pool lined with stone. These were thermal baths, heated from the earth. The hot water filled the room with clouds of white steam.

A bored-looking group of prostitutes gathered languidly by the side of the pool. As the men approached, they dropped their robes to the floor. As always, Francesco felt a little embarrassed by their brazenness, but Raphael greeted them, a few even by name, and gave them a couple of coins to watch his and Francesco's clothes and provide them with towels.

"Only towels, every time. You break our hearts," one said to Raphael. Her smile revealed a chipped front tooth that made Francesco think of Susanna. She caught Francesco looking at her and smiled invitingly, but he quickly turned away.

"You will confuse your biographers, Raphael," Francesco said after they had settled into the steaming pool. The heat soothed his aching muscles.

"My biographers? Why should I have biographers?"

"Don't play modest with me, Raphael. I saw your painting of Julius. You have become the favorite painter of a pope who will be remembered for restoring the glory of Rome. For all his faults— and they are myriad—he didn't take Julius Caesar's name in vain. And you'll be remembered along with him as one of Rome's greatest artists."

Raphael laughed. "And if you are right, how will I confuse my biographers?"

"They'll tell of the beautiful women you painted. They'll tell of your charm, your manners, your beauty, and conclude that you were one of history's great lovers. But they'll be wrong. Instead, you pine for some mythical woman, one you cannot begin to describe, though with every painting you make the attempt. I truly hope you'll meet her one day, and together you'll be very happy. Just be sure you don't let her slip through your fingers."

Raphael laughed again, a little sadly this time. "And how will Michelangelo be remembered?"

"Michelangelo won't be remembered for his charm and beauty, that's for certain. People will look at his paintings of men with the bodies of Roman gods and wonder if he preferred their company over that of women. He will be remembered as your antithesis, and people will fight over who was the greater of the two."

"And his houseboy?" Raphael asked. "How will he be remembered?"

"He'll be forgotten. As will the silversmith's housekeeper."

✦ ✦ ✦

THEY said their good-byes a short time later at Raphael's door. Francesco embraced Raphael, promising to write once it was safe and expressing fervent hopes they would meet again.

With Michelangelo's ill-fitting clothes in a bundle under his arm, he walked through the square, past Imperia's, and toward the Sistine Chapel. The guard refused to let him pass, and it wasn't until Michelangelo's voice boomed out "Is that you, Francesco?" that the man stepped aside.

"I'm sorry," the guard apologized. "But I'm under the strictest of orders from the master of ceremonies not to let anyone in." He seemed afraid to even utter aloud Paride di Grassi's name.

"I understand," Francesco said, giving the nervous guard a reassuring pat on the shoulder. "Keep up the good work."

Francesco made the forty-foot climb up the ladder to the scaffold for what he knew to be the last time. Without a word, he passed Bastiano, who in turn pretended not to see Francesco. The other two assistants nodded at him but said nothing, and he couldn't help but think Bastiano had told them a biased version of their altercation at Susanna's. Francesco thought of the coins waiting for him in the silversmith's chimney. Had Bastiano found them, he'd be a very rich man now, freed from Michelangelo's temper and surely very far away. Francesco could only hope Bastiano would be working as a lowly assistant until the day he died.

Michelangelo was at work on one of the lunettes beneath his new version of *The Flood.* That first fresco had taken so long for him to complete, but he seemed to have learned everything he needed to now proceed at a remarkable pace. Standing in front of the lunette's newly plastered surface, he shifted impatiently from foot to foot as if willing it to dry. In his left hand he held one of his drawings and in the other his brush. At his feet was a pot of black pigment for sketching in the figures. He had become so confident that, instead of tracing the figures' outlines with the use of full-sized cartoons, he was painting them freehand.

Michelangelo ignored Francesco's greeting. "I've been told Raphael bribed the guard the other night in order to get in here," Michelangelo said instead. "What do you know of that?"

"Sounds like the excuse of a guard who fell asleep at his post," Francesco half-lied.

Michelangelo looked at him suspiciously, his gnarled features obliterating all traces of his earlier fatherly tenderness, as Francesco had predicted. "Well, if Raphael wants to sneak around and steal more of my ideas, you tell him he'll have to wait until spring," Michelangelo said, turning his attention back to the wall. "I can't work much longer in this weather."

"And in the meantime, what will you do?"

"I shall finish the drawings and work on my plans for Julius's tomb. This ceiling is but a small matter. The tomb is my destiny."

"As it is to be the destiny of us all." Francesco glanced down the platform to where Bastiano and the others were working and lowered his voice. "I'm leaving Rome and have come to say good-bye."

Michelangelo set the tip of his brush to the plaster. "It has to be just dry enough to form a skin that will take the brush without tearing."

Francesco took this apparent lack of attention to his words as Michelangelo's consent. His father and Michelangelo had an agreement, and it wasn't really up to Francesco to violate the terms. "Thank you for the loan of clothes," he said, setting down the bundle. "You're to have no kind words for me, you understand. I've run off and left you without a houseboy. You'd believe anything of me."

"That shouldn't be difficult. You've been a useless houseboy."

"Exactly," Francesco said, though he was unsure whether Michelangelo was jesting. "I'm only thinking of your safety. Will you write my father?"

"And say what?"

"That I'm sorry."

"And can he expect your return?"

"Should I live. And if he'll have me."

Michelangelo touched the surface of the plaster again, then, dropping the sketch, he picked up the pot of black paint and dipped in his brush. "I shall advise him to do so," he said as he inscribed a long, graceful arc. "And I suggest you stay alive long enough so as not to disappoint him."

"Thank you. As for you, you're right to watch out for di Grassi and Asino. Watch out for Bastiano too. He's a thief."

This short farewell had transpired without Michelangelo so much as glancing at him, but as Francesco started backing down the ladder to the floor, he saw Michelangelo turn toward him. Francesco raised a hand, and to his surprise Michelangelo, holding his brush aloft, raised his too. Francesco smiled the rest of the way to the chapel floor.

✠ ✠ ✠

FRANCESCO was beyond the port when he saw a thick cloud of black smoke curling up from the hills. Worried it was coming from The Turk's home, he picked up his pace. When he reached the great gates marking the beginning of the cypress-flanked drive, there was no longer any doubt. The marble facade was blackened, the roof had caved in, and black smoke billowed from the interior.

Halfway up the drive, Francesco found The Turk leaning on his cane, calmly watching his home burn. "What happened?" Francesco asked just as a loud explosion blew out an entire side of the house, sending up a plume of sparks and debris. Francesco instinctively ducked, but The Turk appeared unfazed.

"There goes my collection of weaponry," The Turk said with a sigh as the boom echoed around the hills. "Surprised it didn't blow before now. All that saltpeter." His great bald head swiveled toward Francesco.

"What happened?" Francesco repeated.

"Blasted monkey was teasing the lion. He'd wait until the lion was asleep and then jump up and down on the cage and pelt him with fruit. Drove the poor beast to distraction. Finally he'd had enough and broke out of the cage, chased the monkey all over the house, smashing and breaking everything in sight. And what a sight it was—over the tables, under the beds, in and out the doors . . . At the height of the madness, he knocked over a stove and set the kitchen on fire."

"Where's your staff?" Francesco remembered Mosa, the little girl who'd waited on him the day before, the one who'd been so afraid of the lion.

"All gone," The Turk said. "Scattered into the hills like scared rabbits."

"And the lion and monkey?"

"Not far behind them," The Turk said with a chuckle, as though the sight had been amusing enough to be worth the destruction of his home. "Now tell me what had you running out of here yesterday like there was a lion on your tail and a monkey on your back? Why all the interest in who was staying at my other villa?"

Francesco shrugged. He thought of Calendula's portrait burning inside, the genesis of all this trouble. Had it not been painted, Calendula would never have come to believe that Agnello was her son, a delusion that surely would have ended with her death at the hands of the Pope's men, had Francesco not led Guido to her. Inadvertently, in leaving Florence, Francesco had altered the course of events in Rome. He had perhaps even saved Calendula, although in her stead, Juliet, Marcus, Guido, and Susanna had all died. Maybe that was why he would get Agnello. To atone. It wouldn't make things right, but this was Rome, and it was the best he could hope to do.

"Will you move to that old villa then, the one you rented to Guido?" Francesco asked, evading The Turk's question. He tried to imagine the meeting between The Turk and Calendula. How would The Turk feel about being duped by her? Then again, he might not get that far before he was wearing Pollo Grosso's dagger in his back.

"No," The Turk was saying, "not there. That would be going back, and my motto is *Never retreat. Always forward. Take no prisoners. No regrets.* To go back is to give up. I have a ship leaving tomorrow for Venice and then on to the east." His eyes were bright with excitement at the prospect of this new adventure, even as his house and all his treasures burned before his eyes. "Turkey, Cyprus, Lebanon, Egypt, who knows where, but I'll be on it. Onward, always onward."

"Any room for me on that ship?" Francesco asked impulsively. He would go to Venice. Unlike The Turk, he would take a few steps back, back to the city he'd visited in his student years, and start again, but this time with a little more wisdom and humility.

The Turk's head pivoted again on its cushions of fat, his beady black eyes sizing up Francesco. "I know not to ask a man why he does the things he does," he said. "But you haven't answered me. You went up to the pyramid to see where Calendula's body was buried, and then you came back, asking questions about my wife's cousin. What did Guido have to say?"

Francesco shrugged. "Nothing. Guido has gone to Naples. Perhaps he's visiting your wife. I'm told Guido's wife is returning to Florence, accompanied by Guido's bodyguard. There was nothing else to be learned. The body was dug up by wolves, as Dante said. There was nothing to be found, and no one saw anything." He stopped, realizing he was rambling. What was the point in telling The Turk anything? He couldn't avenge Calendula's death, as she wasn't dead. In time The Turk would learn that Guido had perished on the way to or from Naples—whatever story Calendula invented. He would learn, too, that Guido's widow wore a veil and resided quietly, shunning visitors. Except for a boy. A boy she had adopted in Rome.

The Turk looked back to his villa as another wall crumpled under the heat of the fire. "And I don't even have her portrait . . . such a lovely girl. But *è la vita,* eh, boy?" he said cheerfully, slapping Francesco robustly on the shoulder. "The ship sails at dawn. I advise you to be there tonight. I wait for no man."

Reeling under The Turk's blow, Francesco thanked him. He'd be there—if he was still alive.

He'd gone several yards when The Turk called after him. "Francesco! That ring Calendula was wearing. Do you think Guido could have taken it from me and given it to her?"

Francesco shook his head hard, a little too hard. Shooting stars blurred his vision. For one moment, he was sure he saw The Turk's stuffed crocodile rise from the smoke and fly away like the mythical phoenix. "Why would he do that?" he shouted back.

"I don't know. Just never really liked the man," The Turk called out, echoing his sentiments of the previous day.

"Neither did I," Francesco muttered as he continued along the drive.

✛ ✛ ✛

FRANCESCO waited in the deepening shadows of St. Peter's for the bells to toll vespers. There were few workmen left in the square. While the foremen often kept the workers late, in the past few weeks, even they'd lost their taste for labor, only too happy to return home early to a warm fire and dry clothes.

It was raining again, a fine drizzle that beaded on his velvet cloak. He'd almost stopped noticing this rain, it had become so omnipresent. Like the wolves. How long had they been howling this evening? He hadn't noticed them until just now.

He would do this one last thing. Then he'd retrieve the money from the silversmith's chimney and board The Turk's ship. In the morning they'd set sail for Venice.

Finally the bells tolled vespers, and he watched as a half-dozen cardinals in their scarlet robes led the way to the Sistine Chapel. An errant choirboy pushed his way through them, no doubt anticipating a beating for being late. A handful of cowled monks and Paride di Grassi came next. Then the Pope himself. Alone.

Francesco didn't hesitate. This was the only chance he'd have. He crossed the square, passing the chapel door, and boldly entered the Vatican palace. The men milling in the great entrance hall were preparing to leave, books tucked under their arms. *No hope of an audience with His Holiness tonight,* he imagined them thinking. *The Pope is at vespers. He will come back and eat his dinner and enjoy the flesh of young boys.*

No, Francesco thought, *they do not think that. Or maybe they do.*

Beyond the great hall, it was relatively quiet. The servants he met avoided his gaze and he theirs, and so he reached the room of the parrot without incident. A servant was in the process of lighting the tall candelabras. He left, head lowered, when Francesco entered. *He'll be questioned,* Francesco thought, but he doubted whether the servant would be able to give much of a description.

"It is you," Agnello said. He held his doll in one hand, a wooden sword in the other. He looked very small, occupying just a tiny square of marble in the vast room. His cloak was crumpled in a heap beside him, while behind him the parrot's roost was empty.

The frescoes had been stripped from the walls, revealing bare stone. Clearly Julius had plans for this room too.

"Where's the parrot?"

"He drank too much wine and fell from the perch."

Francesco could tell Agnello was trying hard not to cry. "I'm very sorry," Francesco said, wondering what ass would give wine to a parrot. "I have a question for you, and you must answer it very carefully. Will you do that?"

The boy nodded. He got to his feet without relinquishing sword or doll. "Can I have your chicken?"

Francesco smiled at him. "I'm asking the question, remember?"

Agnello nodded, the light from the candles dancing in his golden hair.

"I can take you to see the lady in the painting. But if I do, you can never, ever come back here. Is that what you want?"

Agnello nodded again, his expression unchanged. "But she is in Hell . . ."

Francesco bent down and, taking Agnello by the shoulders, looked into his cornflower blue eyes. "I need you to listen to me very carefully," he said. "She is not in Hell, and she is not your mother. She thinks she is your mother, and she wants to be your mother—"

"She is my mother," Agnello said, his eyes now taking on an icy blue resolve.

Francesco picked up the boy's cloak and was fastening it around his shoulders when his fingers brushed against something spongy on the boy's neck. Without saying a word, Francesco lifted one of the boy's long curls and found an oozing red sore the size of a small coin. Quickly Francesco let go of the curl, took the boy's hand, and asked him in a slightly shaky voice if he was ready to go. Agnello nodded. He was a slight child, but Francesco, his arms aching from digging, grimaced as he lifted him. He imagined the questions. *Have you seen the boy?* And they could only reply, *We saw a man in a black cloak. Maybe he hid the boy under it.*

"Hang on tightly and be as quiet as your doll," he entreated the boy. Still grasping his toys, Agnello obediently wrapped his free arm around Francesco's neck and silently laid his head against his chest. "Good," Francesco said as he pulled his cloak around them both.

"Where are you going with him?"

Francesco wheeled around and saw a figure standing in the shadows of the doorway. He'd thought this the insane mission of a man who didn't care whether he lived or died, but his heart now pounded fearfully in his chest. He held Agnello tightly. The voice was faintly familiar, if not friendly, and Francesco struggled to place it as he produced the answer he'd prepared. "I'm taking him to the chapel for vespers."

"Hidden in your cloak?" The man stepped out of the shadows, and Francesco recognized him as the guard who'd opened the Sistine Chapel the night he and Raphael had gone there on a drunken whim. The guard had been drunk too, and Francesco, detecting a slur in his voice now, assumed he was in a similar state tonight.

"Yes," Francesco said, deciding against reminding him of their acquaintance. The man didn't have his spear this time, but his dagger was at the ready, his hand a little unsteady. Francesco's own dagger was sheathed at his waist. With the boy in his arms, he was clearly at the disadvantage. "I thought it best to put him under my cloak to spare us confrontations such as this one."

"The boy doesn't go to evening prayers."

"I know, but there are some fine new singers—" Francesco ventured.

"I'm no fool," the guard said. "You aren't the first man to covet the boy. The last one who tried was hung by his own intestines. The Pope likes to watch his enemies suffer. And the guard who turned him in alive was rewarded handsomely."

"And if the man had offered an acceptable sum to keep his intestines where they belonged," Francesco asked, "would it have ended differently?"

The guard tensed, raising his dagger as Francesco reached under his cloak, but Francesco only wanted to show his purse. He invited the guard to test its weight.

"A ruse to stick your dagger in my eye."

Francesco loosened the string and worked out a couple of ducats, as much as the guard earned in a month. "Perhaps if you could kindly see us to the chapel doors, we could find you several more."

"How many more?"

"As many as you have fingers."

"To the chapel door then, and no farther." He took out a flask and drank from it before replacing it. "And I'll take as many ducats as I have toes too. Let me see them. But throw down your dagger. I know you have one."

Francesco shifted Agnello to one side and, pulling out his dagger, let it clatter to the floor before holding up his purse. "They're all here. But I can't show you and hold the boy at the same time."

The guard staggered forward, grabbing first at the dagger and then at the bag, feeling the shape of the coins beneath the fabric, then nodded toward the hall.

The boy hadn't so much as stirred beneath Francesco's cloak, and Francesco shifted his weight to the other arm. They walked through the now deserted halls with the guard weaving behind them, so close Francesco could smell his stinking breath.

When they emerged into the darkening square, vespers were already under way, and music filtered through the chapel doors.

Francesco looked around, his eyes seizing upon a nearby skid of bricks. "I need to piss," he said, abruptly changing direction and striding toward the skid.

"Not without me, you aren't," the guard retorted. "I'm not stupid. You're going to make a run for it and cheat me out of the money you promised." The guard had guessed right, of course, since Francesco had no intention of giving this fool any of Susanna's money. Besides, he didn't trust the guard not to put up the alarm anyway and double his profits.

"Come then," Francesco said, putting a few precious strides between himself and the guard as he rounded the skid and found himself surrounded on all sides by stacks of bricks and boards. It was better than he could have hoped. Whatever happened here wouldn't be discovered until the workers returned the next morning.

"Quickly," he whispered to Agnello, whipping him out from under his cloak and pushing him behind a couple of boards. Wordlessly the boy ducked down, arm around the doll, his wooden sword held in front of him.

Francesco wheeled to face a wall and pretended to urinate as he curled his fingers around a brick and worked it out to the edge. *Pollo Grosso bringing the club down on Susanna, Dante bringing the rock down on Pollo Grosso . . . and now a brick . . .*

"Aha!" The guard stumbled around the corner, swaying slightly as he blocked the entrance. "I knew you'd make a break for it. But there's no way out here. Hey! Where's the boy?"

Francesco didn't hesitate. He yanked out the brick and swung as hard as he could, feeling a horrible sick lurch in his stomach as the brick met the guard's head. Blood pouring from the gash on his scalp, the man fell with a grunt, his dagger clattering across the stones. Francesco grabbed it and, flipping the man over, found his own as well.

"Is he dead?" Agnello asked, emerging from his hiding place. He held his wooden sword out, its tip pointing down at the guard.

"No," Francesco said, though he didn't know whether the guard would be dead by the time he was found. For good measure, Francesco cut one of the ropes securing the skid of bricks and bound the guard's hands and feet. He then ripped off one of the man's sleeves and gagged him.

"He was the one who gave the wine to my parrot," Agnello said, poking the unconscious guard with his sword.

"He was a stupid shit," Francesco muttered.

Sheathing his dagger, he picked up the boy again and returned to the square. With darkness almost upon them, he traded a man some coins for a torch and, holding it aloft, retraced his steps from early that morning, over the Tiber, and through the fields toward The Turk's garish old villa.

Calendula had been watching them approach from an upstairs window. She came running toward them, Pollo Grosso not far behind. "I knew you'd come," she cried. Tears ran down her cheeks as she took Agnello into her arms, and for a moment Francesco was convinced the boy was hers after all. Who but the child's real mother would display such ecstasy at having her son returned to her? And what child could look happier than Agnello, radiant through his tears of joy? But it didn't take long for Francesco to remember it was all a delusion. Calendula was not Agnello's real mother, but she had killed for him, and while Francesco hardly thought this proved her a good guardian, he couldn't leave the boy with Julius.

His thoughts turned to the sore on the boy's neck. What was it? Did he share the Pope's affliction? If so, how long did he have to live? Francesco looked up through the darkness toward Susanna's grave. If he were a man of faith, he'd conclude God was oblivious to the happiness of men and mocked it whenever He could. But Francesco wasn't, so he had no answers at all. *È la vita*, he thought. *È la vita*. Once for The Turk. Once for Susanna.

The wind was cold, and beyond the walls the wolves howled. Francesco was anxious to be away from here and heading for the docks. He should warn Calendula to watch out for the Pope's men, but with Pollo Grosso beside her it was probably the Pope's men who needed to worry. Somehow he knew she'd make it safely to Florence and Guido's house, and his own father would be there to meet her.

"My father works in Guido's court," Francesco said. "If any harm should come to him, I really will kill you."

Calendula nodded, and he turned and walked away. He'd done all he could, and probably more than he should have. He hoped he never learned how it all played out, because, happy as the scene was now, it could not stay this way.

✤ ✤ ✤

HE returned to Susanna's house by way of the alley. Leaning the torch against the fireplace, he climbed onto the chair, pried out the stone, and reached inside. For one panicked moment he thought the boxes were gone, but then his fingers brushed against metal. Relieved, he pulled them toward him as quietly as possible. He could hear Michelangelo snoring through the common wall.

Francesco placed the boxes in the bottom of a pack, covering them with a blanket from the bed and topping it with the box of honey cakes from the table. He tied the pack over his shoulder and pulled his cloak around it, thinking what a prize he was for robbers tonight. He checked for his dagger, picked up the torch, took one last look around the room, and closed the door behind him.

He walked to the port without incident. The wind had grown colder, and the air was laden with dampness. It was quiet along the docks. A few torches burned on the ships' decks, but other than sullen guards hunched under their cloaks, there was no one around.

The man who let him onto The Turk's boat was the same man who'd given Susanna the bolt of silk, but while Francesco recognized him, he didn't recognize Francesco. Francesco might have left it that way, but he had a question for him. Assuring him first that he had no intention of telling The Turk about the "gift" of cloth, he asked about the boys di Grassi and Asino had come to buy but found too old. "I heard they escaped that same night," Francesco said.

The man looked over Francesco's shoulder out into the night. "Sometimes a hatch doesn't get closed properly," he said slowly. "Don't know how it happened."

After the man had shared a cup of wine with Francesco, he offered him a bunk below, but Francesco found the stench of unwashed bodies so overwhelming he was soon back on deck. He looked around until he found a sheltered spot under some sails that, having come untied from the boom, formed a tent of sorts. The man offered him a few dry sacks, and Francesco spread them over the damp planks.

Francesco sat in his tent, pulled the blanket out of his pack, and wrapped it around himself before leaning back against a barrel. The pack he kept tied over his shoulder, admonishing himself to sleep lightly. However she'd earned it, he would not lose Susanna's hard-won fortune over a good night's sleep.

Shielded from the wind, he was close to being warm and comfortable in his little tent. The rain started again, but it splattered harmlessly against the canvas. He even felt a bit hungry and ate one of the honey cakes, thinking how Susanna would have first licked the honey from the top. He listened to the river lapping against the sides of the ship, the creaking of timbers, the wolves calling to each other in the hills, the rain on the tent, and, unable to stop himself, fell asleep.

✢ ✢ ✢

HE was awakened by shouts and by light creeping in around the edges of his tent. He felt a quick stab of panic when he realized he'd fallen asleep, but his pack was still safe at his side. It suddenly occurred to him that maybe the money Susanna had so generously bequeathed him was not actually hers but the silversmith's. But he had no time for guilt or anything else because the boom over his head was shifting, and his tent quickly resumed its purpose as a sail. He rubbed his eyes, and when he opened them, he was looking at The Turk's massive boots.

"I see we've got a stowaway," roared The Turk. "Welcome aboard, boy."

Francesco bade him a good morning as he staggered stiffly to his feet.

"Been asked to watch out for stowaways," The Turk continued. "The Pope's boy was kidnapped last night." He studied Francesco with his little black eyes.

Francesco stuffed his blanket into his pack. "What did the man look like?" he asked as carelessly as he could.

"He was wearing a black cloak," The Turk said. "It would appear the boy was smuggled out under it, and that this man had a little help from one of the Vatican guards. The poor bastard was found this morning, bound and gagged in the square."

"Alive?" Francesco asked, still doing his best to sound disinterested.

"For now. The Pope is furious, and I don't think he'll let the guard off with a few harsh words. It might have been better for him if the man in the cloak had put a swift end to him. And I'd imagine, too, that the man in the cloak would want to get away as fast as possible. Good thing he decided not to take a boat."

He knows, Francesco thought, but he also knew that, for whatever reason, The Turk was unperturbed.

"Doesn't matter," The Turk went on. "The Pope will just find another boy. Anyway, it'll be a miserable start on this river. One spends more time being hauled over sandbars by oxen than sailing. But once we make it to sea, it's different." The Turk inhaled deeply, as if already breathing in the healthy sea air. "I love the smell of salt air in the morning, boy," he said. "I've taken a liking to you, and I'll make a sailor of you yet. And to be a sailor is to be a man." He leaned over the side, his bulk seeming to threaten the boat's stability. "Untie those ropes," he called down to the dockworkers before walking with the help of his eagle-topped cane to the helm, where he took the ship's wheel.

Francesco watched him go, then found himself a spot in the stern, away from flying ropes, swinging booms, and cursing sailors. From here he looked back on the city, shrouded in gray fog. They passed the Emporium, and he looked over the fields toward the Pyramid of Cestius, where he had buried Susanna among the apple trees.

Before he could dwell much longer on this, he caught a movement out of the corner of his eye. He turned and stared in disbelief, then laughed. "Can it really be you?" he asked. "You know you're breaking Michelangelo's heart."

He was glad no one could hear him, for they would have thought him foolish for talking to a chicken. Of course, the chicken said nothing, just gave a funny hop from one side to the other before cocking its head and giving Francesco that slightly admonishing look he'd always found so unsettling. Francesco scooped up the chicken and held it tightly.

"I can't believe you knew where to find me. You must have the nose of a hunting dog. Stick with me if you don't want to end up in the cook's pot."

Is a chicken with three legs a good or bad omen? Susanna had asked him. Her smile flashed before his eyes as vividly as if she were standing there. Francesco felt a lump in his throat, and as the ship slipped past the walls of the ancient city, he held the chicken close and cried into its feathers.

ACKNOWLEDGMENTS

THANKS TO OUR FAMILIES AND FRIENDS FOR THEIR ONGOING support and encouragement; Ivan "Bud" Caswell, Ian Coutts, Catharine Lyons-King, Susan Neal, June Richards, Andy Ruston, Alexander and Gail Scala, Walter Schuster, and Hannah Silverman for reading drafts and/or giving us valuable input; Christian Catalini for being our Italian language consultant; Cheryl Estrella as well as Krishna and Christine Agrawal for childcare support; and Jessica Tremblay and her "wolves" (Sharayah and Taima) for the author photos.

We are grateful to the staff at Westwood Creative Artists, in particular our agent, John Pearce, as well as to the staff at Harper-Collins Canada, especially Lorissa Sengara, Noelle Zitzer, and Nicola Reddy, and to copy editors Sue Sumeraj, Stephanie Fysh, and Kelly Jones.

Special thanks to Westley Côté for the title and being our all-around Renaissance guy, and to Benvenuto Cellini for inspiring

Dante, as well as the necromancer and the "zombies."

We found the following books to be invaluable and hope the authors will accept our apologies for the liberties taken with their brilliant research: *Michelangelo and the Pope's Ceiling* by Ross King, *Renaissance Rome 1500–1559: A Portrait of a Society* by Peter Partner, *Basilica: The Splendor and the Scandal: Building St. Peter's* by R.A. Scotti, and *The Better Angels of Our Nature: Why Violence Has Declined* by Steven Pinker.

For its generous financial support, we are once again grateful to the Ontario Arts Council.